DREAM HUNTRESS

A DREAM SEEKER NOVEL

*Keep Dreaming —
Michelle Sharp*

Keep Dreaming!
Michelle Sharp

DREAM HUNTRESS

A DREAM SEEKER NOVEL

MICHELLE
SHARP

This book is a work of fiction. Names, characters, places, and incidents are the product of the author's imagination or are used fictitiously. Any resemblance to actual events, locales, or persons, living or dead, is coincidental.

Copyright © 2014 by Michelle Sharp. All rights reserved, including the right to reproduce, distribute, or transmit in any form or by any means. For information regarding subsidiary rights, please contact the Publisher.

Entangled Publishing, LLC
2614 South Timberline Road
Suite 109
Fort Collins, CO 80525
Visit our website at www.entangledpublishing.com.

Ignite is an imprint of Entangled Publishing, LLC.

Edited by Tracy Montoya
Cover design by Fiona Jayde

Manufactured in the United States of America

First Edition June 2014

To my biggest fan, to my greatest source of strength and support, to the one person who has always believed in me much more than I have ever believed in myself...I love you, Mom.

Chapter One

She'd been cursed at, spit on, beaten up, run down, and shot at. And still Jordan Delany found each of those events considerably less repulsive than the grimy hand planted on her butt.

She squelched the fantasy of putting a bullet hole in the center of the drunken cowboy's unibrow and reminded herself to play nice.

"Lewis, you better leave one hell of a tip, since your hand has spent more time on my ass than my underwear has." Okay, so maybe playing nice wasn't her strong suit. But she hadn't permanently rendered his right hand useless, either, so all in all, she'd used admirable restraint.

Slinging beer at Buck's Nightclub wasn't exactly Jordan's idea of a good time, but the intel her team had gathered led straight to Titus—Middle of Nowhere, Missouri. As a St. Louis County Detective who worked on the largest drug task force in the Midwest, she'd been on several undercover operations. This was the first one that had taken her so far outside of the city limits.

About an hour and a half from St. Louis, the rural, backwoods town promised more trouble than any place she'd ever worked. And that was saying something, considering she'd been undercover in some fairly disturbing places, including a meth lab and a crack house. Even the crack junkies hadn't assumed it was fine to stroke her backside whenever the mood struck.

"Come on dollface, let Lewis take you someplace private. I'll teach you what our favorite pastime is here in Titus."

Not in this lifetime or any other, slick.

She forced a smile and politely served him his beer. Her undercover experience, combined with ten years of narcotics and vice work, made her hands down the best candidate for this job, but damn, just once couldn't the job take her to a five-star hotel?

Rolling her head from side to side, she took a deep breath and let it out slowly. There was no one to blame but herself. She was just one of several St. Louis area detectives who had teamed with the FBI and DEA to wage war on the staggering influx of drugs into Missouri. She'd spent the last year attempting to connect local traffickers back to their more powerful Mexican cartel roots, specifically, the Delago Cartel.

But when two cops in deep cover—two friends, two guys she'd shared many beers with—had been butchered and left on display as a warning, she'd had to fight like hell to even remain on the task force.

She swallowed, blinking back the burn that tended to lance through her at the most inopportune moments.

A dirty, callused hand snaked out and grabbed her arm. "Seriously," Lewis said with a drunken slur, "I'd like to take you out sometime."

Seriously, I'd like to cut off your groping hands and superglue your dick to your ass crack.

Realizing that comeback wasn't likely to win any waitress-of-the-year awards, she bit her tongue and struggled for a more appropriate response. "Sorry, we're not allowed to date the customers. Buck's rules." Of course, touching was against Buck's rules, too, but that hadn't put a damper on the number of times her butt had been pinched and palmed. Being stroked by unfamiliar jerks in various states of drunkenness made her teeth itch. She'd pummeled men for less.

But not tonight. Not on this case.

In fact, she'd let the old-school sexist thing work in her favor. She'd bet money that Arlo Buck didn't expect a tall, lanky female with a navel piercing and wild blond hair to be his undoing. A decent ass and pearly pink lip-gloss had opened more than one door to the underworld.

Arlo "Big Daddy" Buck ran a questionable entertainment establishment—strip club—with his son, Warren, on the outskirts of Titus.

The place oozed impurities like an infected boil badly in need of lancing. Illegal prostitution, gambling, and underage drinking were more prevalent than the common cold.

"Kudos to the cocktail waitresses of the world," she mumbled, stalking through the crowd and thinking that undercover narcotics work had nothing on slinging beer for drunk, horny men. She gave her order to the bartender, then turned to study the customers while she waited.

She hadn't worked at the nightclub long, but already she'd compiled a mental list of suspicious people who piqued her interest. Like the man who arrived daily with a duffle, drank a beer, and disappeared into Buck's office. Also, the dancer with red eyes and blackened teeth who spent a hell of a lot more time in the VIP rooms than she did on the stage. And most interestingly, Buck's son, Warren, who liked his whiskey straight up and often. Yes, she'd seen more than enough to know Buck's was a breeding ground of illegal activity.

So, on a chilly November night in Titus, she served drinks, made nice with the customers, and decided that the lingering exhaustion from back-to-back cases was the reason for the red-hot irritation prickling up her spine. Of course, it could've also been caused by Lewis's hand stroking across her backside. Again.

It's just a hand. Don't let it get to you. Serve drinks. Stay calm.

Might as well be back in the Stone Age, where women were nothing more than objects, just playthings for male pleasure. To top off her frustration, the information she'd gathered so far was nowhere near good enough to spring her from the backwoods town. Still, there were a few hardcore truths that were hard to miss.

First, most of the women who stripped in Buck's did so more out of desperation than choice.

Second, customers packed in like sardines, which gave every male in the place an excuse to grope the waitresses as they passed by.

And last, she believed the intel on Buck's Nightclub was spot-on. Arlo and Warren Buck were very likely major distributors of the ultra-pure and deadly form of heroin known as China White.

It wasn't the only drug being pushed, but it had become the fashionable drug of choice among the younger generation. Not only in Titus, but in St. Louis and all across the Midwest.

That knowledge made all the greedy, sex-seeking hands a small price to pay. She could deal with the drunks, the hands, and the come-ons. Because at the end of the day, she'd not only bring the Bucks down, she'd enjoy every last minute of watching them crash and burn. And if she happened to come face-to-face with the son of a bitch who'd ordered the kill on their deep-cover cops, all the better.

If she saved just one person from the gruesome nightmare she'd lived through as a result of drugs, it would damned well be worth it.

...

Tonight was going to be interesting. Tyler McGee knew it the second he stepped into Buck's Nightclub and inhaled the scents of stale beer and fresh sex. He was in a lousy place, with lousy people, and about to grovel for a lousy job he didn't want. Yeah, interesting was about the best way to sum it up.

The half-dressed women were as plentiful as the bottles of beer. Between eight and ten o'clock, it was two-for-one ladies' night at Buck's. The music blared loud enough to take your head off, and the smoke hung still and dense.

A huge T-shaped stage filled the center of the enormous barn-like building. Flashing stage lights and dozens of small, circular tables surrounded the dancers while they stripped. Four VIP rooms were partitioned off behind the stage for private dances.

Arlo Buck's notorious reputation had been well established in Titus for years. Even as a kid, Ty remembered hearing about what a seedy bastard he was. Still, Buck managed to turn a dirty, rundown barn into the hottest nightclub since the Playboy Mansion. *Unbelievable.* Certainly had just as many scantily clad women, though most looked significantly older and less optimistic than Heffner's girls.

Apparently, Buck was smarter than he looked. Because Ty had always thought he looked like a huge, overgrown linebacker who'd had his big, meaty head pounded one too many times. His double chin and thick, round neck topped a six-three, four-hundred-pound body, and his sausage-like fingers usually held a soggy, foul cigar.

But as ugly, round, and mean as Buck was rumored to be, everyone in Titus County hung at his nightclub. Ty's jaw clenched just thinking about the son of a bitch's luck.

He glanced over at Big Daddy Buck, wondering if he could muster enough tolerance for this hellhole to ask for a job. Nerves made his hands sweaty. He smoothed them down his thighs, and his thumb snagged on the ring in his pocket. A ring that would never be worn. His gut tightened against the memories and reminded him exactly where the tolerance would come from.

"Here goes nothing." He headed across the room to Buck.

"Good evening, lucky ladies and gents." The boom of the microphone rattled beer bottles and vibrated off the walls. Peripheral lights faded dark, but the stage flashed bright as the mic boomed again. "Welcome to Lucky Ladies Tuesday, where the drinks are cheap, and the women are cheaper. Only kidding, ladies. Now put your hands together for the lovely Fionaaaa."

Irritating Buck during Fiona's striptease was probably not the best timing in the world. Not when Ty was determined to be gainfully employed by Big Daddy before the night was over. Deciding to wait out the stripper's dance, Ty dropped onto a barstool at the edge of the stage.

He'd barely sat when he heard glass shatter behind him. He whipped around and caught sight of a cocktail waitress bobbling one last bottle before it crashed to the floor with the others.

With a defeated sigh, she turned in his direction and briefly closed her eyes. The moment barely lasted a second, but it was long enough to appreciate her…assets.

Slender. Sexy. Stunning.

Different. Different from anyone he expected to see in Buck's.

"Damn it," she said. Even over the pounding music, Ty picked up on the bristly impatience in her voice. She tossed long, blond hair over her shoulder, but when she bent to pick up the pieces of broken glass, the wavy mane tumbled in front of her again. An impulse to hold the silky strands out of the way almost had him sliding off his stool.

Laughter and applause broke out around her. A quick, sizzling ache enveloped his chest. Probably a sharp pulse of sympathy for the harassment she was enduring.

After plucking the large shards of glass off the floor, she stood. His eyes locked on long, slim legs that trailed up to a strip of denim entirely too small to be considered shorts. Above the denim waistband, a tiny, shimmering rhinestone gleamed in her belly button. His gaze continued the journey up to her breasts. Generous, rounded, spectacular breasts.

"Wrong set of eyes, cowboy. I'm up here." Her brow molded into a scolding arch, irritation plain on her pretty face.

His pride was hurt. He wasn't a typical male who goggled at women and talked to their chests. Not usually. But, okay, this one caught him by surprise. Embarrassed that he'd gawked like a teenager, he tried to redeem himself. "I'm sorry. I was noticing…your rhinestone."

"Uh-huh." She snorted. "That's the first time I've heard them called that."

Busted. He concentrated on keeping his eyes more respectfully on her face, although it was just as intriguing as her body.

She looked him over with attitude and piercing, emerald eyes.

Her wild, wavy hair ended precisely where the bikini top started. Though he damned well wasn't going to shift his eyes to look, not if it killed him. Thankfully, though, he had excellent peripheral vision. Even without so much as a southward blink, he was well aware of the two miniscule triangles of shiny gold material and string barely covering her chest. If she was that good looking and working as a waitress in Buck's, she must not be the sharpest pencil in the box.

Leaning in to be heard over the music, she asked, "What

can I get you, cowboy?"

Her clean, flowery scent overpowered the club's stench of sweat and smoke. His body tensed like an over-tightened guitar string. He swallowed hard. "Do I look like a cowboy?"

She cocked the brow again, probably wondering if he needed alcohol to further diminish his brain function. "Not at all." Her voice strained over the beat of the bass. "The boots and denim shirt practically scream tax attorney."

"Come on, baby, it's a freaking desert in here," a drunk at another table hollered. "How long is it gonna take for your tight little buns to bring me a beer?"

"Keep your pants on, Lewis," she growled back. "Listen, the natives are restless, and the show's up there"—she pointed to Fiona dancing on the stage—"not here." She jerked a thumb back toward her chest. "Can I get you anything or not?"

"A real smile and a beer too much to ask?"

Apparently, he'd finally charmed her, because her full lips tilted toward a genuine smile, until some guy squeezed behind her and slid obscenely against her bottom.

An irritated scowl replaced any hint of a smile. She whipped around to face the man.

"I was only trying to get by, sweetheart. It's crowded in here."

She turned back and rolled her eyes. "I can get you the beer…"

The dancing and music ended abruptly. The house lights edged brighter, and Ty's eardrums vibrated in the absence of the thundering bass.

"…but the smile's gonna be harder to come by." She lowered her voice to a normal decibel. "House draft okay?"

He nodded and grinned, then watched her walk away. It was barely a conversation, only a couple of sentences to judge by, but she didn't seem like the brainless beauty he'd pegged her for.

Her narrow hips swayed away from him and toward the bar, but her head snapped toward a scuffle a few feet away. Ty watched her zero in on a couple of college-aged guys giving Dave, one of the regulars, a hard time. She tossed her tray onto a table and stalked toward the commotion.

Dave wasn't your typical, everyday regular. He wasn't your typical, everyday anything. He was special. There were a million bad things about living in a small town, but the way people pitched in and took care of one of their own was definitely one of the pluses.

Dave had special needs. He hadn't finished school and couldn't read, but he worked hard bussing tables and doing dishes at the local diner. At thirty-four years old, he still lived with his mom, talked with a fairly severe speech impediment, and couldn't drive.

Ironically, he always had a ride; some local usually took him anywhere he needed to go. Ty couldn't have counted the number of times he'd hauled Dave around. Usually, it was home, to the diner, or to Buck's. Dave had an affection for beer and "boobies," as he would often yell out when the girls were on stage.

"That's a lot of cash for a half-wit." College Guy continued to give Dave trouble. "How 'bout we take some of it off your hands for you?" He tossed Dave's wallet to a buddy.

The second jerk laughed and fingered through the wallet. "Look at this—Mr. Big Bucks. We could take your money and invest it for you."

Ty moved, with the intention of taking care of the idiots bothering Dave, but the sexy cocktail waitress beat him to the punch. He slid into a chair and waited, figuring it was only a matter of time before she needed help.

"You better invest in a bulletproof vest and a bodyguard if any of these locals hear about you taking anything from Dave," she suggested with an icy stare. "Give me the wallet and get the hell out. Don't come back until you've figured out how to impersonate a human."

The college kid puffed up his chest. "Blondie, you don't have nearly enough muscle to back up your big mouth. You need to poke your scrawny ass into someone else's business."

"You think so?" She stepped closer until they were nose to nose.

Ty wasn't sure whose jaw dropped more, his or the college guy's she had now backed up a step.

"You see Tiny and Tim over there leaning against the doors?" she asked.

Ty glanced in the direction in which she'd nodded. He smiled, doubting very seriously whether their names were actually Tiny and Tim, but he appreciated the joke. There was at least eight hundred pounds of flesh between the two hulking bouncers.

"When I turn on the water works and tell 'em you grabbed me in the bathroom hallway and had your hands all over me, they'll tear you apart just for the sport of it. I doubt a reattached dick ever functions the way it did the first time around."

Ty eased to a stand. He didn't know if the punk was stupid enough to actually touch her, but given the way she mouthed off, preparing to move quickly only seemed logical.

She fished a crumpled tissue out of a skintight pocket, started the fake sobbing, and turned toward the bouncers.

"Screw this," the punk called after her. "We're out of here. And don't worry, we won't be back to your skanky, redneck bar."

Ty studied her with intrigue and awe. He wasn't sure if he wanted to high five her or take her out back and shake some sense into her. Damn. Was she always like this? No sooner had the thought crossed his mind than she turned to Dave, rolled up a menu, and gently bopped him on top of his head.

"What did I tell you the other night about waving your wallet around?" she said. "Not everybody in here knows you or cares about you. You want someone to take your money? Or worse yet, hurt you and *then* take your money?"

"No," Dave answered, looking down and refusing to meet her eyes.

Her full lips curved into a frown that looked a lot like guilt. She closed her eyes, inhaled a deep breath, then gently pinched his chin and tilted his head up. "I'm sorry, Davy. I'm not trying to be mean, but you don't need any money in here. Buck runs a tab for you and settles up with your momma once a month, okay? I want you to put the wallet in your pocket and leave it there."

Dave put his arms around her waist. "Okay."

Actually, it sounded more like, "O-ay," but Ty understood the sentiment. She ruffled Dave's hair and stalked away.

Ty continued to watch her. So did half the guys in the place. That annoying little fact stirred an overwhelming urge to cover her up. A T-shirt, a jacket, a chastity belt—

hell, anything would've been an improvement. It was just a matter of time before one of the drunks tried something. Only an asshole like Buck would expect a woman to wear next to nothing in a place like this. Ty slid onto the stool he'd been using when she took his order.

She headed to the bar, filled her tray, and returned to deliver drinks, seemingly unfazed by the altercation.

"Six dollars, cowboy." She set the beer in front of Ty. "Oh, I'm sorry, that's right; you're not a cowboy. Six dollars, Mr. President."

A real smile curved her lips, and his chest tightened again. He attributed the rogue sensation to anger. Buck's lucky streak was still going strong; looked like he'd found another pretty victim to lure into a life of sex and drugs.

The Lewis character eased up behind her and slid a hand under her arm and around her waist. Then he slipped it up to her breast and squeezed.

Ty's final string of self-control snapped. He jumped up from his bar stool, but the waitress spun around and clocked Lewis with a right jab that would have made any boxer proud. By the look of the blood trickling out of Lewis's nose, she could hold her own. Then she stepped closer and pushed him hard in the chest.

"Holy crap, Lewis. If you put your goddamned hands on me one more time tonight, I swear to God, I'm gonna have Buck kick your sorry self out of here." She spun back around to Ty. "You need anything else?" No smiles this time, just irritation.

"I'm not judging," Ty said, "but I'd think a beautiful woman like you could make a lot more money doing something a little less…stressful." Okay, so maybe his tone did sound a little harsh and judgmental, but she clearly didn't belong at Buck's.

She glared, as if *arrogant ass* was etched across his forehead. "Really? Well, I'd think a cute guy like you could get a real date instead of getting his rocks off watching women strip. The world is full of mysteries."

The woman had a knack for stunning people into silence. Her sharp, lethal tongue was as dangerous as her fist. *Run away now*, his brain said. Unfortunately, his brain was outnumbered by his other body parts, so he stood there watching her take a deep breath to compose herself.

"I'm sorry," she said. "Really. I didn't mean that. It's just…Lewis is grating on my last nerve."

Ty dug for a ten and then sat on his bar stool. "No, *I'm* sorry. I didn't mean—"

Lewis grabbed the back of her bikini top and yanked hard. The straps snapped. Then he reared back in his stool and kicked the thick sole of his work boot fast and hard into her back.

She lurched forward, busting her head on a table and falling face first and topless onto the floor.

"Damn tease," Lewis hollered.

Ty lurched forward and plowed a fist into Lewis's jaw, knocking him backwards onto a table. Then he hauled Lewis up by his shirt but restrained himself from beating the drunken asshole unconscious. Instead, he shoved Lewis to the ground and twisted his arm behind his back.

Buck flew over like a lightning bolt.

Ty had never seen anyone with that much body mass move so quickly.

"Break it up; no fighting in here," Buck shouted.

"I'm not fighting, just taking down this idiot who attacked"—it dawned on him he didn't know her name—"your girl."

They both looked over at her. With blood pouring down her face, she struggled to sit up and cross her arms to cover herself. One of the other waitresses handed her a towel to catch the blood gushing from her forehead. She looked like she didn't know whether to put it on her head or cover her chest.

A crowd of customers formed around the commotion. The music continued to play, but the noise level dropped considerably. Everyone was too busy gawking at the naked, injured waitress to be loud. Ty looked up and realized all eyes were on her, which made him want to throttle every idiot looking in her direction.

He dropped his hold on Lewis and stripped off his button-down shirt. He kneeled beside her, guided her arms in, and tugged the shirt around her. Sucking in a sharp, involuntary gulp of air, he fastened the button directly over her chest.

Holy shit! No wonder every guy in the place was staring. Maybe somewhere there were breasts more beautiful than hers, but he'd certainly never seen any. Why he was so relieved to cover them, he had no idea.

"Lewis, get out and stay out." Buck hauled Lewis off the floor with one hand. "If I ever hear about you touching one of my girls again, in *or* out of my club, you won't live long enough to regret it. Boys…" Buck waved to Tiny and Tim, who caught Lewis when he stumbled halfway across the dance floor. Buck turned and stared at Ty.

Ty helped the bloodied waitress off the floor, but he

could feel Buck's eyes burning a hole through him.

"You the McGee boy? The cop over in Longdale?"

"Yes, sir, only I'm not a cop anymore. I ran into a little trouble and decided it wasn't quite the right fit for me. Now I'm doing PI work and personal security. Looks like you could add some brains to your muscle around here."

"Maybe, but I don't hire cops." Buck looked at one of the other waitresses. "Get Jordan cleaned up. Let me know if she needs stitches."

Two other girls brought more towels and shuffled her toward the back door.

Ty had to admit he was torn. It was the perfect opportunity to get his foot in the door with Buck. But something about the sexy waitress with the gash in her head wouldn't let go of him. He wasn't sure if anyone at Buck's had enough brains not to let her bleed to death on the back step. She might have even blacked out for a second or two, and blood still gushed from her head.

"Damn it," he muttered as the girls guided her out the door. Then he looked back at Buck. Whether to help a beautiful, injured woman or beg a mean, sweaty asshole for a job he didn't want, the choice should have been obvious. He was truly worried about his own sanity when he took a few steps in Buck's direction.

He walked up behind the human mammoth. "Buck."

Buck turned and squinted his cold, mean eyes.

"Sir, actually, I was serious about a job. I've been out of the cop business for a while now and could use some income. I know how to handle a weapon and take down a drunk like Lewis with one hand tied behind my back. I've heard there's been some trouble here, and I can help with that. If you're busy right now, we could set up a time to talk tomorrow."

Buck turned away as though he wasn't going to answer, but then threw his head around and grumbled over his shoulder, "Three o'clock. You better not waste my time, boy."

"No, sir, three o'clock tomorrow. I'll see you here."

Ty was pleased. He played that just right, and it took no more than thirty seconds. Now he was off to find a beautiful, bleeding waitress.

. . .

So much for having dreams. *Useful* dreams.

Hardly a night went by that didn't include some haunting vision while she slept. Since she'd been cursed her entire life with images of horrible, violent crimes, Jordan figured she should get a little peek at her own upcoming reality, a helpful warning when she needed one. But, no. Nada. Zilch. Not even a little whiff of impending doom.

"Jordan?"

She looked up. *Great.* The cowboy who'd scolded her for working at a strip club leaned against the frame of Buck's back door with a big, fat *I told you so* in his expression.

"You okay?" He moved closer, dipping his hands into his front pockets. "We never got around to full introductions. I'm Tyler McGee. I heard Buck call you Jordan."

She sat on top of the picnic table used for outdoor smoke breaks. The dripping blood from the gash in her head had mostly stopped, but she'd yet to get the trembling under control. Gingerly, she nodded.

As a rule, Jordan wasn't typically at a loss for words, but his intense stare frayed her nerves.

Apparently, he gave up on any meaningful response. Shaking his head, he turned and walked toward the parking lot.

Even injured, she found it difficult to take her eyes off his backside. Man, was he built. Like a heavily muscled upside down triangle. His jeans hung enticingly from his hips. Well-worn denim cradled an ass that was pure temptation. Her breathing hitched, and a rush of heat flared through her.

She exhaled slowly. What the hell caused that burst of insanity? The knock on her head must have triggered a sudden fascination with cowboy boots. Or maybe it was just the solid wall of muscle wearing them. Didn't matter—those kind of thoughts shouldn't even be a blip on the radar.

Closing her eyes eased the throbbing, so she rested her head in her hands and rubbed her temples. Just a few seconds of peace, and she could pull it together. Local backup was only a button push away, but she sure didn't want that kind of shit storm raining down. Explaining how she'd managed to get hurt less than a week into an investigation was not going to boost anyone's confidence that she had the mental clarity to close this case.

Plus there was a small technicality—she wasn't supposed to be working inside the club yet. A minor detail.

Even though Jordan worked for the St. Louis PD, she currently answered to FBI Special Agent, Ted Bahan. He was in charge of the multi-jurisdictional task force known as "Operation China White." He'd assigned her to apply for the job at Buck's and settle into her apartment, but nothing more. The team that would wire her and do the surveillance wouldn't arrive for more than a week.

So she'd applied at Buck's four days ago. Who knew

she'd be hired on the spot and start the same day? Failing to mention the small turn of events prickled her conscience. But Bahan doubting her ability to stay objective and finish a case she'd given countless hours to prickled even more.

Bahan claimed to be a friend, but he sure as hell hadn't hesitated to pull rank. A friend wouldn't insist on watching her like an errant second-grader. A friend would treat her like the experienced cop she was. She'd likely closed more undercover narcotics cases than any other detective in St. Louis, and frankly, the whole damn thing chapped her ass.

"I don't know if it's the bump on your head or the fact that you're barely dressed in forty-degree weather, but you're shaking."

She looked up. Cowboy had returned.

"Do you have some real clothes I can get for you?" Sounding annoyed, he slung a jacket around her shoulders and pulled it tight around her neck.

She shook her head.

His hands gripped the collar of the jacket, and he stepped close enough for her to feel the warmth radiating from his body. Working narcotics had honed her sense of smell. From the pungent aroma of a meth lab to the more subtle odor of marijuana use on breath or clothing, she could identify a scent almost as keenly as a canine.

Cowboy smelled like pine needles and rain.

Even earlier in Buck's, his clean, male scent had penetrated the chaos when he'd offered his shirt. But this second, stronger wave as he slung the jacket around her shoulders was almost like a drug. Obviously, her mental focus had taken a blow, but the buzz in her head ramped up a notch as he wrapped her in the warmth. Either the injury was worse than she thought, or he smelled intoxicating.

"Let me see what this looks like." He gently brushed her hair from her forehead and blotted the cut with a towel. Looking deep in thought, he shifted around, studying her head from different angles.

For the first time, she had a close-up view of him. Buck's was dark and smoky, but under the bright parking lot glare and the full moon, this man's face mesmerized her.

She was all about the eyes. Her whole life, she'd believed a person's eyes told the truth even when their words failed. His were a breathtaking metallic gray with the thickest lashes she'd ever seen. Hard to accept such stunning lashes ended up on a man.

Strong jaw, full lips, dark wavy hair just a tad too long. Definitely a total package. One a woman could easily lose herself in. Only by the time she realized she had, he appeared to realize it, too.

He smiled slowly and knowingly, as if he'd caught her with her hand in the cookie jar.

She was mortified. Her lungs tightened.

He broke the awkward silence to ask, "Headache?"

"Duh," she said.

"Nausea?"

"Every night I work here."

He pinched the bridge of his nose and ran a hand through his hair. "Damn, woman. Are you always this difficult? Any vision problems?"

"Completely blind." She closed her eyes and stretched her arms out in front of her to feel the air. Her hands bumped his chest.

"What color are my eyes?"

"Gray, okay? They're gray." Of course, she realized she hadn't opened her eyes yet. When she did, he smirked with blatant male satisfaction.

"You'll probably live," he said.

So she knew his eye color. Big deal. Any good cop would've picked up on that. Not that she wanted him to suspect she was a cop. Damn, she needed to get rid of this guy.

"Look, you've been really nice coming to my rescue and giving me your clothes. I'll make sure you get your shirt back, and you should take this." She handed him the jacket. "I'm good now."

He didn't acknowledge her words, just moved behind her and gripped the hem of the denim shirt he'd buttoned around her. "I'm going to take a look at your back, okay?" Apparently interpreting her stunned lack of response for a yes, he raised the material and gently skimmed a finger across her skin where Lewis had kicked her. "You've got a bruise starting here."

Heat radiated from the tender spot he touched, like a sip of brandy on a cold night. Great, that's all she needed right now. She edged away from his touch. "Really, you can go enjoy the show. I'm okay."

"I'm not here to watch the show, never was. You need stitches. And I'd feel better if someone looked at your back. Let's get you to the ER." He slipped his fingers under her arm.

"Hold on a minute, cowboy." She pushed his hand away. "I appreciate all you've done, but surely you don't think I'm gonna hop in a car with a guy I don't know, much less let him take me to God knows where, do you?"

"Well, you could sit here and bleed to death, if you'd

rather. And I hate to point out the obvious, but it doesn't look like judgment is your strongest asset."

"What the hell is that supposed to mean? I didn't do anything wrong. The guy kicked me when my back was turned."

He backed up a step and threw his hands up in surrender. "I know. I'm sorry."

He didn't *look* sorry. He looked...pig-headed and irritated.

"I only meant...you, working here. You're just, really... attractive. And all these guys are drunk." He slung his jacket around her again. "And that outfit doesn't leave a lot to the imagination."

He stuffed her arms in the coat and this time zipped it all the way up to her chin. "Plus, you're working for Arlo Buck. I think maybe you don't know what you've gotten yourself into."

"So, you think I need big, strong, handsome you to straighten me out?" Who the hell was he, and why on earth did he think she needed him to play protector? Another verbal lashing began to build, but the nausea and light-headedness returned with a vengeance.

"I'm fine. I am *not* going to a hospital. I *don't* need stitches, and I certainly don't need you to..." Even as she spoke, tunnel vision closed in, black and thick. She felt herself sway sideways off the picnic table. Just a moment before she hit gravel, strong arms closed around her.

Chapter Two

Jordan's mom slid the pan from the oven. The scents of sage and onion overwhelmed the tiny kitchen. Hot and steamy air dripped with the aroma of turkey, stuffing, and pumpkin pie.

Mom's special cheesecake sat on the countertop.

Jordan loved the holidays. Usually. But not today. She swiped the tears away with the back of her hands. "Something terrible is gonna happen, Mom. I don't know when, but I saw it in my dream."

Her mother turned and inhaled a deep, steadying breath, crossed the kitchen, and took Jordan's face in her hands. "And that's all it was, honey. Just a silly nightmare. You've got to stop this."

"I'm not crazy." Jordan stomped her foot. She needed to warn them. Needed to tell them he was coming. Why didn't anyone ever listen? Because she was only ten years old? "You act like you don't even hear me."

Her mom snapped. "Enough. I'm trying to get ready for

Thanksgiving. You and your sister promised to help, but now Katy's in her room crying because of what you told her. You've scared her half to death. I'm sorry you had a nightmare, but I swear to God, Jordan, one more word and you're grounded."

"One more stitch and she's all done. She should be coming around soon."

Jordan didn't recognize the voice.

Something squeezed her arm. A machine beeped. A warm hand touched hers.

Dad always held her hand.

Thanksgiving meant family movie night. "What movie are we watching tonight, princess?" Dad asked. "We've got A Christmas Story, It's a Wonderful Life, *and* Rudolph."

He crossed the bedroom and snuggled next to her when she silently shrugged. He brushed her hair back and tucked it behind her ear. "Your mom told me you had another dream. I guess it was a bad one?"

Jordan nodded.

"You want to tell me about it?"

This time she shook her head. If Mom heard her talk about the dream again, she'd get it for sure.

"Open your eyes, Jordan," a voice said. A pungent, antiseptic smell overtook the sage. She felt a touch on her shoulder. "Come on, open your eyes. Jordan? Jordan?"

"Jordan, open your eyes," Dad said. "I know you're tired, but A Christmas Story *is starting."*

She was tired and couldn't care less about the stupid movie. She closed her eyes, needing to rest, just for a little while.

Violent pounding slammed against the front door. Recognizing the sound, Jordan bolted upright. She grabbed for her dad's arm. Too late. He was already sprinting from the bedroom.

Screaming. Cursing. The front door burst open, and a blast of exploding wood vibrated through the tiny house.

She should have told Dad everything. Now it was too late to save him. To save them all.

She knew what was next. Because she'd seen it just the night before.

In her dream.

The blood pressure machine sounded two shrill beeps.

A hand touched her arm. Then she heard a man's voice.

"Jordan. Jordan, wake up."

She clawed her way back to consciousness, opened her eyes. Fluorescent lights blinded her, and the room whirled like one of those sickening, spinning carnival rides. Squeezing her eyes tight, she fought the urge to throw up.

Fingers moved over her hair and stroked her cheek. "Shh, it's okay. You're okay. A little knock on the head, that's all." The deep rasp of the voice, silky and sure, calmed her like a warm blanket. Comfort spread in all directions.

Briefly, an image of her father smoothing back her hair and holding her after a nightmare centered in her mind. He'd been her hero at one time, quick and skillful at easing her fears. Too bad he hadn't been nearly as noble when it came to the rest of his life. But she'd moved past her daddy issues long ago. Plus, the son of a bitch was dead. So who the hell was stroking her cheek?

She pushed away the hand touching her. The last thing she needed was someone's pathetic attempt at comfort. Especially when she'd been reliving *that* night again. The night daddy dearest had made them all pay for his mistakes.

Keeping her eyes squeezed tight, she drew in a few deep breaths. Sometimes a little air could bridge the gap between the dreams and reality. After a few seconds, she remembered where she was and what was going on. She had a vague recollection of doctors, a scan, stitches.

Her father could always smooth away all the rough edges after a dream. But he was gone. Dead.

So who was here with her?

"The nurse should be here in a minute."

Finally, she dared to open her eyes. It was the guy from Buck's. The one she'd dubbed "cowboy." The last thing she needed was for him to see the aftereffects of a dream, particularly that dream. Thank God she woke before the worst of it.

She lightly rubbed the bandage on her head.

"Seven stitches," he said. "Could've been worse. After they scanned your head and knew everything was okay, they gave you a little something to take the edge off the back pain. It must have made you tired." He smoothed his thumb over the back of her hand.

It might have been an innocent gesture, but it didn't feel that way. Every sensation dulled except where their skin touched. Like a shock from a live wire, a current buzzed from his body into hers. She inhaled sharply and looked at him.

His gaze held her captive.

For several long, mesmerizing moments, she floundered, trapped in his cool, steel-colored stare. If she hadn't been caught in the dregs of the pain medicine, she'd have had the good sense to look away. When noise drifted in from the hall, she jerked her hand back as if she had been scalded.

The odd jolt intensified the thump in her head, and it took a few seconds for speech to return. "I'm sorry. I don't remember your name."

But she very clearly remembered the sinful blue jeans and the dark hair that curled just over his collar. The way his thick chest filled out a plain, white tee would forever be seared in her mind. But his name...his name escaped her.

"I'm Tyler McGee. Everyone calls me Ty. And as far as the nurses are concerned, I'm your big brother."

"I don't have a brother."

He shrugged and smiled. "You do now."

She eyed him from top to bottom and back up again, deciding it was most likely the killer smile, rather than the lie, that had gained him access to her room.

His grin grew wider. He looked amused at her thorough inspection.

Why *had* she studied him as though he was the main course at dinner? Her cheeks flushed hot. "Well, Ty, thanks for everything, but I can manage from here."

Leaning against a countertop, he folded his arms. "Yeah, you're in great shape. You plan on jogging home with your head injury or just taking it slow and hitchhiking?"

Ah, yes. Now she remembered. He was truly as handsome as the devil but also as cocky. He'd probably only said about ten sentences before she passed out, but if her memory was coming back accurately, most of them were condescending.

"I'll call a cab," she snapped.

He chuckled. "In Titus? Sweetheart, where are you from? It sure isn't around here."

He strode to the bed then leaned in close as though he was letting her in on a dangerous secret. "In case you haven't noticed, Titus isn't exactly a thriving metropolis. We don't have taxi service or buses. The closest thing to public transportation is Dan the Scooter Man. He makes a fortune driving people home from the bars. You want his number?"

The laughter and amusement in his ridiculously beautiful eyes could've been contagious, except he was laughing at her. "I'd prefer Dan's scooter over being driven home by someone who thinks I'm an idiot. It's your fault I'm here anyway. Some things are a little foggy, but I seem to remember saying no hospitals."

"You scared the hell out of me." Frustration jumped in his voice. "You passed out behind Buck's. What did you want me to do with you? Leave you under the picnic table?"

He had a point. Didn't mean she had to like it. "I'll call Buck; he's been really nice to me. He'll send someone, so you can go."

"Maybe you'll get lucky, and Lewis will be available." He was quick with the comeback, but all his amusement had faded. Irritation and, if she wasn't mistaken, a bit of anger swept across his handsome face. He leaned against the edge of her bed and picked up her hand again.

She was prepared this time. Just because the man had the eyes of a god did *not* mean Jordan Delany would get stupid.

He held on tight when she attempted to jerk away and silenced her with one finger on her lips.

"Jordan," he said, apology unmistakable in his voice, "I was only yanking your chain, honey. But I'm sorry, because I know you don't feel well. I'll drive you. You wouldn't rather have a stranger from the bar take you home instead of me, would you?"

She raised an eyebrow. "I hate to point out the obvious, cowboy, but you *are* a stranger from the bar."

"But I'm the stranger who brought you to a hospital when you were completely at my mercy. I could've taken you to some remote cabin and chopped you into little pieces. Don't I get any points for not doing that?"

The man's smile just killed her.

"Look, I'm here. I'm not doing anything else. You may not believe me, but I used to be a cop over in Longdale. I'll take you home unless you're truly worried about me being some kind of axe-carrying murderer. If that's the case, I'll call one of my buddies, a policeman, to give you a ride home."

"You were a cop?" Well now, wasn't that interesting? Maybe she'd let Mr. Tall, Dark, and Arrogant take her home after all. An ex-cop probably had several solid nuggets of information tucked away about the good people of Titus. Tyler McGee could be a connection worth exploring.

A nurse walked into the room. "Miss Brooks, Dr. Yew would like to admit you for observation. Your wound was fairly minor and shouldn't cause any problems, but we never take chances with head injuries."

Great. A hospital admission meant paperwork and explanation. It was bad enough being brought to the ER. What kind of idiot got knocked in the head like this? She'd held her own with murderers, drug traffickers, thieves, and addicts, but drunk Lewis had smoked her. It was embarrassing.

She could blow off stitches, but a stint in the hospital would have to be reported. "Well, I'm feeling much better, so I think I'll just get dressed and go home."

"If you do, it'll be against medical advice," the nurse told her. "You'll need someone with you for twenty-four hours, at least."

"Oh, my brother can do that." She smiled at Ty. "Right, big brother?"

The smugness drained from his face, and his eyes opened wide. "Ah...well...Is she going to be okay? What do I need to—"

"I'm fine." She had to stop him before anything really stupid rolled out of his mouth. Apparently, he wasn't a crazed killer. Honestly, the man couldn't even lie himself out of a hospital room. "You don't need to do anything." She turned to the nurse. "Please get my paperwork, so I can leave."

The nurse looked back and forth between them, then turned and left.

Jordan tugged off the blood pressure cuff and tossed back the blanket. "Could you turn around? I'm in a hospital gown here."

"Turn around? You've got to be kidding me. That's the most clothes I've seen you in."

She glared.

"All right, all right." He turned away.

"You suck at lying." The ground shifted side to side as she slid to her feet. She grabbed the bed's side rail to keep from falling.

"Some women might consider that a good thing." He peeked over his shoulder and whipped around, steadying her with his hands on her hips. "Are you kidding me? Damn, woman, you ever been tested for a balance problem? Inner ear issues, maybe?"

"Shut up, cowboy," she snapped. "It's been a hell of a

night."

"Tell me about it." He chuckled. "*You* certainly didn't have any problems ripping off a convincing lie." His hold relaxed, but his fingers lingered on her hips. "Seems to me like you've had a lot of practice at it."

...

The success or failure of undercover work rested solely on a cop's ability to become someone else, to completely morph into an alien persona. And sometimes, particularly in a small town like Titus, the living arrangements could prove as tricky as the new identity. Everything had to fit.

As such, Jordan's driver's license now read Jordan Brooks rather than Jordan Delany.

Her cover was a college student waiting tables at Buck's. Of course, college students didn't typically own homes or drive expensive cars. She had no problem with the four-year-old Accord. She also didn't care that her wardrobe had been overhauled for a younger, sexier appearance. And bravely, she'd endured the sting of the piercing in her navel.

What had come as a shock was the apartment. Turned out that furnished living arrangements—available in Titus and conducive to her cover—weren't all that plentiful. The result was an odd little place in a small complex that leaned toward the lower end of the income spectrum. The place wasn't fancy, but it worked.

"You still with me?" Ty asked, pulling into her parking lot. "You look tired."

"Yeah." Jordan forced a smile. She was tired, but rest wasn't going to come easy tonight. Her back had been hurting, and the hospital had offered her a mild pain reliever. She should have known better than to take it; even a simple aspirin tended to screw with her dreams. And true to form, she hadn't even made it out of the hospital before the ugliness began. "Ty, thanks for the ride and the trip to the ER and the shirt. If I see you in Buck's, your next couple of drinks will be on me. Good night."

She opened the door to make a clean getaway.

He turned the engine off and was on her side of the truck, easing her out, before she had a chance to protest.

"Look, I appreciate everything, including letting me stop by Buck's to get my purse and keys. You've been more than generous, but I've got it from here. Good night."

There. That should settle it. Even Mr. Arrogant couldn't have missed *that* subtle goodbye. Or so she thought. Damned if he didn't cuff a hand around her arm as though she'd melt to the ground at any moment.

She stopped at the flight of stairs that led to her apartment on the second floor. Was it possible that the number of steps had doubled since that morning?

Before her brain could process the move, Ty swept her up.

"Put your arms around my neck."

He left her no choice but to grab hold. With her head so close to his chest and her arms locked around him, it was impossible not to breathe him in. God, he smelled good. A shocking tightening of muscles clenched low in her stomach.

She trembled as he put her down at the top of the stairs.

"Ty, really, I know I owe you big for all you've done"— she put her key in the deadbolt, but didn't turn it—"but you need to go."

He laid his hand on top of hers and twisted the key, then

pushed the door open and stepped inside. "You're gonna owe me bigger by tomorrow. If I can't leave you alone for twenty-four hours, you better have cable. Or some other way to keep me entertained."

Jordan heard the suggestive grin in his voice. She flipped on the lights.

After another five or six steps inside the door, he stopped abruptly, as if he'd hit an invisible brick wall. He looked around the one-bedroom apartment in much the same way she had when she first stepped inside.

A ninety-two-year-old woman had passed away a few weeks earlier. The apartment manager offered the place fully furnished, claiming the older woman's family didn't want her personal items. It didn't take long for Jordan to figure out why. The apartment's color scheme was avocado green and burnt orange. The colors had apparently been popular decades ago, and this place had never progressed with the times.

The television looked like an antique. So did the mattress and the giant, rust-colored couch. But at least the couch was comfortable—if you could get past the smell of Pine-Sol and pot roast. Despite the mildly strange aroma, she slept on it most nights to avoid the lumps and broken springs of the mattress.

The old woman had also collected roosters. Big roosters. Little roosters. Rooster clocks. Rooster canisters. Rooster bookends. Rooster coasters.

Jordan had died and gone to rooster hell.

To steady herself, she put a hand against a wall and kicked off her shoes. She shrugged out of the jacket he'd put around her. "You're probably a nice guy, and I get that you feel some sort of misguided responsibility for bringing me home, but I'm not comfortable having you stay here. I just need to rest."

Turning toward him, she caught his gaze traveling up her body. His intense stare scorched her as effectively as a branding iron. From her ankles to her eyes, her skin flushed hot.

For several long heartbeats, silent heat radiated between them. It was entirely possible that her breathing had stopped altogether. Just when she thought her legs might give out, he whipped his head in the opposite direction, turning his interest to a rooster cuckoo clock hanging on the wall.

He scratched his forehead and turned back to her. The sexy mischief in his eyes made her stomach tumble again. "Look, the nurse said someone needs to be here to check on you. I know you're uncomfortable having a man you don't know well in your...um...*place*."

He poked his tongue at his cheek, no doubt trying to control his amusement as he took in the crappy furnishings. "But I'm not comfortable being the guy who took you to the ER and ignored very specific instructions not to leave you alone."

The jerk was all but laughing at her, or at least her roosters. It would never have been the kind of place featured in *Better Homes and Gardens*, but it was spotless and functional. *Mostly*. He didn't need to be rude.

"I hate to break it to you, cowboy, but you staying here was never in the cards. I only told the nurse that so she wouldn't give me any trouble about leaving the hospital."

"You put it in the cards when you said I'd take care of you. If something happens, I'm responsible. It'll take someone in town about two minutes to finger me as the guy who took you home. If you have a girlfriend you can call to come over, then I'll go." He plopped down on her couch. "Otherwise, I'm staying."

Man, she wanted to stick a pin in his over-inflated ego. *No*, she didn't have a girlfriend to call, nor did she want one while she was on a job. Bahan was enough of a pain in the ass.

"Fine," she said. "Suit yourself. But if you're staying"—she gestured to the kitchen—"I need coffee."

Half an hour later, they sat on opposite ends of the sofa, sipping coffee, but Ty's voice had lost most of the good-natured charm it held earlier. Perfect. With exhaustion closing in on both of them despite the caffeine, it wouldn't be long until she convinced him to leave.

"You've been really nice, but I'm fine. Go home and get some rest. Don't you have to work or something?"

He exhaled. "This is not the most flattering admission, but I'm in between careers right now. When I was a cop in Longdale, my chief and I didn't see eye to eye. Long story, but I'm moving on."

She glanced at him. Mr. Controlling had walked out on a police career with no backup plan? Must've been one hell of a fight with his chief. Or he was lying. She let the silence hang between them. When he didn't speak, she said, "Sorry. I know it can be frustrating, especially financially, being unemployed."

"Well, I'm good there. My whole family lives in town, so I'm not planning on living out of a cardboard box anytime soon." He grinned, but his finger tapped nervously on the arm of the sofa. "I'll always have a roof over my head. But to answer your question, I don't have anywhere to be. How 'bout you? What do you do when you're not serving drinks?"

"I'm a business student at Lincoln U in Cooper."

"A student?" He smiled and shook his head. "I hadn't pictured you the number-crunching type."

No kidding. She couldn't picture it, either. Eager to ignore his insight, she said, "So, do you hang out at Buck's much?"

"Not really. It wouldn't be my first choice of places to hang out." He fidgeted and turned to face her.

Something was off; his eyes wouldn't quite meet hers. He was working up the nerve to say something, she'd lay money on it.

His jaw clenched. He raked a hand back through his hair, and his eyes went flat. "I realize you don't know me well, but I've lived in this town my whole life, and…well… you need to reconsider working at Buck's. Especially after last night. It's not a good place for a woman like you."

Geez, she must have been playing the part well, because he thought she was an idiot. "Ty, despite what happened, I can take care of myself. I'm not helpless. It's a fine place for a woman like me."

"It's not. You need to get the hell out, the sooner, the better."

She tilted her head and studied him. No gentle persuasion in his voice. No polite suggestion, just anger. Hmm. Interesting. And then it hit her.

He knew something.

The devastatingly handsome guy who almost passed for caring and noble fucking *knew* something.

It was those eyes that had slipped right under her radar.

She'd been trying to figure out why he sent her composure into a tailspin, but now all the red flags made sense. He was a cop—ex-cop—who'd worked for the Longdale Police Department and hung at Buck's. The FBI suspected the local cops were in league with Buck. Could Tyler McGee be one of Buck's protectors?

Her chest ached at the thought of him involved with a drug ring. He'd been so kind, so caring, but she had to push. "Okay, I'll bite." She sat her coffee mug down and shifted to face him. "Exactly what kind of girl do you think I am?"

"Damn it." He rubbed the back of his neck.

Frustrated. Nervous. Angry. It was all there. How the hell had she missed it?

"The people who hang out and work at Buck's? Let's just say it's a rough crowd." He stood and started pacing her tiny apartment. "Have you taken a good look around there? The place is nothing but trouble."

"Why? Because the women strip? Since I wear a bikini top, I must have asked for what happened tonight?"

"I'm a man, Jordan. I've got no problem seeing a beautiful woman wearing a bikini top and waiting tables. Or dancing, for that matter. But surely you're not naive enough to think Buck's control ends when your shift does."

What did this guy know? He was trying to warn her about something. His anger was palpable; she could feel it as sharply as the pain radiating through her back.

"Is that how you want everyone in town to see you? As one of"—he made quote signs in the air—"Buck's girls?"

"I haven't been there long, but most of"—she imitated his finger quotes—"Buck's girls are pretty nice women. Some maybe have a few problems, but that doesn't mean they're bad people."

"I'm not saying they're bad people," he corrected. "I'm saying Buck has sucked them in. One way or another, he owns them like property. That's what he does. First, he pretends to be a friend. Gives them money, drugs, anything that will indebt them to him. Then the threats come."

She made a conscious effort to play dumb. "Well, I don't use drugs, and I haven't borrowed any money from him, so I shouldn't have a problem. I like it at Buck's. School can be expensive. I make great tips, especially on weekend nights."

"Seriously? You've got to be kidding me. The money's good enough to risk your safety? What do you think would've happened if Lewis grabbed you on the way to your car?"

Jordan stood and faced him. "I'd have protected myself. The way I've always done."

"Yeah, right," he said. "Like you did tonight? Naked and bleeding, face down on a strip club floor. Wake up, Jordan. Do you need me to draw you a picture of the danger inside that place?"

"You know, not everyone gets to quit their job and run home to Mommy and Daddy when things get rough."

"Running home would be a lot better choice than the one you've made. Do your parents live around here? Do they have any idea what you're doing to earn money?"

She drew back at the mention of her family. He'd struck the one nerve, even after all these years, that continued to be raw.

"My parents are dead. They've been dead for twenty years. So guess what? Nobody gets to tell me what I can do or where I can work. Least of all, you."

He opened his mouth but obviously struggled with what

to say. After a long, awkward moment, he said, "I'm sorry. How did it happen?"

She beat down the memories and faked composure. "Car crash." She never wavered on the lie, never even blinked. But their conversation had turned in a direction that had become much too personal.

He stepped close and reached out his hand.

She moved back, throwing her own hands up to stop him. "My choices are all mine." The last thing she needed was to feel the pity roll off of him when he touched her.

He dropped his arm but spoke softly. "I just want you to realize there are better choices out there."

"I just want you to realize not everybody has the golden-boy, small-town upbringing you seem to have had. Not everybody has the safety net of family."

"If this is about money, there are a few other places in town that I could check into—"

"Stop. You've only known me a few hours. I don't need you to fix me. But you were right about one thing: I do need to rest. And you need to leave. Please lock the door on your way out."

She hugged her arms close against her body and headed to the bedroom before her hard-won composure slipped, and the sting in her eyes betrayed her.

Shit! She'd lost it. She'd never lost it on the job. Never. It was the headache and exhaustion and back pain that gave her such a stupid, irrational reaction.

The front door slammed. She jumped, but a huge wave of relief rolled through her.

Tomorrow she'd track him down and get back in his good graces. She could do that, right? Find him, talk to him.

Figure out if he was connected to Buck in any way.

But tonight, all that she wanted was a few hours of sleep. "Screw it," she murmured as she grabbed the aspirin bottle. She'd taken meds at the hospital, which meant her dreams were already likely to turn ugly. Might as well curb the pain if she was doomed anyway. And who knows, maybe she'd get lucky and just this once, there'd be no dreams.

...

A huge party. Hundreds of kids. Graduation decorations everywhere.

A beautiful girl twirls like a ballerina in the center of the room. Maybe fifteen or sixteen years old, with perhaps the longest, darkest hair in the world. Her smile glows almost as bright as her eyes.

She hasn't graduated yet — not old enough — but some of her friends are graduating. A night filled with dancing and laughing and alcohol. A handsome guy in a ball cap hands her a beer. She laughs and bats her eyes at him, then flips her long, silken mane over her shoulder.

She walks past a group of boys, notices some are smoking. Others snort something through a small, clear straw.

The girl looks at the clock when it strikes midnight. She hugs a few friends and heads toward home.

Across the road.

Through the cornfield.

Up the stairs.

Her baby blue bedroom struggles between little girl and young lady. Dolls and teddy bears on the bed, but bras and panties litter the floor. Pennants hang on the wall with a cheerleading picture underneath them.

She smiles into the mirror, as if recognizing how perfect life is. Young enough to be a child. Old enough to drive a car.

Snuggled in bed, she barely hears the faint pinging at her window. Brushing the curtain back, she sees him: Mr. Handsome and his irresistible smile.

He must have followed her home. Now he stands in the shadows of moonlight and motions for her to come down.

She glances at the clock, then sneaks out to talk to him.

He pushes her on the wooden plank swing tied to the giant old oak tree behind her house. She sails through the air as if it's her favorite spot in the world, as though swinging under the stars makes her feel like an angel.

He kisses her gently, hands her a beer.

She winces at the taste.

He laughs and calls her a lightweight, so she drinks.

Minutes pass, and she can no longer balance on the swing. Her feet drag through the grass, and her head falls back.

Like a spider snaring a moth in its web, he catches her as she slumps toward the ground.

Struggling to wake up, she opens her eyes. She's in a car. A back seat. With the boy from the party. Nothing but trees and woods surround them. So dark, even the moon has lost her.

Her arms and legs no longer move, but he shifts her around, tears at her clothes, and rams himself inside her innocent, young body.

"My daddy will kill you." She tries to scream, but the words are hollow and weak. Regaining some muscle control, she claws at the hands clenched around her neck. His ear grazes her lips, and she bites him. Hard enough to draw blood.

Almost over before it began, the high is wearing thin, and he has to hit her to quiet her moans. Once, twice, the third time he succeeds. In the silence, he twists and turns to pull up his pants, but an unused condom falls to the floorboard.

"Oh, shit." Blood from his ear drips on her chest. "Shit. Shit. Shit." He uses his shirt to soak up the blood.

"It's not going to matter now," the girl whispers. "You'll pay. I know who you are. I'll always remember what you did."

He's the one crying as he pulls her out of the car and drags her behind the trees. "I'm so fucking sorry, but you left me no choice." Then he chokes the last bit of breath out of her.

Chapter Three

Ty tried to walk away from Jordan and leave the whole damn mess behind. He even stood cursing in the hallway for a few seconds before walking back inside and slamming the door.

Lord knew he had his own objectives, and babysitting the puzzle in the next room wasn't on his to-do list. He even tried telling himself he stayed because of the orders from the nurse. But the truth was, in spite of her being a pain in the ass, he liked her.

Actually, *like* was probably too tame a word to describe the live wire of attraction that buzzed between them. She certainly stirred something he hadn't felt in a long time. Not this strongly anyway. He was still on the fence about whether it was blinding insanity or just bone-deep lust.

Probably lust. It had been months since he'd felt anything but a thirst for revenge. It figured that his body would pick now to spring to life.

Jordan certainly wasn't the only eye-catching blonde

who'd crossed his path. In fact—he looked around her weird, little apartment—he had no idea how she'd burrowed so deep under his skin in only a matter of hours. She had a maddening stubborn streak, a tongue she wielded like a well-aimed sword, and possibly the worst taste in decorating he'd ever seen.

So why the hell couldn't he leave her alone?

Probably because he knew all too well what dangers lurked inside Buck's.

Plopping down on her sofa, he slipped the small ring from his pocket and hooked it on the tip of his pinky. He twisted it around and around as light arced off the shiny metal. The ring never failed to remind him of what could be lost when a whole town chose to bury its head in the sand. Even he had ignored the danger lurking right under his nose.

Never again.

He couldn't change the past, but he'd change Arlo Buck's future if it killed him. First, though, he was getting Jordan out of the nightclub. Even if nothing transpired between them, he'd be damned if Buck was going to suck her into his seedy world.

He leaned back on the old, musty couch. It was surprisingly comfortable in spite of how ugly the damn thing was. Resting his eyes, he started to doze. It couldn't have been longer than an hour before he was startled awake.

Jerking upright, he focused on the sounds in the building.

A door slammed. A car rumbled through the parking lot. Nothing unusual.

Then…moaning. Crying. Something crashing to the floor. Those sounds were coming from Jordan's bedroom.

He sprinted to her door and opened it. In the shadows, he saw her huddled in a corner of the bed. He crossed to her nightstand and turned on the bedside lamp.

Her cheeks glowed bright red. A sheen of sweat covered her face and dampened her hair. He bent to feel her cheek for fever. As soon as he touched her, she began to thrash, tossing side to side, crying, tearing at the sheets, clawing at her throat as if she were choking.

He grabbed her hands to pull them from her neck.

A shrill scream tore from her throat. Jerking free, she swung a fist that connected with his cheek.

Startled, he pulled back but noticed her eyes were still closed. "Jordan. Jordan, wake up." Was it the head injury? Maybe she needed an ambulance.

"Jordan," he said louder, grabbing her wrists again. He pinned her arms against the bed to keep her from hurting herself. "Jordan, stop it. Wake up."

Her eyes sprang open, but the blank, empty stare and motionless body disturbed him more than the fighting. She looked terrified, as if she had no idea where she was.

He said her name, soft enough to soothe but forceful enough to bring her back.

She took a couple of sharp breaths, then struggled against his grip. Twisting her head to look at her restrained hands, she screamed, "What are you doing? Don't touch me, let go. Let me go!"

He released her, and she shot out of bed, but her legs folded underneath her. She dropped to the floor, gagged, then clamped a hand over her mouth.

"Jesus. Fuck. I'm calling an ambulance." Ty hopped up, dashing into the next room searching for his phone. His hands shook. Sweat slid down his temple. "Damn it." He couldn't find his phone.

"Ty, no. Stop. No ambulance. I'm okay."

The words came from her bedroom and were barely audible, but he heard them, and they stopped him dead. It was the first fully coherent thing she'd said. He sucked in some air and walked back into her room.

She was silent now, the only noise was his breath heaving in and out. "What the hell was that?"

She didn't answer.

He crouched beside her. "Can you move? Can you stand?"

She nodded but then slumped back against the bed and closed her eyes. She looked like a broken doll. Tears streaked her cheeks, and blood oozed from the scratches on her neck. A good portion of her hair had been wrestled from its ponytail. Her teeth chattered, and what began as slight shivering quickly morphed into a full-body tremor.

He couldn't stand to leave her on the floor any longer. He slipped one arm under her legs and the other behind her back. In one quick swoop, he lifted her and then set her gently on the bed.

Her eyes, glassy and unfocused, stared straight through him.

"Jordan, look at me." He laid a hand against her cheek and eased her face toward him. "Look. At. Me."

• • •

Jordan clenched her jaw, attempting to control the way her teeth were knocking together. She ordered herself to choke down the nausea and think through the dream. A few moments of clarity started to fuse into meaning.

It was a new dream. A new victim.

God, she hated when the dead invaded her dreams with their cryptic messages. Just once, couldn't the vision be straightforward instead of hazy and incomplete?

The beautiful girl had been raped and murdered, that much was clear. But who was she? And who was the boy?

"Jordan, is it your head? Are you all right?"

Ty said something. She replied with an automatic nod, though she wasn't entirely sure what he'd asked. The girl's face, she would never forget—classically beautiful, long dark hair, soft eyes. But the boy appeared out of focus. Damn it, she couldn't remember the boy. Not even his height or hair color.

"Jordan." Ty pulled a blanket around her shoulders and squeezed. "Talk to me." He reached for the cordless phone by her pillow and clicked it on.

The dial tone drew her back to the moment. Grabbing the phone from him, she clicked it off. "C-c-cold. I'm just so, so cold." She pulled her arm into the cocoon of the blanket. "But I don't need an ambulance. I told you that."

It wasn't unusual for the visions to hold on for several minutes after she woke, but tonight she wasn't alone. She glared at Ty. "You were supposed to leave. Why didn't you leave?"

He stood and paced the room. A humorless laugh surged from his throat. "Gee, I don't know. I thought maybe you'd wake up feeling kind of rough. Just not *that* rough. Damn."

He turned toward her, too many questions in his eyes. She'd never be able to field them all. The smug tough guy who'd pushed his way into her apartment and raked her over the coals for working at Buck's looked like he'd just discovered the Grim Reaper in the room with them. "I'm sorry," she said. "I had a bad dream. I ju—"

"Okay. It's…okay." He drew his hand across his face, pausing to rub his eyes. "I've had kind of a strange night myself. And I've had bad dreams, too. A lot of them lately. But that was no bad dream. I thought you were having a seizure."

He continued to pace, probably freaked out by what he'd just witnessed.

She understood how scary the dreams could be, but tonight she'd managed a new low. She'd allowed someone else to be affected. He had bright red spots on his cheek and scratches on his chin. Scratches she knew were her fault.

"If you're not going to let me call an ambulance," he said, "I at least want to take you back to the hospital to be checked out. You need another brain scan. Maybe you're injured more than they thought."

She couldn't control the slight grin. He thought she had brain damage. Maybe she did. But if so, it had started about twenty years ago, not last night with Lewis's boot. And she sure wasn't getting another "brain scan."

"Can you come here and sit down for a minute? You're making my headache worse, pacing like that."

He let out a long sigh, walked to the bed, and eased down next to her. "Are you warming up? You were shaking like you were freezing to death." He ran his hands up and down her arms.

Her breath hitched, and her gaze locked on his. He pulled his hands back, as if the impact of the connection startled him, too. She wasn't sure if chemistry was the right word, but something foreign, and not altogether unpleasant, crackled in the air when they touched.

Oddly compelled to test the theory, Jordan reached out and ran a finger over the scratches on his chin. "I'm sorry, I hurt you."

He continued to hold her in that dangerous gaze, and when she pulled her hand away, he swallowed. Hard.

Definite chemistry.

He offered a thin smile. "You almost gave me a heart attack; my blood pressure was probably high enough for me to stroke out. I thought you were dying. Probably took ten years off my life, and you're sorry you scratched me?"

He was attempting to lighten the mood. But his humor only made her throat swell and her eyes burn. She'd put him through hell, and he was still being sweet.

"Well, then, I'm sorry for the stroke and heart attack, too," she teased, managing to yank a knot in her unraveling emotions. "I thought you left, and I took something for the pain. The doctor at the hospital said it would help if my back started hurting again, but I should have known better. I have bad reactions to most drugs, even the mildest ones. They help with the aches but also give me weird nightmares. Usually, I don't even take aspirin, but tonight I thought it might help. Guess it backfired."

"You think?" He lifted his hand to her face and tucked a strand of hair behind her ear. "Okay then, no more drugs for you. Trust me when I say you won't even get a baby aspirin out of me."

He let his knuckles fall against her cheek, and the zing of chemistry returned. Then the pad of his thumb smoothed across her bottom lip and stalled there. Along with his gaze.

There was no escaping the fact that he was contemplating

kissing her. And she was seriously contemplating letting him. The invitation must have shown in her eyes, because he leaned close enough that his warm breath teased her lips. Then his mouth brushed hers in a whisper of a kiss.

Her chest tightened. Her stomach tumbled. She laid a hand on his chest and felt the gallop of his heart beneath her fingertips. His kiss was such a soft, soft touch, but it unleashed a flood of unbearably intense sensations.

One spiraling emotion ebbed into another. Her hand slid into his hair, tangled in the thick, dark waves, and pulled him closer.

God, she wanted to taste him.

Not just his lips, but the corded strength of his neck, the solid lines of his chest. He smelled good enough to eat. Did he taste that way, too? She eased her tongue into the heat of his mouth.

A hoarse growl erupted from him.

He tasted her, savored her as though she was a last meal. Long, demanding stokes of his tongue against hers left her boneless and nearly as off balance as the dream. His muscles tensed as the kiss spun further and further out of control. Finally, he wove his fingers into her hair and tore his lips away. "I think you need to sleep now, baby. You're tired."

That's when she realized she'd crossed about ten lines too many. She'd connected with Ty. Not physically, but mentally. Not in the way of a lover's touch, but in the way a voyeur would sneak into a mind and steal the most private thoughts. She felt the powerful forces raging through him. Lust. Desire. Need. All of it pushing against a crumbling wall of decency.

Thank God he had more restraint than she did. She was

terrified to think she might have said yes to anything when he kissed her like that. Embarrassment flamed in her cheeks.

A few deep, calming breaths helped put the barriers back in place. Her guarded instincts not only surged back but shifted into overdrive. *Danger* flashed in her mind like a warning sign at a construction site. He could be working for Buck. Or more probable—and more frightening—he could be a good man with the innate ability to scale all her carefully placed walls. Neither option was good.

She still had questions, but that questioning clearly wasn't going to happen tonight. "You've been amazingly kind, but I think it would be smart if you left now."

He pulled her against his chest and leaned back against the pillows. "You can't keep me up all night and then kick me out when I'm too tired to drive. Besides, my brother's the smart one. I have to get by on my looks."

It was a huge mistake, but she allowed herself to be pulled into the comfort of his arms. The danger sign flashed neon now. Despite the sleepy calm washing through her, her mind fought for the right words to make him leave.

"Stop thinking everything to death," he said, as if reading her thoughts. He kissed the top of her head. "Go to sleep, babe. It's been a bad night, but it'll be better after you rest."

No one but her father had ever held her after a dream. Since his death, nobody had ever put their arms around her just for the sake of soothing. Did Ty realize he was giving her the one thing she'd never had in her entire adult life? For that alone, he could have taken whatever he wanted from her.

The danger sign blazed once again. Only this time, Jordan didn't think it had anything to do with the case.

. . .

When Ty woke, his arm was numb. Jordan's head still rested on his shoulder, and she'd curled against him like a cat nestled into a warm blanket. Everything inside him wanted to melt closer to her, touch her, stroke her. He suppressed a groan when he checked the time. If he didn't get up, he'd be late. Needing a shower and fresh clothes, he slipped out of the bed and away from her warm body.

It had taken every ounce of willpower he possessed not to let the night progress beyond a kiss, but he hadn't wanted to take advantage of the state she was in—scared from the nightmare, hurting from her injury, confused from the pain medicine. There would be a first time between them; he'd known it the second their lips met, from the moment she'd vibrated under his kiss. Hell, from the moment he'd vibrated under hers.

He hit his apartment for a quick shower and shave, then headed to Buck's for his three o'clock appointment. The guilt for sneaking out while she slept was eating him alive. He would've canceled if it wasn't so important, but the desire to get hired at the club was now twice as intense as it had been last night. Not only did he intend to destroy Arlo Buck, but now he was determined to keep a close eye on his sexy waitress, as well.

At ten to three, he pulled into the parking lot. He hopped out of his pickup hoping the nerves didn't show. This interview needed to be played completely cool and straight. He had one chance to get inside, and screwing up wasn't an option.

"I have an appointment with Buck at three," Ty said to a

younger, slightly taller version of Buck sitting at the bar. Ty hadn't seen the guy in a long time, but it had to be Warren. Same meaty head. Same huge body. Ty and Warren had played football against each other, Ty for Longdale High and Warren for Titus. They had never been friends, but Ty had heard plenty of stories. Warren was notorious for always being in trouble, and Buck was just as notorious for bailing him out.

Warren glared, stood, and stalked into a small office behind the stage. He reappeared about two minutes later with his old man.

Buck didn't say anything, only walked to a table at the farthest end of the nightclub.

Ty followed.

Motioning for one of the girls to bring two beers, Buck plopped down into a chair.

"Thanks for seeing me, Mr. Buck."

"Just Buck, no mister. I'm not your fucking high school principal. Why'd you quit the Longdale PD? Bouncer at a nightclub is a big step backwards."

The waitress set down two beers.

"Thanks, babe." Arlo winked at her.

"Long story, but Commander Davis and I had a few issues we couldn't work out."

"I'm gonna tell you what I heard. I heard you failed a drug test, and Davis let you walk instead of firing your ass."

Ty had rehearsed all the answers, so he was prepared. Buck had checked him out thoroughly, just like he figured.

"That's bullshit." Ty shook his head. "I was set up by Davis and Tom, that prick of a nephew of his. I was at a party; Tom was there, too. He kept pushing one beer right after another at me, and then some chick was all over me. She left and came back after a few minutes with a joint."

Ty shrugged. "I didn't want the joint, just the woman. Couldn't figure out why she was practically cramming the damn thing down my throat. I took a couple hits to keep the peace. Go figure, a surprise drug test the next day. Coincidence? I doubt it." Ty drank the beer, looking up at Arlo.

"I heard you were tight with Davis."

"We were. Our families have been friends for years. But his nephew is an asshole and a serious liability to the Longdale department."

Buck sat silent for several moments before speaking. "I could use a guy with a few skills when it comes to keeping the peace around here, but I'm not crazy about inviting any more cops around than I have to. I haven't seen eye to eye with Davis myself in a good many years. Fucker always sends his cops around to poke in my business. If I didn't know better, I'd think he sent you to nose around."

Ty focused on his beer, deciding how to answer. He knew Buck wasn't an idiot, but he hadn't expected him to cut to the chase so quickly. Ty decided to go for the move that would look like an early fold. "I get it. I guess, if I were in your position, I might think that, too. Thanks for your time and the beer." Ty stood and offered a hand to Arlo.

"Sit down, boy, before I knock you down."

An appropriate amount of anger would be prudent here, Ty thought. He sat slowly and let a little heat glare from his eyes.

"You tell me why it would be smart for me to let an ex-cop in my business, one that has family ties to Longdale's chief."

"I don't care who you let in your business, but you won't find anyone in this town more willing to make Davis and his asshole nephew look like idiots than me. Seven years I put in with them. Then he screws me out of my badge and blackballs me in town with every business lead I pursue."

Ty was reasonably sure Buck was at least paying attention. He let his face go a little wild and uncontrolled. The words weren't truthful, but the anger and intention to make someone pay for what Ty's family had been through were absolutely real and humming on the surface.

"Tom's an idiot," Ty continued. "Couldn't hit the broadside of a barn if his life depended on it. I responded to that robbery about eight months back, you know, at Jed's Gas Mart."

Buck nodded.

It had been big news in a little town. Two college kids were strung out and strapped for cash. They'd held up a local gas station, and Ty had responded to the call, been grazed by a bullet.

"Tom was supposed to back me up. I knew as soon as I walked in they were just a couple of teens who needed to score. They weren't looking to shoot anyone. I was about done talking 'em down when one pointed his gun at Tom instead of me. Tom flipped, started shooting up the place. Killed one of the kids, almost got me killed, and then put in his report that the kid fired first. No fucking way I was backing up that story."

Ty leaned back in his chair. Rage and frustration had his hand not quite steady, but Tom and the incident at the gas station weren't the cause. The truth of it was that Tom had handled the situation by the book. It was the knowledge of Arlo Buck's criminal operations and being this close to getting inside that had Ty's nerves standing on end. This was it. If Buck turned him away now, game over.

Buck drained the last half of his beer and slammed the empty bottle on the table, making no attempt to hide the fact he was debating his options. He drilled his dark gaze into Ty and leaned both elbows on the table. "I want someone who does exactly what I tell 'em, when I tell 'em. You're a big boy, so that'll buy you a little respect, but I need a guy in charge of the bouncers who can handle their attitudes and their stupidity. I'm not screwing around with idiots like Lewis who come in here and hassle my girls. No petty drug exchanges, either. You got a license to carry?" Before Ty could answer, he said, "If not, get one. No one screws around in here with drugs or sex."

He never said it out loud, but he didn't have to. Ty could read between the lines perfectly: Buck had security issues and went to a lot of trouble to cover himself. He wasn't getting busted for stupid college kids dealing drugs in the nightclub.

"I'm not sure how I feel about an ex-cop working security, but I'll assume you're smart enough to know you're either all in or all out when you work for me. I take care of my people"—Buck smiled with all the warmth of the devil—"and their family and friends when they work for me."

To anyone less savvy, that might have sounded like a declaration of loyalty to his employees. Ty recognized it for the threat that it was—*Fuck with me, and I'll take out everyone you care about.*

"We'll give it a few weeks, see how it fits for both of us."

Ty let a smirk take the edge off his nerves. "You hiring me?"

"Yeah. Start tomorrow. I'll meet with my guys tonight. I got seven bouncers you'll be in charge of. A few of the boys are strong as hell but none too bright. A couple more, cocky and hotheaded. If you can't handle them and keep 'em in line, you're out."

"I won't let you down. Thanks, Buck." Ty extended a hand. Buck reluctantly shook it. Ty turned to leave.

"McGee."

Ty turned back.

Buck leaned back in the suffering bar chair that looked like it wanted to collapse underneath him. "No one crosses me and lives to tell about it. That's how you work my floor, with that level of arrogance. You get rid of the small side drug deals. You kick the shit out of the bastards feeling up my waitresses. Make sure no one gets rough in the VIP rooms unless they've properly paid for it. And make damn certain you understand I'll be watching you closely. No one crosses Arlo Buck."

Chapter Four

After a few peaceful hours of dreamless sleep and a long, hot shower, Jordan felt almost human again. Only then did she allow herself to think about the vision and the drama with Ty that had followed.

She couldn't fault him for slipping out while she slept. If he'd been smart, he'd have left a long time before that, when she'd passed out behind Buck's or when he got stuck in the ER half the night. But he hadn't. He even stayed after she snarled at him when he mentioned her parents.

And then there was the kiss. Good God, what had she been thinking?

It was pretty obvious she hadn't been thinking at all. How could she be so stupid? Head injury or not, her behavior was inexcusable. Any cop who worked undercover knew exactly how dangerous screw-ups could be. She'd screwed up big time last night.

The way McGee affected her bordered on insane. Keeping

a good, healthy distance from him might be the best move. Then again, was it ridiculous *not* to explore a valuable connection simply because he sent her hormones into overdrive?

How would she explain that to her superiors? *I'm sorry, Captain, I didn't pursue a valuable source, because I couldn't keep my tongue out of the subject's mouth long enough to question him.*

She blew out a disgusted sigh. Instincts that had guided her through several successful undercover missions were screaming at her to find Ty and press him for information. Only an idiot could deny the attraction between them. Maybe if she used that attraction, pretended to need him, need to be taken care of. Shower him with a few soft kisses… Maybe he'd confide everything he knew about Arlo Buck in no time at all.

Taking a look at Ty's professional records might help, too, although she couldn't just waltz in to the Longdale Police Station and demand his file. But the FBI could. Bahan was a master at gathering data. She'd send him an email requesting the information, because she sure as hell wasn't risking a phone call. It wasn't a mere coincidence that she checked in and left voicemails at times he'd be unavailable. No reason to risk an inquiry about her progress inside Buck's.

Jordan grabbed her laptop and eased onto the sofa. Now for another unpleasant task. Time to do a little digging of her own. Who was the mystery girl in her dream? She couldn't pawn that off on Bahan; he'd ask too many questions. Questions she had no intentions of answering.

She didn't remember a time in her life when there were no dreams. But she remembered a time when she didn't fear them. Back when she was too little to understand what they meant.

Then there had been the dream about her family—the one that had opened her eyes to real terror. The one that had driven home the very real consequence of ignoring the message inside the dream.

Now she knew better. "Come on, mystery girl. What were you trying to show me?" she muttered as she tapped her security code into the laptop.

Most of the time, she'd convinced herself the spirits were seeking justice for what they'd suffered. Other times, she believed their desperation to connect with her had more to do with closure for their families. On very rare occasions, a spirit would show her a precognitive event—something that hadn't happened yet—usually attempting to save a loved one, but those visions were the hardest to decipher.

Combining visions with police work seldom followed a straight line of logic. Interpreting what each victim wanted her to see was tricky, yet becoming a cop was the only way she knew how to give purpose to the freakish ability. As for the latest dream, every angle would need to be checked. She'd start with the missing persons database because everything in the dream told her the girl had family and friends that would be looking for her.

While the computer popped up results, Jordan reached for her journal. Habit almost had her dragging it out while Ty had been in her apartment, but luckily, common sense had rushed back in time. What would she have said to him?

Excuse me, could you hand me that notepad? Dead crime victims tend to visit me in my dreams, just need to jot down a few notes.

After escaping as efficiently as Houdini, she was quite

sure Ty had already put her in the "whack-job" category. Sharing her ability to connect with the dead would no doubt earn her a one-way ticket to Freakville.

"Been there, visited that part of town, cowboy—not likely to go back," she murmured, scribbling the date in her journal. "Not even for an ass as fine as yours."

Now, hours later, she was concentrating twice as hard to recall a fraction of the details. Even through the suckish aftermath, she'd always been vigilant about writing down the facts. It was important to log every visual element as soon as possible. Each minute that passed blurred the fine edge of detail that she could recount. Often, it was the smallest of those details that made all the larger ones fall together.

She tapped a pen on her journal a couple of times, then took a few cleansing breaths and played back the vision in her mind.

Victim—White female. Middle teens. Long dark hair. Raped. Murdered. A party, graduation likely.

Male suspect—A ball cap? Green? Brown?

Damn it!

She slapped the journal shut. How frustrating to remember so little. The only positive aspect of her dreams was that they gave her information. In this case, there just wasn't enough.

But consistently, the dreams had been tied to whatever case she was working on at the time. It was likely the girl was local and, with enough digging, Jordan was betting on a tie to Arlo Buck.

As much as she hated to think it, she needed more. And she could bet—there would be more.

She'd barely logged in when someone knocked at her

door. After closing her computer, she moved to the hidden gun on the bookshelf next to the door. She put one hand on the doorknob and one on the gun. "Who is it?"

"Pizza delivery."

Fairly confident she recognized the voice, she cracked the door open, leaving the chain in place. "Ty, what are you doing here?"

"Bringing you dinner if you'll take the chain off."

The pizza smelled like heaven. It hadn't occurred to Jordan that her last meal had been the day before, not until the pepperoni hypnotized her.

After slipping the gun behind the books, she slid the chain off the door and opened it. "Wow, it smells amazing. What's in the bag?"

"Salad and Antonio's world famous cheesecake."

He caught her off guard, and she didn't know what to say. She liked to be prepared. *This* she was singularly unprepared for. Did she have enough wits to deal with him tonight? She was undercover. He needed to be checked out. The conversation wouldn't be on her terms, but it could work.

Stepping back, she gestured toward the kitchen. As he passed, she smelled the pizza, but the more enticing aroma followed in its wake—freshly showered male. Was it soap? Cologne? Who the hell knew? But her treacherous body inhaled deeply while his back was turned.

He headed to the kitchen and started scrambling around as if he'd lived there all his life. "Oh, man. I forgot sodas."

She watched him, frankly bewildered that he'd come back. "I've got diet soda in the fridge."

"I know. I hate that stuff." He stared into the nearly

empty refrigerator. "Why do women do that? It's so stupid."

She couldn't decide whether to be insulted or amused. "Do what?"

"Eat pizza and cheesecake, then wash it down with diet soda. I was at the burger joint in town yesterday. Some woman in front of me, honest to God, ordered a double half-pound burger with extra mayo and a giant-size fry. Then got a diet soda. I mean, come on, what's the point?" He shut the fridge and turned to her. "Do you have paper plates? We don't need to dirty the real ones if you do."

"Ah..." She tried to remember if she'd seen any. *How do I know?* is what she wanted to say. She'd only been in the furnished apartment a short time. There was a coffee pot and coffee cups. Everything else was just overkill.

"No paper plates." She faked it. He wouldn't know.

"Are you sure? I thought I saw some when I was looking for coffee filters this morning." He opened up a couple cabinets, finally swinging open the large one in the corner. Three different sizes of paper plates practically fell on top of him. There were napkins, plastic utensils, and even paper cups with lids. A virtual smorgasbord of disposable dinnerware.

Damn. She hadn't planned on entertaining. How was she supposed to know—or care—they were in there? She shrugged when he shot her a confused look. "The woman in the apartment before me must have left them."

She continued to watch him as he set the tiny two-person table. He started a pot of coffee, tossed the salad, and served them both a piece of pizza.

"Have a seat. I'll get us coffee in a minute," he said.

If the man had a shy or reluctant bone in his body, she'd

yet to see it.

He looked over to where she stood rooted to the floor. "I'm such an idiot. I haven't even asked how you're feeling. Are you doing okay?" He walked to her, tilted her head up, and brushed back her hair to inspect the stitches on her forehead.

A sharp intake of air flooded her lungs. Her skin heated, and her heart thundered so loudly, she wondered if he could hear it. "Yeah, I'm much better."

"I had an appointment I couldn't get out of." His eyes drifted to her chest before he blinked them back up to her face. "I hated to leave you, but…"

"It's okay. You're not my keeper." Glancing down to where his gaze had landed, she realized her old tank top was quite thin. She no longer needed to worry if he could hear her heart pound. Her erect nipples took the embarrassment over how her body reacted to his touch to a whole new level. "I'll be right back. I'm gonna grab a sweatshirt."

By the time she came out of the bedroom, he'd poured coffee.

He pulled out a chair for her. "Have a seat."

She nodded, deciding it was time to start the business end of the dinner. "I'm beginning to wonder about you."

He lifted a brow. "Why is that?"

"I figured after what I put you through last night, you wouldn't be back. And here you are, with dinner no less."

"Technically, I'm still on duty until about midnight."

Confused, she narrowed her eyes.

"My twenty-four-hour watch over you still has six hours to go. I noticed you only had two apples and a half-eaten yogurt in the fridge. Thought maybe you wouldn't be up to getting dinner, so here I am. I wasn't going to let you starve on my shift."

"I wouldn't have starved." She rolled her eyes defensively. "I have chips in the cabinet, too."

"Yeah, well, you'd probably be hard-pressed to find them," he said. "I'm beginning to think you don't have a clue about what's in those cabinets." He waved an extra paper plate at her.

Ignoring his comment *and* the way his eyes sparkled when he teased her, she picked up the pizza and bit into it. "Oh, God, this is good. I think I may be in love."

He grinned at her low, appreciative groan. "I try."

She laughed. "Not with you, with Antonio."

He clutched his chest. "May I remind you that if it weren't for me, you'd be eating old, crusty yogurt tonight?"

"And I might have bled to death on Buck's picnic table," she added with a smile.

"You're right. So you best start stroking my ego better, or I'm taking my world famous cheesecake and getting out."

Propping her head on a fist, she watched him eat. He was impossibly gorgeous and very sweet. She desperately wanted to scratch him off the list of suspects. "So, why'd you give up being a cop? I'd think that would be a pretty good living around here."

No mistake, the glittering shine in his eyes turned a shade darker. He dropped his crust onto his plate and proceeded to serve them both another piece of pizza. "It's a small town. When bad blood starts flowing in a police department as small as Longdale's, there aren't a lot of ways to diffuse it. You live with it or quit. I quit."

"What caused the bad blood?"

He paused. "A disagreement."

She kept her eyes fixed on him and hoped he'd succumb to the silent invitation for more information.

"About a promotion," he finally admitted. "One that I should have had, but the police chief's nephew got. It's all about who you're related to in this town."

"So instead of trying to move to another department like Titus or Cooper, you just quit?" His actions didn't make sense. Someone would take her badge when they pried it out of her cold, dead hands.

"You went through training, got your badge, worked for eight or nine years, and then just walked away?" She'd spent a great many years reading people, and she already knew a few things about Ty. He loved playing protector, had been doing it since she'd met him, which made the fact that he'd turned in his badge over a missed promotion unlikely.

"You ask a lot of questions for someone who's more attracted to the guy who made the pizza than me."

"Sorry, occupational hazard."

"For a business degree?" His head tilted as he stared at her. He appeared to be mentally weighing her words. "Do they make you interrogate people to get your business degree?"

Stalling, she stuffed another bite of pizza in her mouth. It *had* sounded more like an interrogation than a friendly conversation over dinner. "Cocktail waitress," she said around the pizza. "The more you talk, the more interested you are in people's lives, the better the tips. I ask a lot of questions, chat a lot. It seems to be an asset at Buck's."

He scowled, instantly annoyed. "Good ol' Buck's."

She watched him crumple a napkin and tap his fingers

on the tabletop. Something had him ticked off.

"When do you think you'll go back to work?"

"Today was my day off, so not until tomorrow."

He shook his head. "You really think you're up to carrying trays and fighting off idiots like Lewis?"

The agitation in his voice escalated. Even if he turned out to be one of the cops—or ex-cop, in his case—protecting Buck, the toxic atmosphere inside the club seemed to drive him nuts.

"I'm fine. I can't afford to be off anyway. Are you done?" she asked.

When he nodded, she picked up their plates and threw them away.

"What if I could get you a job at Antonio's? His family has been good friends with mine for years. It's a really nice place." He tossed the leftover pizza on the kitchen counter and grabbed the dessert bag. "And now you know their food is awesome."

So dinner had been a well-planned move to get her to quit Buck's. She had to give him points for strategy and persistence. "Look, Ty, I know you don't like Buck's, but do you have any idea how much money I can make there in one evening? I start at four, and it's pretty steady until about nine, and then it just completely opens up. On the weekends, I can walk away with a couple hundred dollars a night."

"Yeah, but the place is a hole, and you know better than anyone it can be dangerous."

"Only if I turn my back on Lewis." She knew her lack of concern about the danger prickled under his skin. "Cheesecake now or later?"

She turned to look at him when he didn't answer and got

the distinct impression he had more to say on the subject of her employment but had apparently decided to drop it.

He moved the bakery box to the table, opened it, and served up the dessert. "Come here, you've got to try this."

Guiding her into a chair, he pulled another one intimately close and sat. He scooped up a bite of cheesecake and fed it to her. "Tell me that's not the best thing you've ever had in your mouth."

With her eyes closed and the slightest taste of heaven on her tongue, "hmm" was all she could manage. And not in a sweet, agreeable way, but in a low moan of delight.

"I told you so." He chuckled and fed her another bite.

After she swallowed—and licked her lips—she said, "My mom made the best cheesecake. Thanksgiving meant pumpkin pie to everyone else, but my sister and I would beg for Mom's cheesecake. God, it was good. I remember helping her make it. We'd try to shape the whipped cream on top into a pumpkin, in the spirit of pumpkin pie, you know. But we were artistically challenged." She smiled. "Most years, we just ended up with an odd-looking smiley face. This is truly the best thing I've had since…"

…her family's last Thanksgiving together.

Words turned to ashes on her tongue. Stunned, she glanced at Ty. The hot sting in her eyes jolted her. Had she really just talked about her mom and sister? She never mentioned them. Not to anyone. Not ever. Images of their last morning together ignited and spread through her like a brush fire.

Ty dropped the fork and picked up her trembling hand, enveloping it in his large, warm grip. The icy claws of the flashback thawed when his fingers stroked her skin.

"You're shaking." His brows drew together. "I'm sorry, Jordan. I didn't know. I mean, I never would have…"

"Don't be stupid, it's fine." She pushed the words out, scrambling to shift into autopilot. *God*, she hated that her past could still grab hold of her like this. "The cheesecake *is* amazing."

He moved a hand to her face, turning her head toward him. "I never meant to bring back bad memories or hurt you. I'm sorry." He leaned in and touched his lips to the spot where a tear had streaked down her cheek.

The simple gesture, hauntingly intimate, undid her. Fighting the burn in her throat, she averted her face. She wanted to die. This man had been screwing with her emotions since the first moment she laid eyes on him. Why couldn't he have let it go, pretended she hadn't just made a fool of herself, the way any other man would have done?

"My mom and sister aren't bad memories; it's just hard sometimes." She forced the words through the constricting pressure in her lungs. "I overreacted, so I'm the one who should be sorry."

Framing her face in his hands, he tilted her head up, forcing their gazes to meet. "Don't do that," he said. "You don't have to pretend that it doesn't hurt. I know what losing someone you love feels like."

She looked into his eyes and couldn't quite bring herself to look away. He did know. Somehow—he did know. Pain. Anger. Embarrassment. Raw emotions hung in the air like a dense fog, thick enough to suffocate in.

His lips brushed her forehead, then shifted and settled lightly against her mouth. The gentle, intimate connection stole her breath. Shaken by the fierce tightening in her body, she moaned.

At the soft sound, his grip tightened, and his lips grew more demanding. One of his hands dipped to the small of her back, the other tangled in her hair. His tongue edged into her mouth and stroked hers.

Confused, captivated, completely off balance—she was overwhelmed by sensations. There were good, solid reasons to stop, but this kiss was the nirvana she'd sought for twenty years, spurring a deep pull in her core that curbed the heartache and left behind something much more pleasurable in its wake.

Common sense waged a small battle. She needed to think. Needed to breathe. Needed to stop.

Just like everyone else—he'd already be gone if he knew your secrets.

Determined to step back, she lifted her hands to his face to push him away, but he turned his head and captured one of her fingers between his lips and sucked. The yearning flared hot and deep this time, driving a sharp, involuntary breath into her lungs.

Again, her thoughts spun. The desire to be taken, to be greedy and satisfy a need she'd denied for a long, *long* time exploded through whatever compartment she believed it safely locked in. A wicked tremble racked her body. Desire begged for her to open up just long enough to grab a screaming release.

But opening up is the worst kind of danger for someone whose world hinges on remaining closed.

His mouth captured hers again with long, languid strokes of his tongue mixed with short, ravaging licks. The hand he had splayed on her back slipped under her sweatshirt to stroke flesh. Panic filled her when his quick fingers slid to the front of her body, skimmed up her torso, and gently cupped her breast. But the alarm gave way as his fingers closed around her nipple, teasing and taunting. An uncontrolled groan of pleasure rose from her throat.

It had gone too far. She had to stop. "Ty...We need...I should—"

"Take the damned shirt off and come here? Yeah, I was thinking the same thing."

He yanked both shirts over her head and tugged her toward him.

In a moment of complete insanity, she straddled him. None of the material left between them could hide the erection pressing against her.

Ty groaned long and deep when she settled on his lap. He splayed his hands on her bare back. "Damn," he whispered while taking in her breasts. "There's just no part of you that isn't gorgeous." He leaned in and ravaged the tip of her bare breast with his lips.

This time, when she grabbed his face, there wasn't a chance in hell it was to push him away. His tongue flicked, caressed, expertly drew from her nipple in a way that seared a heated path straight to her core. Her response was basic and all woman. The cop fell to the wayside.

Need won.

Dampness flowed from her body. She peeled off his shirt and let her hands explore and discover. Her fingertips traced the hard planes of his chest, sliding over smooth skin and a dusting of hair that covered firm muscle underneath. Quite simply, Ty was beautiful.

The next thought brought terror. Sheer blistering terror.

She wanted him.

And not in a way she could ever remember wanting any man before. She needed his hands on her and her clothes off. Needed to feel him, his body, his weight—not just his lips and chest, but every part of him driving inside her.

Pulling back, she sat, dazed.

"Let me take the edge off, baby." He drew her closer, whispered in her ear. "Please."

Taking advantage of her silence, he smoothed his fingers across the skin low on her stomach, brushing them inside the waistband of her shorts. Fingering the rhinestone on her navel, he said, "What do you like, Jordan?"

The gravel in his voice scraped across her skin, raising a fine layer of goose bumps. Her thoughts spun out in all kinds of crazy directions, but she couldn't have put two words together to save her soul.

His hand slid lower and cupped her. Her breath caught. He didn't move, just allowed the heat of his hand to sear her. The man was a sadist; it was torture to have his fingers so close to where she needed to feel them. *God*, did he want her to beg? She started to pant. When she did, she felt his smile against her neck.

And then he moved.

He stroked her, just the faintest, slightest touch of his finger, and she jerked as if she'd been shot. God, it had been a long time. Way too long if one slight touch sent her nerve endings into spasms.

"Jordan." Her name rolled from his tongue with a low, male groan. Twisting his free hand in her hair, he tugged her head back, devouring her throat with lips and tongue and teeth.

She couldn't think. Not when he crushed his mouth to hers and slid one skilled finger into her while gently stroking his thumb over her swollen mound.

"Ty." Her gasp for air turned hitching and jagged. She couldn't remember how to breathe. "Ty, God, ah..." He was using her body against her, sliding his fingers over...in... out...

Her body shattered, convulsed. She drew him tighter, scrambling for something solid to cling to. Her breath heaved as if she'd just crossed a finish line. But they weren't done. She knew in her heart, knew from his low, throaty growl, they weren't done.

"Christ, I want you." He stood and crushed her body between his and the wall, cupped her bottom, and lifted her.

Her legs reflexively circled his hips. He felt so good. So solid. So strong.

An unwelcome notion sat somewhere in a dark corner in her mind—*this is wrong*. She was here on an investigation and had crossed a line. It was professional suicide. And if the orgasm he'd shot her to in less than a minute was any indication, she suspected he was capable of knocking her private world completely off its axis, too.

Ty stumbled his way into her bedroom and fell on the bed while tugging at the tiny cotton shorts she was wearing. They were the only thing standing between her and the biggest mistake of her life, and even so, as he eased them down her legs, she didn't stop him.

Her phone rang somewhere in the background. The answering machine kicked on.

"Jordan, it's Bahan. Come on, pick up. Why aren't you answering your cell? I'm sorry I missed your call, but I got your email."

Reality snapped back with a big, ugly, ferocious bite. She opened her eyes and popped up on an elbow. Ty's fingers smoothed along the inside of her thigh—and, oh man—she wanted those very talented fingers doing exactly what they'd done to her only moments ago.

"I need specifics on that info you wanted." Bahan's voice echoed through the room again.

She leaped, fumbled in the dark room, and turned on the light next to the bed. Fumbling again, she grabbed the phone.

"Hi, Ted, it's me." Turning to Ty, she held up a finger as she stood, then pulled a blanket from the bed and walked to the other room.

She cut Bahan short, telling him she'd be in touch tomorrow. But the brief conversation was enough to clear the fog and let her normal, rational thinking spring to life. Not once since she'd had her badge could she remember being this impulsive or reckless.

She took a deep breath, prepared to go back into the bedroom and send him home.

By the time she returned, Ty sat on the edge of her bed. She sat next to him, but he didn't look at her.

"Not a good sign when another man is on your recorder sounding so desperate to speak to you."

"Hey." She turned his head toward her. The brooding gray of his eyes pulled at something inside her. No one had ever scrambled her senses like this man. "Ted's an old friend. He's helping me with"—she stumbled all the way—"a project at college. I'm not involved with him, if that's what you're thinking."

A small smile lit his face.

"I'm not involved with anyone, because I don't get involved. Ever. I'm sorry I led you to believe otherwise tonight."

His eyes narrowed. "What do you mean you don't get involved ever? No one has that kind of restraint, baby."

She shrugged. "I do. I have very little free time, and I just find it easier this way. No expectations or obligations. No disappointment." She looked at him, but he didn't appear convinced. "I'm sorry I let things get out of control. I don't know what happened."

His handsome face morphed into an evil grin. "I think we just happened. Almost. I won't push you, but you can't live like a nun just because you're busy." He slid a hand up her cheek and leaned in for a kiss.

She backed away, not at all sure she could stop if things started again. She couldn't use him, not like that. If he turned out to be a dirty ex-cop, she couldn't stand the thought of being this attracted to him. If he turned out to be a good guy, she didn't want to hurt him that way, either. "Look, relationships are complicated. I prefer my life simple. Finding Mr. Right isn't a priority."

"I suppose I'd lose points quickly if I told you I'd be happy being Mr. Wrong?"

She couldn't stop the laugh that escaped. "Are you offering to be my booty call?"

"If that's what it takes. I could live with that. For now."

She could damned well live with that, too.

But instead she thought about Arlo Buck and his greedy ambition to make a dollar at the expense of children. She had a job to do and couldn't afford a distraction. She'd made a life, albeit a solitary one because of the dreams, but it was a life that had meaning now.

Why would she ever risk it for a man? Why risk having him turn her world upside down and then walk out when the truth surfaced?

Her life wasn't perfect, but it worked.

"How about just a friend?" She got up to put some space between them, went to her closet, came back, and handed him the shirt she'd borrowed the night before. "I washed it today. I think all the blood came out."

She walked him to the front door. In one quick maneuver, he kissed her, slid his hands down to her butt, and pulled her against him. Her breath hitched, and her thoughts scrambled. The lust he could ignite in a few short seconds teetered on baffling.

He smiled, cockiness all over his face. "Just think about it. I'm not asking for a commitment." He leaned in close to her ear. "But I think, together, we'd really be something."

"Out," she managed with a huge gulp of air and an enormous degree of willpower.

"But I didn't get any cheesecake." He pulled his head back and grinned.

She went to the table, grabbed the cheesecake, and then shoved the box at him. "Good night."

"Good night, Jordan." He winked. "I'll be in touch."

She heard him whistle when she closed the door.

It was a goddamned train wreck.

"Well done, Jordan," she muttered to herself, crawling into bed a few minutes later. "You really couldn't have screwed this one up more if you tried."

Her long, dark hair danced on the breeze as the beautiful girl swung in the moonlight under the huge, old oak tree.

The boy watched, then walked to his car and cleaned football gear out of his back seat. After stashing the athletic bag in his trunk, he grabbed two beers from a cooler and a small vial filled with clear liquid.

Looking unsure, he poured the liquid into one of the beers, then added a little more and a little more.

"Free sex, no strings," he murmured. "Wear a condom. Put her clothes back on. Dump her by the swing and let her sleep it off like it never happened. She'll never remember."

He opened a small plastic vial, stuck in a pinky, brought a crust of fine white powder to his nostril, and snorted.

Walking back to the swing, he smiled at the girl. Then he handed her the tainted beer and teased her for drinking too slowly.

When she felt dizzy from the swing, he caught her. Laid her unconscious body in his car and drove to the middle of nowhere. When the car was safely hidden in the trees, he killed the engine.

He moved to the back seat, but she began to groan a woozy protest even before he had her clothes off.

"Shut up." Covering her mouth with a hand, he plowed into her quickly. He squeezed her throat to stop her sobs while he rutted like a wild animal.

She clawed at his wrists and bit his ear. "My daddy will kill you."

One blow, then two, the third finally hard enough to stun

her into silence. When it was over, he collapsed on top of her. But as he pulled up his pants, the unused condom fell from his pocket.

"Oh shit." He'd forgotten the condom. Blood from his ear dripped on the girl's chest. He swiped at it with his shirt. He'd left his signature at the scene of the crime. They'd have his DNA.

The girl groaned again. "You'll pay. I know who you are," she whispered. "I'll always remember what you did."

"It wasn't supposed to end this way, but fuck, you left me no choice." He pulled her from the car, put his shaking hands around her neck. "I'm sorry," he said as sweat streaked down his face. "You can't remember. I can't let you remember."

Chapter Five

"You can't even get a good cup of coffee in this stupid, flipping, one-horse town." Jordan ranted and slurped down an energy drink after the teenage disaster with a nose and tongue piercing at the Stop and Go said, "We stop selling coffee at three o'clock."

"Idiot," Jordan rambled to herself as she walked back to her car. "It's like three-oh-four, honest to God."

After her rotten luck with Lewis, her rotten judgment with Ty, and the rotten nightmare that apparently wasn't going to go away quietly, her mood was, well—rotten. God help the drunken ass who laid a hand on her today.

Her eyes felt gritty and swollen with fatigue. The nightmare had started the second her head hit the pillow. In the past, she'd normally get a couple hours of sleep before they'd begin. Not willing to risk an encore performance of the gruesome vision, she'd stayed up the rest of the night, searching the database.

Nothing.

She didn't usually feel this out of sorts so early in an investigation. Maybe by the end of a case, she'd find herself down a few pounds and on the verge of exhaustion. That was to be expected. But she'd only just begun this mission, trying to get a feel for the town and the people, and already the mental and physical fatigue were whispering in her ear.

The injury and concussion were unexpected. So was the disturbing and graphic nature of the latest dreams. Normally, they came slower, in bits and pieces, but these had shot right out of the gates with a powerful, sickening vengeance.

Victims communicated with her, it was just a fact. A reality she couldn't escape.

It followed that the more violent and disturbing the crime, the more violent and disturbing the vision. But this girl, the beautiful one in the dream, just wouldn't let go of her. Even after she woke, the girl's soft, innocent eyes and long, dark hair were constant visuals in her mind. It was bad enough dreaming about these people, but it was something else entirely to realize she felt a connection with this girl. A bond she'd never had before. Some kind of link that went deeper than the murder.

Jordan pulled into the parking lot of Buck's at three-twenty. Her shift didn't start until four. Since she'd never had a dream in a car, she figured maybe she could get through a ten minute power nap without the beautiful mystery girl staring her in the face. She dozed off until her cell vibrated.

"Hello." She wasn't completely coherent when she answered.

"Explain."

"What? Who is this?" Jordan asked.

"Who the fuck do you think it is?" The angry slap shot

through Bahan's voice and stirred Jordan awake. "It's the person that's getting ready to end you if you don't have a damned good reason for ignoring my instructions."

FBI Special Agent Ted Bahan had to remind her he was in charge. *Again.* It wasn't necessarily a bad thing. Bahan was skilled, connected, organized, and had more experience and seniority than just about anyone she worked with. She had complete confidence in his ability to be in charge.

The fact that he had worked with her for almost ten years and didn't return the sentiment still rankled. Not once had she given him a reason to doubt her capabilities. But when two of her guys—cops from her department, men she worked side by side with—had been killed in St. Louis while in deep cover on this China White investigation, Bahan had tried to pull her from the task force.

She'd busted her ass for the last year, hunting the prime source of China White, while Bahan had been content on the bureaucratic outer edge until her colleagues had been killed. And unfortunately, understanding his argument that she was too emotionally involved to continue did absolutely nothing to fix the betrayal in her gut.

"Chill, Bahan," she said. "First of all, you're not my captain. We're supposed to be partnering on an investigation."

Silence. Bahan's mouth could cut just as sharply as hers, so she knew the silent treatment was not a sign of good things to come.

"Second," she continued, "you may be heading up this thing, but that sure as hell doesn't mean I've surrendered all authority and my right to make a decision on the fly when I feel it's necessary. I've been doing this kind of work damn near as long as you have."

Still more silence. He'd be sitting at his desk, knee bobbing like a jackhammer, jaw clenched. She'd seen him like that before, but his temper wasn't usually directed at her.

"Okay, look," she said. "We agreed that we couldn't all roll into town at the same time without throwing up red flags. It's a small community; people notice things. You need to trust my judgment. We also agreed I could apply for the job at Buck's just to see if he'd hire me. I had no way of knowing he'd ask me to start immediately."

"Really? I thought we agreed that if he hired you, you were going to tell him you couldn't start until after Thanksgiving, until I had time to safely integrate my surveillance team."

"That was your plan. Mine was to get my foot in the door any way I could. He was short-staffed and wanted someone right away," she explained. "I couldn't take the chance he'd find another girl for the job."

"And it simply slipped your mind to update me? Listen, hotshot, I don't roll this way. I know you're pissed at me. I get it. And I've seen you pull some risky stunts before, but this is over the top, even for you. This borders on asinine. You're in a strip club, in the middle of nowhere, not wearing a wire, with no backup. I'm not sure what it is you're trying to prove—"

"I have backup." When she realized she'd yelled at him, she took a deep breath and choked back the emotions. "I saw an opportunity, and I took it. The two local cops involved with the case said they'd back me up, just until you get here. We're talking what, a week until Thanksgiving?"

"Oh, well, fuck me then. What in the world am I worried about? Two country cops and a renegade detective. What could possibly go wrong?"

His sarcasm made her temper flare. "You know, the FBI always claims they'll partner with local law enforcement, work as a team, but there's no partnering with you guys. It's your way or no way. It was *my* information that led us here." She took a breath, trying to level out her voice. "It was *my* two cops who were killed trying to pinpoint where the flood of China White was coming from, and knowing all that, you still tried to yank this case away from me."

They were both silent, the only sound Bahan's heavy sigh. "It won't bring 'em back, Jordan. You can fuck yourself up seven ways to Sunday, and it won't accomplish a damn thing other than one more dead cop. I won't sit back and let that happen. I fought for control of this task force, because I was worried about your objectivity. Looks like I had just cause."

He sighed into the phone again. "You lie to me one more time, and you're done. Completely done."

"I didn't lie to you," she growled, knowing full well that she had. "Buck asked me to start. I said yes."

"But you didn't tell me, Jordan."

"I'm training. Just a few hours a night, a couple nights a week. You have no reason to worry, and he has no reason to be suspicious, because I really am only waiting tables at this point."

"Still, you ended up in a hospital and didn't report it."

Damn. The information the man could gather was just scary. "I didn't need to. I'm fine."

"So that's the game we're playing now?" Someone who didn't know him might have said the question sounded calm, almost passive. But Jordan recognized the danger lingering in the cool words. "You want to challenge me, hotshot? I'll be in your chief's office so fast, you won't have time to blink. How's he going to like it when I tell him his golden child has been removed from a federal task force for being unwilling to follow simple safety procedures?"

"You wouldn't dare. This is *my* investigation."

"Wrong. This is *our* investigation, *partner*. While you're in Titus, I'm responsible."

She was familiar with this particular tone of voice, knew she wasn't going to win. Better to cut her losses and suck it up. "All right, all right. Let's both just calm down. I got pushed by a drunk customer and stumbled and hit my head. That was it. Some guy drove me to the hospital to get a couple of stitches. I don't know where you got your information, but it wasn't anything more than that."

"Hello, McFly. You're still not listening. The lab confirmed the heroin confiscated in Titus matches the stuff your people confiscated in St. Louis last month. Arlo Buck has a nasty and powerful connection. His drugs are fingering off into bigger cities. He'll have a game plan. He'll have plenty of people watching his back. More than likely, a few of them will be local cops. Trust no one."

"Bahan, I get it. I have about ten minutes to get somewhere, and I can't be late."

"Buck's? Are you planning to work at the club tonight?"

"No." She stared up at Buck's huge neon sign. "I'm... doing something else. Look, I need you to shut up and listen for a second. Did you get my email? I want every last detail you can put together on Tyler McGee. I'm sorry I don't have specifics yet. But he's an ex-cop for the Longdale PD. Around thirty. Probably lives in Cooper or Longdale."

"Jordan, I'm telling you to be careful."

"I'm always careful. Are you writing it down?"

"I don't need to write it down, I already have wheels in motion on that information. Now *you* shut up and listen to me. I want you to stay out of Buck's for the next week. Tell him you're leaving town for the holiday. Tell him you're sick. I don't care, just fix it."

"Yeah, yeah. Okay. I'll figure something out." She disconnected.

She studied the back door of the nightclub. Her back still ached from the Lewis incident. She could use it as an excuse, but she didn't want to. She knew how quickly things could go wrong on an undercover, knew she was probably being stubborn, but she was only waiting tables.

She walked inside the bar with a throbbing headache. The jolt of caffeine from the energy drink had done nothing to wake her up but *had* succeeded in giving her a nice case of the jitters. In all honesty, she probably should have stayed home. Working here wore at her patience when she was in good form. Tonight, she'd be lucky not to kill someone.

"Jordan, over here."

Warren and Arlo Buck were sitting at a table near the bar. They motioned for her. *Great*. She mentally prepared herself as she walked toward them. Warren would pull her down onto his lap, put his hands somewhere inappropriate, and make all sorts of suggestive comments. Obviously, sexual harassment training hadn't made its way to Titus.

Warren's attraction to her had been anything but subtle. She tolerated it. Most of the time, she even encouraged it and made an attempt to flirt back. Getting close to him was the next best thing to getting close to Buck. In fact, he'd probably be much easier to get past. His old man's radar always seemed to be on alert. Warren was too self-absorbed to even have radar. But today had largely sucked in all directions already.

"You doing okay?" Buck asked.

Before she had a chance to answer, Warren picked up her hand and spun her around until she tumbled onto his lap. She jolted as a sharp pain shot through her back.

"I'm sorry, honey," Warren said. "Are you still hurting? Holy shit," he said when he lifted the back of her shirt. "That's some bruise."

Buck even raised an eyebrow as he looked at the bright, colorful spot that had formed across the center of her spine. "You gonna be able to work?" he asked.

Decision time. She could play up the injury, take a few days, make Bahan happy. Instead she said, "Yeah, I'll be okay."

Warren stroked her back with the tips of his fingers, gentle circles around and around the bruise. "If Lewis ever shows his drunk, stupid self around here again, I'll kick the shit out of him."

"Aw," Jordan cooed, "you'd be my knight in shining armor? You're so sweet." She shifted and put an arm around his neck, then kissed his cheek. "Such a good friend."

Warren ate it up like a starving man, and his hands suddenly seemed to be on a mission to touch as much of her bare skin as possible.

"I better get to work," she said.

"Wait." He wrapped his arms around her and spoke softly in her ear. "I was wondering if you had plans for Thanksgiving?"

"Turkey potpie and a bottle of wine." She smiled. "I don't really have any family."

"Yeah, I thought that's what you said. I wondered if you'd like to come to our house for Thanksgiving dinner?"

Maybe today was her lucky day after all. She knew Buck's main office was in his home, and she was dying to poke around in there. She'd wondered how she'd ever score an invitation to their house.

"Warren, that's so sweet, but are you sure it's okay?" She looked at Buck. "Thanksgiving is for family."

Buck had an ever-so-slight smile on his face. "It's the least we can do after letting you get roughed up last night."

"Well, I'd love to. You guys are just the best," she said, hugging Warren again. "Should I make a dish?"

...

Ty was huddled in a corner of Buck's, introducing himself to his crew of bouncers. He turned when he heard the back door open and slam shut.

Jordan walked in and slipped off her jacket. Everything inside him tightened. She wore a little black tank top and black denim shorts. Her hair was pulled back into one long, sleek, blond ponytail, with just enough left in front to cover her stitches.

Her hair was styled completely different, but the same ache that had surfaced the first time he caught sight of her flared again. Like a sucker punch in the gut, it caught him off guard. Recognizing how deeply she affected him from even thirty feet away was not a good thing. He had an agenda, a reason for being here that shouldn't have anything to do with a sexy cocktail waitress.

He was nervous about what she'd say when she finally saw him. After giving her so much grief, he'd taken a job at Buck's himself. She probably wouldn't see the wisdom in that logic. He smiled thinking about the verbal abuse she'd probably let loose on him. It was different for him, though; he knew what he was getting into. Anyway, she should be grateful to have someone here who actually cared if the girls were harassed.

Turning back to the guys, he said, "We're done for now. I appreciate everyone coming in. If you're not working tonight, I'll see you in a day or so. Let me know if you have questions."

Looking toward Jordan, Ty caught sight of Warren pulling her onto his lap, lifting her top, and touching her back. What the hell right did he have to do that? Ty watched the other man put his arms around her and glide his fingers under her shirt.

Instantly annoyed, he tried to ignore the surge of anger and the unfamiliar ache that bubbled in his chest. He wasn't jealous, and she was a big girl. If she wanted to fall all over a pathetic excuse of a human like Warren, more power to her.

He couldn't see the whole picture, so he shifted. It looked like Warren's hand was positioned somewhere between her thighs. Killing Buck's son on his first day of work would most certainly get him fired, but seriously, if the bastard didn't stop touching her…

No, screw it. She'd made it clear last night she didn't want any kind of relationship.

Then why was she cozying up to this jerk, of all people?

Damn, she put an arm around the man's neck and kissed

his cheek. What the hell? This was just too much to sit back and watch.

Ty walked over to where Buck's son and Jordan were flirting and laughing. She sat in his lap while his filthy hands slithered across her skin.

"Hey, how's your back and head?" Ty asked.

Jordan twisted and met his gaze. All the color drained from her face, leaving her damn near as pale as the night she fell off the picnic table.

That's right, I busted you, sweetheart.

"Ty, what are you…? Why are you here?" she asked.

He was pretty sure she'd just spoken, but the visual of her wrapped around Warren temporarily seized up his brain. It was perfectly clear now. Last night had been one big, whopping mistake. Even after she'd thrown him out, he would've sworn there was something between them. Apparently, he'd been wrong.

"What are you doing here?" she asked again.

"I work here. Running security for Buck."

She eased to a stand but said nothing.

Buck called Warren into the office. When they were alone, Ty stood face-to-face with her for a few miserable seconds. She looked stunned, shocked into silence. That was a first. In fact, she opened her mouth to say something and then snapped it closed and turned to walk away.

Ty followed her. "What, no congratulations on my new job? I thought maybe you'd be happy to see me here, but I didn't know I'd be cutting in on your thing with Warren."

"Really?" She spun around, coming at him like a lion springing toward its prey. "You thought I'd be happy to see you working for Buck, security no less? Well, think again."

She pinned him with a hot look of anger. "You know, you basically accused me of having no pride." She looked around at the other waitresses, who were already there, and lowered her voice. "Told me how stupid I was for working here, that this was a bad place nice women didn't work in. Now, here you are. A bit hypocritical, don't you think?"

He leaned in until they were nose to nose. "Is it uncomfortable having two guys you're messing around with in the same building?"

She shrank back as if he'd hit her. "What?"

Ty folded his arms across his chest and continued to glare.

"I am *not* messing around with anyone."

"Really? You keep telling yourself that, sweetheart. Who knows what would have happened last night if we hadn't been interrupted by a phone call. Now I find you in Warren's lap, letting him run his hands all over you. My mistake. I thought you were different from the rest of the women who work here. I thought you didn't get how much trouble there could be in a place like this. Stupid me, I thought maybe you'd be happy to have someone watching your back."

"If that's why you're working here, I tried to be perfectly clear last night. I don't need you or anyone else watching my back. This is precisely the reason I don't want a man in my life. One stupid kiss and you think you have a right to bitch about what I do and who I do it with."

"One stupid kiss? Really?" He looked around. The bartender and another cocktail waitress were looking in their direction. He leaned close and whispered in her ear. "I guess I really was the one who didn't get it. You're obviously exactly where you belong, doing exactly what you're good at."

The night dragged slowly and without mercy. Jordan had more body parts that hurt than didn't. The loud, pounding music and flashing lights were doing a number on her head. Her feet hurt. Her back throbbed. Even her heart ached—Ty's harsh words had stung more than she'd ever dare admit.

His physical presence alone seemed to stir something inside her, but every time the man opened his mouth, she ended up stumbling over some stupid emotion. If he had the power to trip her up every damn time he came near, she'd avoid him like the kryptonite he was.

They'd known each other about three minutes, and he expected what? Some sort of commitment? Her undying love because he was the first guy to bring her to a mind-numbing orgasm in…Well, it was none of his business how long it had been for her. That's probably why it had felt *so* good. A long abstinence could make even the most mediocre encounter feel like bliss.

He hadn't even given her a chance to explain. Not that she *could* explain. But the things he said, the way he had looked at her…

Probably similar to the way she'd looked at him. She was still reeling over him being Arlo Buck's head security man. That couldn't be good.

Even so, she couldn't stop watching him. But not once this evening had he allowed his cool gray eyes to meet hers. Now she needed to figure out why that stung so badly.

Determined to ignore Ty, she loaded her tray and headed back to her section. It was slow in the club tonight, but she had a table of seriously drunk young men who were tipping extremely well. She was lost in thought, half debating whether her income was better as a cop or a waitress, when an uninvited hand touched her ass and snapped her back into reality.

Great. A drunk old man with fast fingers and warm beer breath, spouting obscene sexual innuendos. How could she resist? She was fully prepared to let it go, but the old coot grabbed her hips and gave a sharp tug.

She stumbled back and dropped onto his lap. Her tray and five full beer bottles toppled to the floor. When she turned to glare at him, he was smiling, but he had no front teeth. None. At all. On the top or the bottom. He also sported the worst comb-over she'd ever seen, plus a scraggly, long beard.

Rubbing two ten-dollar bills together, he winked. "You. Me. A VIP room. Come on, sugar."

Was that his idea of a big payoff for getting to grope a woman half his age in a dirty, little room for a few minutes? The thought was absurd, but she decided to blow him off with a friendly smile. "I'm sorry, but I'm a waitress, not a dancer. The dancers are the only ones permitted in the private rooms."

After the Lewis incident, she needed to avoid a scene. She had no desire to explain why she'd been fired from the nightclub before the mission technically started. The old man seemed fairly harmless, so tonight was his lucky night. She'd let him off with a warning glare. What the hell, he didn't have any teeth to knock out anyway.

She'd save all her hostility for Tyler McGee.

• • •

Ty watched Jordan all night. Every time her back was turned, that is. Never when she'd look at him. He wouldn't give her the satisfaction of that.

"Jesus, the woman is just a magnet for trouble," he grumbled when he whipped around to see she'd been the one to drop another tray full of beers. His heart tripped when he saw her wrestling with a very drunk customer.

He stewed for a minute, wondering if he should let Jordan get a solid glimpse of how her life would be if she was dumb enough to continue to work at Buck's. Every instinct in his body was screaming for him to snap the old, grimy hairball in half. But before he knew it, a crowd had formed around her.

"You want me to take care of that?" Big Tom asked, pointing in Jordan's direction.

"No. I'm on it," Ty growled, dashing in her direction.

He broke through the crowd, then stopped abruptly. She had apparently decked the old guy, taken him down, and was now kneeling on his back.

"What are you doing?" Ty pulled her off the old man.

"Your job, apparently." She sneered and stalked off.

Five young guys, who were likely from the college in the next town over, were hollering, teasing, and in general, laughing their asses off as they marveled at the old man who'd been knocked down by a waitress.

Ty pushed the old man over to Tom to have him escorted out and then turned back to the table of young men still in awe of what they'd seen.

It was unlikely that a drunk who'd caused trouble would take legal action, but Buck had made it clear he wanted to be covered against anything that resembled a lawsuit. Ty grabbed an incident report and approached the table next to "Old Floyd's." That's what the college guys were calling the loser who had manhandled Jordan.

A skinny, blond guy well on his way to being obnoxiously drunk spoke first.

"Dude, Old Floyd tried to snag himself a feel." They all laughed hysterically, punching each other in the arm. "Looking for a freebie, I guess. I mean, he was all hands with her for a while. She was trying to blow it off, but we all saw it coming."

Another guy blew beer out of his mouth trying to choke back his laugh.

"Yeah, Old Floyd went for the golden ticket, and she ninja'd him right to the floor." He wiped his mouth on his arm. "It was awesome. She must be like a black belt or something. I'm going for the golden ticket when she comes back, 'cause I want her to hurt me." He made an obnoxious thrusting motion with his hips. "Please baby, please. Hurt me."

Ty scrubbed a hand down his face, holding back his temper. He remembered being pretty drunk and stupid in college, but these guys needed a serious ass-kicking. Of course, so did about fifty percent of the idiots who walked in the door of Buck's. But Jordan *liked the tips*.

Fuck that.

If she wasn't smart enough to walk away on her own, he was just going to have to give her grief until she quit.

"I'm going to write up the incident. It will say the customer inappropriately and repeatedly touched the waitress. I'll be back, and I'd like to get your names. Oh, and I'm going to suggest you boys behave with the waitress, or Old Floyd won't be the only one dropped to the floor."

Great. Now there was paperwork. Now he'd have to talk to her. Now he'd need to find the restraint not to shake sense into her. And he was seriously annoyed at himself, because the only thing he could really think about was whether she was okay or not.

He found her in the parking lot, heading to her car. "Where are you going?"

"Home. I've got a headache, and we're slow. Warren said I could leave."

"Buck's got new rules. I need a statement from you in case there's trouble. You knocked a customer flat. His lip was bleeding." He stepped between her and her car, folded his arms.

"That's right. I already took down one jerk tonight; I got no problem doing it again. You don't want to look like a fool in front of your buddies, do you?"

"Well, while I'm trembling in my boots, you're gonna need to come back inside and sign off on the trouble you caused."

"The trouble I caused?" She took a half step back and narrowed her eyes. "You want my statement? Fine. I had to deal with a customer who stuck his grimy fingers in my back pocket, because you were too pissed off and thickheaded to do your job. You took your sweet time coming to help me out. You're a sorry-ass excuse of a bouncer and, apparently, a sorry-ass excuse of a cop since you've lowered your career ambitions to the likes of Buck's. Put that in your report and shove it up your—"

"Hey, hey, hey! Don't blame me because you sit in strange men's laps and then get all high and mighty when they expect something more than a beer. This is your dream job, remember? You like it here. 'It's good money. I make good tips,'" he mocked in an obnoxious, girly voice. "That's what you told me."

As soon as the last word left his mouth, he regretted saying them. Even as mad as he was, he could hear the petulant tone of a jealous five-year-old in his voice.

Fury rolled off Jordan in thick, hot waves. "Titus really does have its fair share of village idiots running around, but I got to tell you, cowboy, not one plays the part better than you. Let's get it straight," she growled, ramming a brightly colored fingernail into his chest. "Buck's is not anyone's dream job, is it? I didn't willingly sit in anyone's lap tonight. I was harassed by a drunk customer. I work here. It happens. I accept that. But it's your job to keep things like this from happening. I know you could have come to help me faster than you did."

Guilt welled inside him. In his fleeting moment of stubbornness, she could have gotten hurt again.

"If you don't want to do this job, why are you working here?" she argued. "I'm sure you could find—"

"I'm sorry." He grabbed her pretty face and silenced her with a kiss. Not a sweet, gentle kiss. A dominating, fry your circuits, I-want-you-more-than-my-next-breath kind of kiss.

At first, she pushed against his chest, but by the time he finished with her lips, she clung to his shirt as if it was the only thing holding her upright.

And she was quiet, too.

• • •

Well, that certainly took the wind out of her sails. Only a

moment ago, she had a long, painful list of insults she was dying to let loose on him. Now she couldn't even speak.

A kiss like that could stop time. End wars. Bring world peace. Maybe even get her to forgive him, because really, any anger after that just seemed stupid.

"I'm sorry," he said again, breathing heavily. "You're right, I should have helped you sooner."

Jordan took in a few deep breaths of her own, trying to steady herself. Her hands were still clutching his shirt. She pried them open and backed up, putting a few well-needed inches between them. Good God, she couldn't allow herself to be kissed like that. What if Warren had seen them? Just when she was getting him to trust her?

She had to make him understand that he needed to leave her alone. "Look, I know you're trying to get me to quit, but I'm here because I have to be. I don't have a choice."

Of course, he wouldn't understand why. Sure enough, he rolled his eyes. She decided to try another approach, using a truth she estimated was fairly universal for most of the women who worked there. Much more calmly she said, "Maybe in your perfect world, with a perfect family, you have a safety net. If you can't pay your rent or bills, someone can step up. It's never been that way for me."

It wasn't a lie. In fact, the harsh reality of it lodged a lump in the middle of her throat. She'd been hugely alone since the night a crazed drug addict had killed everyone she loved. She knew exactly what it meant to be by yourself, struggling to make ends meet.

"I make more at Buck's in one night than I could make in a week at my last job. It's nights, it's flexible, and I only have to do it until…" *Until I throw Arlo Buck in jail.* No, she couldn't say that. "Until I'm done with school this year."

He trapped her between his arms and leaned against her car. Even after he'd been in a smoky bar half the night, his scent arrowed straight through her.

"Maybe I just lost my head when I saw you with Warren." He shifted closer and blocked most of the air chilling her skin. Ironically, along with the warmth came a vicious outbreak of goose bumps.

"Are you dating him?" he asked.

She choked out a laugh, but there was absolutely no humor in it. She let her eyes drift to his, and knew, or at least felt, he couldn't be a part of Arlo Buck's drug mess. God, he had the most beautiful face. Was that an insult for a man? She couldn't help it. Every time she looked at him, she was struck by it. The wicked lips, the chiseled chin, and for God's sake, the eyes that danced between a hypnotic silver and a dark, dangerous gray, depending on his mood.

"Look, you have to trust me when I tell you I know how to handle myself," she said. "I've been doing it since I was ten. You're right, this is a bad place, and some less-than-honest deals are being made here. I'm just a waitress, and I intend to stay neutral with Warren and Arlo, even very friendly if need be. They're not people you want to cross."

Heaven help her, but she was going to try to save him. God only knew why. It wasn't a good decision. It wasn't smart. It probably wasn't even based on gut instinct that he was innocent. It was a decision based solely on the fact he made her insides curl every time he stepped close. If he had even an ounce of cop instinct left in his body, he'd take the hint.

"Ty, you need to find a different job. Don't ask me

questions; I can't elaborate. I've become friendly with Warren, and I've overheard a few conversations I shouldn't have. You need to listen to me. Tell Buck this isn't for you. You've had another offer, a change of heart, whatever, just get out." She turned to escape into her car.

He caught her upper arms and pulled her back against his chest. His lips nuzzled against her ear. "What do you know?"

His demanding, husky voice penetrated down to her bones. She spun around, seething, hoping to cover desire with anger. "I know I've had the last private conversation with you I intend to have. I've told you what I can. Now be smart. Stay the hell away from Warren and Buck. Stay the hell away from me. I mean it."

She turned and opened the door of her car, only to have him slam it. He snagged her arm again, much less gently this time.

"If there's something going on, I need to know."

She twisted and looked up at him. "You'll walk away from all of this, me included, or the next time you touch me, you'll end up in a lot worse shape than the old man who put the moves on me tonight. And just for the record, if you're not smart enough to quit on your own, I can have you fired in a heartbeat. He already hates you." She tilted her head toward Warren Buck, who was approaching quickly.

"You're supposed to be watching the floor, McGee, not hassling the girls. I told Jordan she could leave." Warren's gaze fixated on Ty's hand, the one still wrapped around Jordan's arm. "Is there a problem here?"

"No problem. Just your dad's pit bull growling about how I haven't signed the incident report. Heaven forbid that would wait until my next shift," she said, sneering at Ty.

"Get back inside, McGee. The only employees you worry about are your crew. I'll take care of the girls. You got a problem? You come to me or my dad. Now get lost."

...

Ty decided it would be better to walk away. Beating Warren Buck bloody would have been, in the short run, very satisfying. But his goals ran a bit more long-range. He stepped back and walked inside but never left the window where he could watch for himself every move Warren made with Jordan.

Warren played with her hair, smoothed a finger down her arm, slipped his hands around her waist, and leaned in to steal a kiss.

The look on her face said it all. She shrank back, lightly tapped his chest, and pushed him away.

Ty thought back to last night when he'd kissed her. They'd damned near torn each other apart. He rubbed a finger over his lip, still tingling from their kiss of a few moments ago.

Jordan wasn't interested in Warren. She brushed him off like a piece of lint.

Ty's jealousy diffused quickly but was replaced by something equally as uncomfortable. A feeling that she might be in a lot more trouble with the Bucks than he first thought.

"So what the hell is she up to?" He eased back from the window. Something about her didn't make sense. She must know something about the Bucks. Or maybe…maybe they had something on her. God, could Warren be blackmailing her?

He'd tried to warn her the other night, but maybe he'd been wasting his breath. Maybe Buck had already gotten to her.

"Damn it." He didn't have a clue what Warren could be holding over her, but finding out was his new number-one priority.

Chapter Six

Jordan had barely been home long enough to change and wash her face when she heard the knock. She looked through the peephole to see Ty standing there. *At two in the morning.* Geez, the man was honestly clueless. She toyed with the idea of ignoring him and going to bed.

"I know you're home, Jordan. I saw your car in the lot. Will you open up for a few minutes?" he called out. "Please. I'd like to talk to you privately. Not while we're standing in the middle of Buck's parking lot."

Silently cursing, she leaned her head against the door and mentally listed all the reasons to keep it shut. Not the least of which was the way her stupid body reacted every damn time she looked in his direction. She reached for the doorknob but decided the chain was staying firmly in place. The big muscled chest and the seductive eyes were staying exactly where they belonged—locked on the other side of a thick slab of wood.

"What are you doing here?" she asked through the tiny opening. "I think we already said everything that needs to be said."

"Maybe you did, but I want to talk to you. Can I come in?"

"No." She kicked the door shut, but somehow *knew* that wasn't going to be the end.

"Fine. Okay, fine. You're right, it's really late." His voice vibrated through the small crack between door and frame. "I just wanted to apologize for earlier and ask you a few questions. But we can talk tomorrow. In Buck's. In front of everyone. I don't mind apologizing or maybe asking you out in front of a strip joint full of drunks."

He let the implication hang silently in the air.

The son of a bitch was good. Jordan shook her head and bit down on her lip to stop the thin smile that was threatening. He *knew* the very last thing she'd allow was for him to embarrass her at the club tomorrow. The threat may have been idle, but with Tyler McGee, one could never really be sure.

"I think it'll be nice for Buck's customers to see a little romance playing out in front of them. I'll see you tomorrow," he said. "Sleep well, baby."

See? That's why he's toxic.

But he'd made his point. If he had something to say, she damn well wanted him to get it out of his system tonight, in private. And stay far, *far* away tomorrow.

She steeled herself for the inevitable surge of...insanity... that would zing through her when she caught sight of him. Rolling her head from side to side, she inhaled a steadying breath.

Tonight's strategy called for cool disinterest.

She slid the chain loose and opened the door. His eyes were the first thing that usually screwed with her resolve; tonight was no exception. She avoided the trap by glancing away and waving him in. "What do you want, Ty? I'm tired."

As dangerous as the eyes were, his body held another kind of appeal that defied all logic. He'd skipped the jacket tonight. Nothing to hide the black shirt tucked into snug, low-riding jeans. The polo molded to his body as tightly as the pants. His chest and arms looked like they'd been melted and poured into it.

With his hair a bit too long and the hint of a beard on his face, his normal appearance edged toward dark and dangerous. But tonight, even with the easy movement of his body, she sensed his mood had turned a bit darker, too. He was carrying a chip on his shoulder about something; it didn't take ten years of experience as a cop to figure that out.

"I've been trying to make sense of it all." He paced away from her, drifting around the room. "Trying to figure it out. Figure *you* out. Why you'd give a drugged-out loser like Warren Buck a second glance." He turned back toward her. "Sit in his lap and let him kiss you."

She shrugged. "It clearly sounds like you need a hobby. Something more interesting than poking your nose into my life. There's no mystery here, Ty."

Slowly, he strolled toward her, tilting his head a little. "I think you're nothing *but* one big mystery." Apparently, he'd worked out a strategy of his own. His tone remained even, his body language mirrored hers—the picture of casual indifference—but his eyes gave him away. The dark, predatory stare betrayed a heat simmering just below the surface.

Her body responded with a sharp inhale. Damned if there wasn't heat kindling in her own blood, too. But she knew exactly how to douse the flame. "I like Warren. Did it ever occur to you that I might want to be with him?"

"Actually, it did. Then I saw Warren pull you close in the parking lot." His eyes shifted, taking in every nuance of her expression. He'd slipped into cop mode and was waiting for a tell to pass across her face. But then his gaze dipped to her lips and stayed there. "It didn't look like you appreciated his kiss too much to me. Remember," he whispered, "I know what your face looks like when you enjoy it."

An eerie silence flooded the room, and a sharp sexual twist pulsed between them. She closed her eyes. It was a pathetic last line of defense, but if she couldn't see the dark desire burning in his expression, maybe her own stunning ache would ease.

"Am I wrong?" He murmured again. "Did you like Warren's kiss?" His hand slid into her hair and tangled. He tugged, gently, so she had no choice but to tilt her head back. "If you feel something for him, now is the time. Tell me, and I won't bother you again."

She stood silent, unresponsive, and kept her eyes closed. It was one short, simple lie. But every time she tried to push the words out, they died in her throat. What the *hell* was wrong with her?

He tugged again until her eyes slitted open. "Is he blackmailing you?"

"No. Let go." She refused to make eye contact and attempted to shake free.

"Is he threatening you?"

"I don't have to tell you anything."

"Damn it, Jordan, don't you understand how dangerous he is? You *will* tell me what's going on if it's the last thing I ever accomplish."

This time, it wasn't the arrogant tone or questions that bothered her, but rather the concern in his voice that pierced something deep in her chest. What little determination she had to push him away was fading quickly. He had to go. Right now. In pure frustration, she brushed past him to show him the door.

He reached out and caught her arm.

With a move that bordered on uncontrolled, she whipped around to face him. They stood eye to eye, both too stubborn to look away and diffuse the tension. Fighting to level out the jagged hitch of her breath, Jordan looked down at the hand on her arm, then trailed her gaze back up to meet with his.

He released her. Just when she thought she'd survived the worst of his anger, he laid a hand against her cheek, sliding his thumb over her bottom lip. Heat from his large, hard body scorched hers, and that's when she felt it strongest—want and desire punching through her like a fist through tissue paper. Need mixed with her blood, coursing through her veins like a drug.

He smoothed both hands down her arms and entwined their fingers, then backed her up until his body had hers pressed against the wall. Raising her arms above her head, he said, "I'll tell you what, you humor me and tell me what it is about Warren that makes you fall all over him, and I'll walk out your door. No questions asked."

Their eyes connected in a moment of raw truth, and Jordan knew—just knew—that the way he affected her was more dangerous than any criminal element she'd ever gone up against.

"Nothing to say?"

He wanted her to talk? She was lucky she could draw enough air to stay coherent.

One hand cuffed her wrists, the other slid down her body until it settled on her bottom and drew her hips flush against his. "Don't tell me the woman who uses her tongue like a carving knife is speechless. I'm gonna tell you what I think."

That wicked hand held her firmly against his hard length.

"I don't think Warren makes you shiver like this when he touches you." He bent his head close to hers and murmured, "I don't think Warren is who you want to be with."

His whiskered cheek scraped against her skin. Warm breath feathered down her neck. "His looks? His career? Which is it? Or do you like his hands?" All of his attention focused on her breast now. He cupped it and stroked a thumb across the sensitive tip.

She gasped, trying to decide whether to slap him or plead for more, but a betraying shiver convulsed through her body.

"Do you like his eyes?"

Of course, she couldn't help looking into his piercing, spell-like gaze at precisely that moment. Tyler McGee knew damn well what those eyes of his did to women. He counted on it.

"His lips?"

Slowly, ever so slowly, he took her face in his hands and leaned close, pressing his smooth, soft lips against hers.

She groaned. For the first time in her life, she had a sympathetic pang of understanding for addicts, a glimpse of what addiction must be like—facing something so utterly destructive and wanting it badly enough not to give a damn about the consequences.

The kiss spun out. Desperate. Intoxicating. Their hands and limbs moved, entwined, touched. He broke off the kiss long enough to come up for air. His chest heaved, and his lips were moist and red from kissing her. At least she had the satisfaction of seeing him equally affected.

"Maybe it's just me," he said, "but there seems to be an awful lot of chemistry in this room for you to be so hung up on Warren Buck. Tell me I'm wrong."

Right. Telling the man anything was a lesson in futility. In just a few blurred moments, he managed to have her world tilting wildly off balance. She wanted him. Pretending otherwise seemed ridiculous.

He nuzzled into the curve of her shoulder, nipped at her neck, then soothed the sensitive skin with a heated lick.

She shivered, and the ache in her core turned to thick, hot liquid need. Her arms slid around his waist. Her fingers ran up his back and dug in with a desire she didn't understand. A few days ago, no one could have convinced her that her own body was capable of this kind of betrayal. She knew better. *Damn it*, she knew better.

With his mouth hot on hers, he dropped his hands to her butt and lifted her. Her legs circled his hips. His thick, rigid arousal pressed against the apex of her thighs, and her body tightened and strained. She moaned against his lips. It felt good, so damn good, but it wasn't enough. It was never enough with him.

Every kiss, every touch lured her farther away from everything she knew to be right. She tore her lips away from him and pushed at his chest. "Stop," she moaned breathlessly.

"Stop it." Her head pounded back against the wall.

They both stilled. Ragged breaths panted wildly out of sync with the staccato tick of the clock hanging on the wall next to them. He threw his head back, and a frustrated growl tore from his throat.

Setting her down, he broke all contact and stepped back. He scrubbed a hand down his face, then plowed his hands through his hair. Shaken, Jordan decided, almost as badly as she was, he squeezed his eyes tight as if the next words were painful. "Do you want me to go?"

"I want…" Desperation crawled through her. She didn't understand it. She blinked her eyes, searching for a clue in his face. When he looked at her, she saw the mirror image of her own desire and need. "I want you to touch me. I want your hands on me. And I want to feel you inside me."

The words surely didn't come from her mouth, from her brain, but there they were. A truth she had muttered without caring about any repercussions.

In less than a second, his body had hers pressed against the wall, his lips and tongue ravaging her. Their teeth clashed as the kiss turned into something desperate and urgent. Tugging the straps of her tank top off her shoulders, he pushed them lower and lower until her breasts were exposed.

Then everything stopped. His hands stilled, dropping away from her body.

Fear that he'd changed his mind rolled through her. She opened her eyes and saw him staring, almost reverently, at her chest.

"Dear God," he whispered. "Do you have any idea what seeing you like this does to me?" He moved his hand to her breast, gently caressed the skin, tracing around the nipple, lightly, as if treading new waters, as if exploring something magical and precious for the first time.

The soft, sensual touch almost buckled her knees. She'd always found her breasts more annoyance than asset. Until right now. Until this very moment when he leaned in, drew one nipple into his mouth, and gently clamped the stiff peak between his teeth. She arched into the sensations, and it was female pleasure, pure and simple, that brought a desperate moan for more to her lips.

"I want you," he murmured in a faint whisper on top of jagged breathing. "I've never wanted like this."

Her mind barely registered the words, but for a fleeting moment, she wondered if maybe *this* wasn't normal for him, either. Her reply was lost somewhere in an incoherent moan. She had no idea what she murmured, but her hands were greedy and trembling. She slid his black shirt up his torso and tossed it aside. If she didn't get her hands on his bare skin in the next few seconds, she was sure she would die. The desperate need to touch him wouldn't go away. She unbuckled his belt, opened his jeans, and curled her fingers around the burning hot, well-endowed length of him.

"Ah, Christ," he groaned.

He made quick work of her shorts and panties. Sliding his fingers underneath the fabric, he pushed at them until they pooled at her ankles. Lifting one of her thighs, he hooked it around his hip. His fingers glided against her, into her, with a precision that left her helplessly bowing into his touch.

She clenched a fistful of his hair as her body coiled and pulsed against the movement of his hand. *"God,"* she cried, not just breaking, but crumbling beneath his touch.

"God," she murmured again, slumping back against the wall, hands and arms splayed, scrambling for purchase against the onslaught of sensation.

He gave her no time to regroup, no chance to recover before he kneeled in front of her. Her eyes slid shut, but she felt his hands on her hips, felt his lips lightly grazing nerves that were still reeling. She heard him inhale deeply and groan, then his tongue began to move against her.

The man had turned her into nothing but sensation and greed. And as talented as his hands and mouth were, they weren't what she wanted. She put her hand under his chin and tilted his face up. Their eyes met. No words passed between them, but he seemed to have no trouble understanding her non-verbal plea for more.

Standing, he unleashed one more blinding kiss before reaching into his pocket and pulling out a condom. He held it out for her to take.

Maybe it was his way of asking if things should go farther, but she didn't acknowledge the small interruption, just ripped open the foil pouch and rolled it onto him before logic could catch up with the driving need to be taken—hard—by Tyler McGee.

The feel of him, the hard length of him in her hand, was enough to stir the need into desperation. "I want you inside me. I need to feel you." She pushed his pants lower and fisted a hand around him. With her back braced against the wall, she guided him into that first, breathtaking thrust.

Her body yielded easily, eagerly, despite his size and strength.

Appearing as lost as she was, he pumped into her with several hard thrusts and groaned. "Are you okay, baby?"

Don't you dare give me time to think.

"Don't you dare stop," she said.

From that point on, he didn't. The rhythm, just this side of frantic, hung between desperation and primal need. Every stroke, a new, deeper tangle of sensation. A magnificent sensory overload after a long, lonely sleep.

The way he moved, the way her body drew him so deeply inside, it was too much. Too pleasurable. Too frightening.

"Ty. God, Ty." She shuddered and clawed at his skin as she cried out. The orgasm built, rippling at first, then growing fangs and shredding apart anything that resembled feminine control. She pistoned wildly with him, felt his teeth on her throat as he bucked into her with a violent climax of his own.

Her ears roared. Her eyes swam. Her skin was on fire. Her throat clenched fiercely against the need to sob. She tried to let her legs untangle from where they had been locked around his hips, but he leaned against her and held on tight. She pushed at his chest and felt a damp bead of sweat slick down between her breasts.

A cold, prickly reminder of the mistake she'd just made.

•••

Moments later, Ty was still inside Jordan's trembling body, wishing to God he was lying in a bed with her instead of pinning her against a wall. If he could have gathered even a morsel of control, he would have been gentler, made it last longer, taken better care of her.

He wrapped his arms around her tighter, holding her still when she tried to move. He wasn't ready to let go yet, wasn't quite to the point where he could separate from her body and survive. He let his lips travel her neck, graze her ear, and then slide into a kiss tender enough to show her everything he hadn't taken the time to show her before.

At least he hoped it did. He hoped she could feel it, too. He wasn't great with words, but whatever lightning had just struck between them would probably lose something in translation anyway. It was the most unexpected, superb sexual experience he'd ever had. One he very much wanted to repeat in about ten minutes, body willing.

"My God," he said, kissing across her collarbone. "That was amazing. You're so damn beautiful, Jordan."

Her silence tipped him off that something wasn't right. A slow-motion untwining of bodies followed.

"Are you okay?" he whispered in her ear, still trying to hold her. But her withdrawal was clear. Not just physically, but emotionally, too.

She pushed at his chest. "Ty, I think you need to leave."

"What?" Leaving was nowhere near the agenda his mind had mapped out. He lifted her chin with a finger and saw tears glistening in her eyes. "Come on, don't cry. I wasn't that bad, was I?"

"I could describe what just happened in a lot of ways; bad wouldn't be one of them." She made a half-hearted attempt to smile, but tears began to roll. "You have to go now."

Puzzled, he backed up and studied her. She quickly tugged on her clothes and tossed him his shirt. He disposed of the condom, pulled up his pants, and stepped toward her. By the time he wrapped his arms around her, she was fighting a full-blown sob.

"Shhh, baby. It's okay."

"Don't." She lashed out at him, pushing out of his arms.

"Don't do that. It's not okay. I don't have sex with random strangers. Maybe you live your life this way, but I don't. This isn't who I am."

A quick bolt of anger lanced through him. She wanted to reduce what just happened to casual sex with a stranger? Damn! No one had ever pushed his buttons the way this woman could. "Did it feel like random sex to you, Jordan?"

She avoided eye contact. Her tears made his chest hurt, and guilt kicked his anger quickly to the side.

He'd wanted her from the first moment he saw her picking up glass from Buck's floor. The fact that she'd wanted him in return had gone to his head tonight. There was no getting around the fact he'd lost control like a damned rookie.

Softly tugging her arms, he pulled her against his chest. "Don't cry, baby. Please. I don't usually jump this quick, either, but there's something between us. There has been since the moment we saw each other. It's more than sex. I care about you."

She shook her head. "You don't even know me. You have no idea who and what I am. What we just did had *nothing* to do with caring."

He started playing it back. Did he push her to do something she hadn't wanted to do? Damn. He could deny it, deny what he was feeling when he'd walked into her place tonight, but it would be a lie. He moved closer again, lifting a hand to touch her, but she backed away.

"Jordan, I'm sorry. I didn't mean for it to happen quite this way. If I pushed too hard or—"

"Ty, stop." She said it harshly, as if she were scolding him, trying to snap him out of his guilt. "There were two of us participating, both quite eagerly, as I recall. I'm not fragile.

You didn't push me, for Christ's sake, and you're not stupid. At any point tonight, did I look like I was doing something I didn't want to do?" She swiped at the tears.

"Okay," he said. "Then I guess I don't understand the problem."

...

The problems—as in plural—were many. *I'm an undercover cop. I had sex with you. You work for Arlo Buck.* She wanted to scream, "Pick one."

She'd had sex with him. Mind-blowing, blood-curdling, vibrating sex. With a stranger, more or less. With someone who could be involved in foul play, although every cop instinct she possessed said that wasn't the case. She wasn't sure how many rules and moral boundaries she'd broken, but she could pretty well bet if he ended up arrested on any charges, she'd find out quickly. "I just can't do this. You need to leave. I'm sorry."

He reached for her one more time.

The insanity of it all was that she'd clearly made a mistake but desperately wanted to make it again and again. Instead, she avoided his touch, shot into the bedroom, and slammed the door.

When she finally heard him let himself out, she broke down. Checking to make sure he was gone this time, she struggled for answers and reasons. There had to be an answer as to why she'd chosen to throw away years and years of good, respectable police work. There must have been some reason for giving into lust and need, but at the moment, she couldn't think of even one.

Chapter Seven

Sometimes sanity felt like a judgment call.

Jordan didn't consider herself crazy. Of course, dreaming about dead people, hearing them, feeling what they felt just moments before their deaths was not something most people would consider sane.

Allowing herself to be fucked mindless by an employee of the Bucks wasn't leaning heavily in the direction of sanity, either.

Guilt. Regret. Anger. Humiliation. If it was a self-destructive emotion, she'd wallowed in it since the moment Ty walked out of her door several hours earlier. It all boiled down to one thing.

Shame.

She'd cared more about sex than she had about her badge. The entire case was in jeopardy now, not to mention her career. Even if they arrested Arlo Buck and he ended up on trial, her involvement with Ty could be the one thing that set Buck free again. The thought of it was sickening. It had taken approximately ten minutes to negate over ten years on the job.

Stupid. Stupid. Stupid.

McGee had better not push his luck and try to score an encore performance of last night. The sooner both of them moved on, the better.

In just a few short days, how had a lazy, sexy smile and two hypnotic, silver eyes done so much damage to her status quo? She wasn't some idiot who had sex without thinking first. Well, last night she had been, but usually—no. Never.

Then he'd had the nerve to apologize. As if he cared. As if it was all an innocent mistake.

Damn Tyler McGee.

He'd made good time with her, she'd give him that. Him and his stupid I'm-going-to-take-care-of-you charm. What, three days she'd lasted against it, and she was an undercover cop. Most of the idiot women in Buck's would probably just surrender the first night and save themselves the time and trouble.

Does that make them the idiot, or me?

Unprepared to face anyone until her shift started at four p.m. sharp, she took every long-cut possible on the way to Buck's.

Whether to confess to Bahan or not was another huge dilemma. He'd trusted her, worked with her, come up with her cover, and she'd blown it. If the situation were reversed, she'd have never forgiven him. She didn't expect anything less.

However she spun it, sleeping with a suspect, or a witness who might have vital information—no matter how remote the possibility—was inexcusable. Not that she'd gotten any of that vital information before she jumped him.

No, she told herself. *He jumped me.* That was the story, and she was sticking to it.

Oh, God, did it matter who jumped whom? They'd dived into each other like starving wolves with one tiny sliver of meat between them.

On the surface, it had appeared to be just good, *okay great*, sweaty, toe-curling sex. But it was everything that lay under the surface that was beginning to bother her most. The genuine concern she knew Ty felt over Warren Buck. The way he'd stepped back and offered to leave when she herself couldn't find that kind of resolve. The complete shock on his face when she'd kicked him out.

Her heart told her that those weren't the actions of a man pushing drugs for Arlo Buck. If she were wrong, if her instincts had veered that badly off track, she had no business carrying a badge any longer.

As luck would have it, Ty was in the parking lot when she pulled into Buck's. His muscular arms were folded over his chest as he leaned back against his truck. The taut black material of his shirt stretched across his broad shoulders. He wasn't handsome in that classic boy-next-door kind of way, Jordan decided, but if you liked big and rugged with fuck-me eyes and a country swagger, he'd be your crack cocaine of choice.

Apparently, she liked fuck-me eyes, because her mouth nearly watered as she pulled up next to him. She took a deep breath, scrambling for some form of composure. It was damn hard picturing Ty as a suspect. Harder yet to cut him loose, especially now that she had intimate knowledge of what lay beneath the shirt and jeans.

But it had to be done. Right now.

"We need to talk," he said before she'd even gotten out of her car. "Jordan, things got out of hand very quickly last night, and for that, I'm sorry. Please give m—"

"Stop saying you're sorry. I was there, too. I'm a big girl." She stepped out of her car and glanced at her watch. "It's over now. Let's just forget it happened. We both better get inside."

He caught her wrist but dropped it quickly when she shot him a warning glare. "Warren and Arlo won't be here for another hour," he said. "We have plenty of time."

He stepped closer, narrowing the distance between them to just a few dangerous inches. His face was marred with stress and emotion. "What the hell is going on with you?"

Of all the damned men in the world, she had to find the one who wouldn't want to have hot, mind-blowing sex and then walk away with no strings. He wasn't going to make this easy. The throbbing pound of her heart shot into high gear.

She sucked in some air, then let it out slowly, searching for the right words. "Last night...Well, I shouldn't have let it happen, but after it did, I didn't handle the whole thing very well, and I'm sorry."

"Jordan, I understand if you hate me."

His hair was a mess. His beautiful eyes were smudged with dark circles. His clothes were rumpled. He looked like he'd had a hard, sleepless night.

God, he was gorgeous.

Why tenderness washed through her so deeply at that moment, she couldn't have said. "Ty, I don't hate you—"

"No, let me finish." He covered his eyes with one of his hands and then rubbed it down his face. She noticed the unconscious routine, knew he would then drag his fingers back through his hair. And he did. It was his classic one-two move of frustration. She'd seen it a lot in the last few days. Which was an accurate, if not promising, summation of their relationship.

He reached out and took her hand. "I don't have a very graceful way of saying this, so I'm just going to say it. I feel like I should apologize for what happened." He lifted her fingers to his lips and tenderly kissed them. "But I bet if we both were truthful, neither one of us would be a damn bit sorry. Still, I didn't come over with the intention of things happening quite like they did. I want a chance to show you who I really am." He flashed the brilliant Tyler McGee smile. "I can be downright romantic if you let me."

Christ. All she could think was that Jordan Delany—immune-to-love, take-no-prisoners, justice-to-the-death cop—had a horrible, destructive crush on a man whose eyes were nothing short of mesmerizing. And he was working at Buck's as head of security.

"Ty, you didn't do anything wrong last night." In fact, he'd done everything just a little bit too right.

"Sure, that's why you kicked me out."

"There were two of us. I'm perfectly able to hold my own when I need to. The truth is…Well, the truth is I didn't want to say no. I could have. I didn't want to." Looking at him stripped her of the ability to lie. "I wanted you as much as you wanted me. It was—"

"Incredible. Amazing," he offered.

Her lips curved, and she shook her head.

"Mind-blowing, life-changing," he continued with his trademark smile.

"Shut up, you idiot." He actually had her grinning in spite of the train-wreck of a mess she'd made. "I was going to say mutual. You don't have anything more to feel guilty about than I do, but I'm sorry—it can't happen again."

"It will happen again," he said without pause or question. His rapid-fire response raised her hackles.

"It won't." She volleyed the words back.

"So, you snap your fingers, and it's over. Just like that?"

"Just like that."

"I really thought you were smarter." He leaned cheek to cheek with her. His warm breath caressed her skin. "I don't think you're any better at controlling this thing, attraction, or whatever it is, than I am. Are you, Jordan?"

She shivered and closed her eyes. The manipulation was obvious. Unfortunately, so was her body's reaction. Her heart ached to tell him he was right.

But then he said, "We can make this work."

That brought it all into focus. He thought there was a "we." She stepped back and took a deep breath, attempting to clear her senses of everything Tyler McGee. "I can't do this with you. I told you there was no room in my life for a guy."

Looking disgusted, he narrowed his eyes, propping his hands on his hips. "Yeah, I can see how those twenty minutes you gave me would really take a toll. What aren't you telling me?"

The man was a fucking dog with a bone. "There's nothing to tell. You want more, I don't. It's over."

He clearly wasn't interested in her half of the conversation. He wagged his finger as if she hadn't spoken at all. "I've got a bad feeling there's something going on between you and

Warren. Something a whole lot uglier than some simple, harmless flirting. If you need help—"

"I can't have this out with you right now." She held up her hand to cut him off. "Whatever *is* between me and Warren is my business. My shift was supposed to start a couple of minutes ago. I need to go."

"Damn it." His eyes could change like a bloody damned mood ring. Right now, a cold, hard concrete gray snapped out at her. "Jordan, he's a spoiled brat, not to mention an alcoholic. He's got a hell of a temper, and he's lit every night of the week. I've asked around about him; he's bad news."

He cupped the back of her neck and drew her close. The move was quick; she looked up, inhaling sharply at his intense glare. He leaned in and covered her lips with his.

The kiss was soft, a shocking contrast to the hard lines in his expression only moments ago. Her legs began to melt like candle wax under the heat of a flame. Her head tilted back, allowing the smooth, gentle stroke of his tongue better access to her own. It should have been a short, simple kiss. One she should have dodged. But it turned out to be neither short nor simple.

The man's lips could coax any reasonable thought right out of her head. But it was the soft bite and tug on her bottom lip that had her arms springing up around his neck. Every single nerve craved him. The roar of a car barreling down the road finally made her peel herself off him and inspect her surroundings.

After the car passed, he stepped closer again, murmuring into her ear. "Warren Buck can't make you feel like that."

Nothing had ever made her feel like that. And it was reason enough to end whatever this was before it began.

"This *won't* work. I *cannot* have this in my life." She pushed away quick and hard. "I'm not with Warren, but I won't make him angry, either. He does seem to have feelings for me, and I need this job. If you care about me at all, you won't come between us. I can't afford for Warren to think there's something going on between you and me."

"He can't fire you because you're interested in someone else. That's completely childish."

"And just the kind of thing he would do, don't you think? I have to go. Don't come near me in there. I mean it."

...

The woman made his blood boil. In good ways. In bad ways. He'd known her less than a week, and quite possibly, she'd be the death of him.

It didn't make sense. She didn't make sense. There was more to her story than met the eye. He'd bet everything he owned on that fact. She was smart. Good personality. Sexy as hell. And she no more belonged at Buck's than he did.

Don't come near me in there; I mean it.

Her words tore at him. She claimed she wasn't interested in taking things farther, but her body spoke a truth she couldn't possibly deny. She wanted to dismiss what happened between them as a primal, sexual mistake. Maybe it had been primal and sexual, but mistake? Not likely. She'd admitted to the attraction, and he knew they weren't over.

But he'd give her time to come to terms with it all. He'd play it slow. Steady. Controlled. Give himself time to figure out what the hell kind of hold Warren Buck had on her. He hoped she hadn't done something illegal with the

Bucks holding proof. Warren Buck would love nothing more than to have a woman like Jordan in his bed, even if it took blackmail to achieve it.

Ty was with his crew in the corner of the club, going over proper takedown procedures, when Warren sauntered in. He was loud and obnoxious and carrying on with a couple of his friends. By the time the place closed, Warren could work up a good drunk. Apparently, he'd gotten an early start today.

Determined to ignore the idiot, Ty continued working with the bouncers. He'd finished the official meeting and was talking about scheduling problems when a couple of the guys lost interest and started mumbling.

"Warren is seriously drunk," Big Tom whispered. "And he has a major hard-on for Jordan."

Ty's gaze zeroed in on Warren.

"Jordan, come here, darlin'. Take a load off those amazing legs." Warren's obnoxious voice echoed off the walls of the mostly empty club.

Ty stared in Jordan's direction; he couldn't help himself. Warren Buck had his hands on her hips. Ty's jaw clenched hard enough to grind his teeth into dust, but he'd choke down the anger. If this is how Jordan wanted it, so be it. He turned back to his guys, determined to ignore anything Warren said. The problem was, he could hear everything the bouncers were saying.

"She ain't giving it up to him," the other bouncer whispered. "He ain't in her league."

"This is my girl, right here." Warren boasted loudly in front of his two friends. "She likes to play hard to get, but she's gonna come around real soon to the idea of the two of us together."

"See what I mean," Big Tom said. "Depends on how bad she wants to keep her job. I've seen his moves when he comes in drunk like this. He'll pull her in the office or a VIP room in a couple of minutes. If she likes the money here enough, she'll give."

With that, Ty felt the top of his head lift right off his body. "We're done here." The look he pinned on the two mumbling bouncers was sharp enough to cut diamonds. He stepped toward them. "Is Warren like this all the time?"

"Not usually. But only because he's scared of Arlo. His old man damn near drop-kicked him the last time he was this drunk in here. They had a huge fight, and everyone in the place heard Buck tell him he better straighten his ass out or he was cut off."

"A lot of good that did," Ty muttered.

He watched Warren brush Jordan's hair to one side and start nuzzling her neck.

Game over. Ty was pretty sure a blood vessel had just burst inside his head. So much for slow, steady, and controlled. Did Jordan think he was just going to sit and watch?

Not fucking likely.

He wove through the sea of tables toward the other end of the nightclub. The end where Jordan's station was and probably the spot where Warren would take his last breath.

Warren stood and tugged Jordan out the back door.

Fine with me. He didn't need a nightclub full of witnesses when he beat Warren unconscious.

Arlo Buck walked through the front doors of the club and almost collided with Ty. "McGee, follow me."

Ty stopped midstride and stared at Arlo.

"You deaf or just dumb, boy? Get your ass over here."

Buck plopped down at a table next to the bar.

Ty backtracked to Buck. He was still debating the wisdom of ignoring him and heading out the back door to kill Warren, but Jordan's voice played like a recording in his head. *"Stay away from me in there."*

"You legally covered to carry a gun?" Buck asked.

The question caught Ty's interest.

"Yes. I haven't needed one in here, but I'll make sure it's visible if you want me to."

"I'm getting some important deliveries of alcohol and food for the Christmas and New Year's parties. I want security, so all of the bouncers working. I want you armed. I don't trust them delivery guys. If they can find a way to screw you, they will."

Ty's focus shifted solely to Buck for a moment. Guys who delivered food and alcohol weren't notoriously untrustworthy, but guys who delivered drugs certainly could be. He nodded. "Okay. When?"

"Couple weeks before Christmas. Probably that Monday while we're closed." Ty nodded again and turned to walk away.

"McGee, what's wrong with you?" Buck called out.

On a flash of brilliance, Ty decided the best way to save Jordan was to fuel the fire between Arlo and Warren. "Warren came in about a half hour ago. He's pretty drunk, hitting on the waitresses and being loud. I know it's a bar, but he's obnoxiously loud. Hands all over the girls. He just pushed one of them out the back door."

Buck turned red, as though his blood pressure spiked about fifty points. Of course, that was precisely the intended reaction. For one brief moment, Buck looked almost human, more like an angry dad than a mean, nasty, drug-dealing son of a bitch.

"Go get him. Tell him to get in my office. Now."

Ty didn't have to be asked twice. He shot toward the back door like a bullet.

...

It wasn't so much the whiskey on Warren's breath or even the stale smell of sweat that made Jordan want to heave. It was the hand he cupped over her breast while pushing her up against the back wall. Not to mention it was freezing, and she was in shorts. All in all, not a position she hoped to find herself in. Not today anyway.

She was perfectly aware she'd been playing a dangerous game with Warren, and now the shameless flirting was beginning to backfire. The plan, her plan, was to dodge any serious moves for at least a few more weeks. Warren obviously had a timeline of his own.

He squeezed her breast and whispered in her ear. "Kiss me, Jordan."

The whiskey on his breath could have knocked out a lesser woman. She angled her face to the side.

It was a sticky situation at best. She would *not* insult him; a friendly line of communication with the Bucks was a must. But God, she wanted his hands off her body. She tried to let him down easy, but the subtle hints didn't seem to be registering.

"I'm sorry, Warren. I don't want to do this here. You're drunk. I'm freezing. Anyone could walk out the door at any moment. I know these outfits look like an open invitation, but I do have some standards."

The back door opened, and Ty flew out. He stormed up to Warren and got in his face. "Your dad wants you in his office. Right now."

"Scram, McGee."

Warren didn't bother to look at Ty, which was his first mistake. Not bothering to take his hand off her breast was probably the second.

Ty shoved him. But it was the fist he powered into Warren's stomach that dropped him to his knees and made him puke.

Jordan stood still and silent. Emotion told her to step between them and knock their heads together. Instinct told her to stand clear. She'd asked Ty to back off. The fact that he ignored her should have infuriated her, but being rid of Warren's hands was a definite bonus to his interference. And she hadn't had to break cover to save herself. So she just stood there.

Warren struggled upright. "You sealed your fate here, McGee. You're fired."

"Your dad hired me. If he fires me, I'll leave. But not before I tell him I found you assaulting a waitress in a parking lot while you were drunk. I heard a rumor that he doesn't like it when you come to work trashed. We can go in there and cause serious trouble for one another, or I can forget that I found you out here mauling an employee. Your call."

Warren glared at Ty as he stumbled past Jordan and back into the nightclub.

Jordan took one deep breath to compose herself. She swallowed hard, rubbing her hands up and down her arms to generate some warmth.

"It was no big deal," she said, although Warren probably outweighed her by two hundred pounds. Still, she was no pushover and had been trained well. With a weapon, she could have certainly dropped him. But alone, one-on-one, as tough as she believed herself to be, she knew it wouldn't have been a fair fight.

Apparently, Ty saw her moment of uncertainty.

She expected anger, a lot of anger. Instead, he put a hand on her chin and tilted her head up.

"Are you okay?"

His words were soft and sweet, but she'd be damned if she'd tear up like a helpless female because some big, drunk ape put his hands on her. But that had been as close as she'd like to get to a very large, very drunk man who took whatever he wanted and never suffered any consequences.

Ty pulled her close and wrapped his arms around her trembling body. He was warm and smelled…Well, as he always did. Amazing. The contrast between Warren's rough hands and Ty's gentle caress made her body wilt against him.

It struck her, profoundly, just how attracted she was to him. It was so much more than anything she'd ever felt, so much more than anything she'd ever wanted to feel. Definitely more than anything she *should* be feeling.

"Shit," she mumbled into his chest as her arms slid around him. "I'm fine. Go back in. I just need a moment here."

"Go home, Jordan. Get out of this place. If you need financial help until we find you something else to do, I'll help. You need to—"

"Stop, Ty. Just stop." She found the strength to push away from him. "Unless I go in and Buck fires me, I'm not quitting. You're the one who just hit Warren. You're the one who may not have a job much longer."

"Job or no job, I can help you. You said you never had a safety net; I'm offering to be yours. You don't have to put up with this crap. I want you out of here. Now. No arguments."

Her head began to swim. She wasn't sure if she wanted to laugh or cry. Instinct told her to take his head off for the utter stupidity of what he was demanding.

"Maybe you don't want to be taken care of, fine. You can pay me back. Can you honestly stand there and tell me you wouldn't like to walk away from this place?"

How did it all get so complicated? Huh, as if she didn't know. *Sex* complicated everything. She was in new territory. She'd never done anything quite so stupid. And yet, as much as she wanted to regret the whole thing and hate herself, hate him, and walk away, she was quite honestly having a hard time getting there.

"Look, I can't deny that I, you know, feel something. But damn it, Ty, I told you from the first day I met you that this"—she motioned between them—"whatever you think it is, can't happen. You can't go chasing me around or even look in my direction. I need you to pretend I don't exist."

"Yeah? Tell me this doesn't exist for you." He pulled her into his arms and crushed his lips over hers, kissing her roughly at first before letting it slide into a simmer of tenderness and passion.

Her knees buckled, her fingers dug into him, and her heart thundered. Her heart always thundered when he touched her.

He stroked his tongue across her bottom lip. Breathless, shivering, and almost incoherent from the kiss, she stepped back and stared at him.

"Maybe that doesn't exist for you," he said, "but it sure the fuck does exist in my world. Why are you here? Why are you scared of them? What do Warren and Arlo have on you that's trapping you in this godforsaken hellhole?"

She wasn't sure of the best way to answer and needed time to think, so she simply turned to walk away.

He snagged her wrist and pulled her close. "Neither of us is moving from this spot until you come clean. Since you're about to freeze to death, you better start talking fast. I mean it, Jordan."

Instinctively, in one slick move, she broke his hold, swept both of his legs, and tumbled him to the ground.

"The men in this town need a serious damned lesson on how to treat women," she said, stomping back into Buck's.

...

Ty half smiled at the way she'd taken him down. She had some moves he hadn't expected. Must have been how she took down the old man the other night. Almost like she'd had self-defense training or something.

And with that thought, he got it.

Jesus, I'm an idiot.

Never saw it coming, just like a bullet between the eyes.

She had moves, intelligence, beauty, and, it looked to him, very possibly...

A badge.

Chapter Eight

Jordan hadn't yet put the key into her door when she noticed it wasn't latched. "Son of a bitch," she mumbled under her breath. Someone had been there and done a slop-ass job of breaking in. They hadn't even bothered to cover their tracks.

Her hand instinctively slid to a holster that wasn't there. Being accustomed to carrying a gun, she found working without one on her person was the thing she hated most about this particular undercover. Being weaponless was a risk, but carrying while wearing short-shorts and a bikini top was a logistical impossibility.

She opened her purse, grabbed her Glock, and popped into the apartment with a low, fast sweep. No visible intruder, but the bedroom light was on. She paused to listen. No noise. No footsteps.

She whipped around the corner. Again, nothing. Another quick sweep into the bedroom proved uneventful, but the window was open. She walked to it and looked down, noticing some dirt that could have come from a shoe on the windowsill. A jump from the second floor wasn't impossible. Not one she'd voluntarily like to take, but if someone had been in the bedroom when they heard her come in, they might have done it.

Content with the knowledge she'd at least scared the intruder into an ugly jump for freedom, she'd clear the apartment and take inventory. Hopefully, it had just been a college kid looking for cash. She'd left precious little about her real life lying about, nothing that should feed anyone's suspicion. But the idea that someone was interested enough to break in was disturbing and something she'd need to report.

A peek in the closet showed her clothing untouched. If a thief had been looking for electronics or valuables, he'd have been sorely disappointed. Unless he collected rooster knickknacks, there wasn't a damn thing inside the place worth carrying over the threshold.

She stepped back into the hallway, her instincts kicking in just a second before large, powerful hands grabbed her from behind.

She rammed an elbow into a rib cage. When the guy crumpled over, she landed a sharp, vicious blow to his head with the butt of her gun.

He dropped to the floor and didn't move as she drove the barrel of her Glock into the back of his neck.

The takedown had been much too easy for an intruder of his size. Not a single protest, no fighting back. Jordan blinked in the dim light filtering in from the bedroom and immediately recognized the dark, wavy hair and expansive shoulders. Her gun was burrowed squarely into the neck of

Tyler McGee.

"You really are some kind of an idiot, aren't you?" Stomping a foot on his butt, she stepped over him and raged off into the other room. "Honestly, what the hell are you doing here? Do you have a death wish? I could have shot you."

He stood and followed her. Saying nothing, he folded his arms across his chest, and his lips curved into one of his smug smiles.

"Really? You think this is funny?" She raised the gun, it at him. "I ought to shoot that stupid grin right off your conceited face."

"Shooting an unarmed man at point-blank range seems like a bad move for a cop." He leaned casually against the back of her couch, not at all bothered by the gun aimed at him. "They'd probably take your badge if you killed an innocent man."

Her eyes opened wide as her brain fully absorbed the impact of his words. She made a sound very similar to a cornered, rabid animal. "You are a lot of things, McGee. Innocent is *not* one of them."

He'd figured it out. Figured her out. She took a few steps and kicked over a dining room chair, then whipped around and threw a rooster saltshaker at his head like a missile.

He ducked.

"Damn it all to hell. You've been a royal pain in my ass since the moment you walked into Buck's," she said.

She'd blown it. For the first time in her career, she'd blown it. A huge multi-jurisdictional investigation, and she'd been made as a cop.

This whole hellish undercover had been one big, hairy

disaster from the moment she'd crossed into the little flea-infested, two-bit, rat-hole town. And given the fact she'd messed the whole damned thing up so thoroughly, screwing with McGee's mind felt like the only reasonable thing left to do.

If she was going down and had to give up this undercover, she was at least going to give him as much grief as she could inflict. She stalked to a small desk in the corner, unlocked a drawer, and pulled out her badge and handcuffs.

Deadly serious, she walked back and looked him squarely in the eyes. "Down on your knees." With the wave of her gun, she motioned for him to drop.

His face sobered. "What?"

Ha. That knocked the smart-ass grin right off his face. "I said get down on your knees. Put your hands behind your head."

She watched as confusion and skepticism dawned in his eyes. He had no idea what to make of her now. Oh, yeah, she was going to enjoy this. And she was going to find out once and for all what his connection to Arlo Buck was.

"Funny. You're real funny, Jordan. Come on, I'm not getting on my knees."

She tossed him her badge. "I'm Jordan Delany, a narcotics detective with the St. Louis County PD. I'm working on an interagency drug task force team based in St. Louis. We're investigating a trafficking ring believed to be operating out of Buck's Nightclub. Because you broke into my place tonight, you're under arrest for breaking and entering. And because of your involvement as Arlo Buck's head security guy, I'll do my best to throw in suspicion of drug trafficking with intent to distribute."

It was a bluff, but a decent one. Watching the color drain from his face was satisfying. Very satisfying. She could see him reeling from the insult, but she knew better than to think he'd quietly cave. She'd bet every last dime on the fact that the man had never quietly caved on anything in his entire life.

"You can't arrest me. I didn't do anything."

"At the very least, you broke into my apartment. You can't deny that, since I caught you in the act. B and E alone can get you time, McGee. Add assaulting an officer, resisting arrest, drug charges—you're in deep."

Jordan was pleased her bluff had the intended effect. His eyes were wild with anger, but he swallowed it quickly. It was a nice recovery. And such a smooth one that she suspected he was plotting his countermove.

"Drug charges? Against me? That's ridiculous." His tone was dangerous and even, his body language implied, "I'm not worried." The man wore his arrogance like a finely made suit, but his eyes were a dead giveaway. He'd never be able to hide a damn thing from her in those overly expressive eyes. They spoke volumes in complete silence. Right now they said he was livid.

"I only broke in to get you to admit to being a cop. It finally sank in when you took me down in back of Buck's. Your moves were too powerful, too practiced, too precise for a cocktail waitress who'd simply taken a self-defense class. I knew you'd never come clean unless I forced you, and here, you defended yourself like a cop, gun and all. Case closed."

"Let me get this straight." She stepped closer. "You figured it more logical to break into my apartment and possibly get a bullet put in your ridiculously smug ass than to just confront me? You really are some kind of stupid. Get down on your knees. Now!"

Vibrating with anger, he assumed the pose—the one she'd seen him use on Warren. The one he'd whip out on any customer who dared to challenge him. The arms-folded, chin-set, I'm-not-budging stance.

"I'm not amused with your game, Jordan. I'm inside Buck's for the same reason you are. I've spent six months embarrassing myself and my family, letting the rumor circulate that I lost my badge because I failed a drug test. Now that I'm inside, no one is going to screw this up for me. Not even you, sweetheart. Sorry."

Jordan leaned casually against the wall and raised an eyebrow. "Wanna bet? Last time I checked, a federal investigation trumped the hell out an unauthorized, half-assed local one. I'd be happy to call my FBI contact and let him come sort this out."

An interesting shade of pissed-off red flushed his face. "You can't be serious. Everyone knows Arlo Buck is a major distributor of drugs, and not one person wanted to risk crossing him. It's about damn time someone did something about it. I'm on the same side of the law you are. Don't screw with me. If this is a joke, it's not funny."

"No joke, cowboy." Jordan stood straight, let every bit of emotion drain from her face. Bahan had dubbed it her *ice bitch* face. It had the intended effect when she was working over a junkie in one of the interview rooms. Ty certainly wouldn't be a pushover, but she hoped it would set him off kilter for at least a minute or two. "I'll ask for your cooperation one more time. Down. Now. Put your hands behind your head."

He dropped, laced his fingers, and nailed her with a look

so dangerous, it almost unnerved her enough to blow her game.

She walked around behind him and slapped the cuffs on. "Start talking, cowboy. Everything you know about Arlo Buck."

Stepping back in front of him, she bent slightly to get in his face. "If I get the teensy- tiniest inkling that your story is off, I'll have a dozen federal agents here before I get done reading you your rights."

"I'm a damn cop, too, Jordan. My chief authorized me to do some poking around on Arlo Buck. I've only worked for him for a couple days. This is bull. You can't touch me, and you know it. You need to call my chief."

Relief buzzed all the way to her toes. Having sex with another cop was considerably better than sleeping with a criminal. It still wasn't good, but if he was telling the truth, maybe last night's indiscretion wouldn't threaten her badge.

"I don't need to do anything but make one simple call and wait for the special agent in charge to come haul you away. Spill it now, McGee. If you're really trying to bust the Bucks, lay it all out for me. Your suspicions, your research, your hunches."

Sparring with another cop was never as easy as yanking the chain of some street thug. The problem being, he knew the law, too.

"See, you keep threatening me, but you've made no serious attempt to read me my rights. No call for backup." His smug smile returned. "I think you believe me."

"Don't think. Just talk." She was channeling her ice bitch, but she needed to study him in order to get a really good handle on whether he was telling the truth or not. And therein was the catch-22. Looking at him seriously screwed with her instincts.

"You know why you're not calling for backup?" His smile grew even more cocky and self-assured. "Because you already know you don't need any. You know I'm on your side."

He sighed as if digging deep for patience. "Look, I'm sorry I set you off by busting in here tonight, but I needed to know if I was right. I needed to know if we could work together and trust each other."

She choked out an incredulous laugh. "Whoa, whoa, whoa. Back the hell up. We are *not* partners. We are *not* working together. This isn't going away just because you want it to. You wanted to find out if I was a cop by breaking in here tonight? Well, congratulations, I am a cop, and you're in serious trouble."

Dropping onto his butt, he began to shift around, the irritation of being restrained clear on his face. "Is all this really necessary?" He jerked against the cuffs. "I get it, you're pissed. But quit screwing around. I know you're a cop; so am I. I want to help you. We can do this together. If there's an investigation going on, I want to be a part of it."

"Well, that's going to be tricky to pull off from jail," she answered coolly.

Without a doubt, the man had more balls than brains. She could totally see him trying to be the single protector of Titus; it was just like him. Stupidly cocky and unbelievably dangerous. Vigilante cop, taking on a drug ring all alone. No backup, no contacts, no FBI or DEA. She actually bought that scenario more than she bought into him being a dirty cop.

"Come on, take these off. We need to talk this through. I can help you, Jordan. If you're going up against the Bucks, you'll need help. You'll need me."

"Listen, sport, I didn't fall off the turnip truck yesterday. As much as it may shock and amaze the pig-headed, chauvinistic attitudes so deeply engrained in this godforsaken town, I'm more than qualified for this job. I do not, under any circumstances, *need* you."

"Yeah, darlin'," he mocked, pure country drawl in his words. "You're doing a bang-up job so far. And hell, you're right, you didn't need any local hick cop when Lewis kicked you face first onto the floor at Buck's. No, sir"—he laid the drawl and the sarcasm on thick—"you and your fancy investigation didn't need me to cover your naked breasts or take you to a hospital or stop Warren Buck from having his way with you out behind the club tonight."

"You're an ass," was all she could manage through the blinding rage.

He dropped the sarcasm and the drawl but continued to glare. "Maybe I am, but I know a hell of a lot more about this town than you do, things your big-city training can't teach you. I don't care how many agencies you claim to be working for; they don't know this town. They don't know Arlo Buck. And none of you know me. So take the cuffs off now. Settle down, and get over your snit because I surprised you tonight."

Jordan was pretty sure her brain had just seized up. Settle down? *Snit?*

Her head began to pound. Or maybe it was mini-strokes from the spike in blood pressure. He was going to kill her with smugness and stupidity. It was a new technique, one she hadn't seen before, but damned if she wasn't one step away from an aneurysm.

The fact that he was local and no doubt did have a perspective on the town that she would never have throbbed like a rotten tooth.

She paced, tamping down the desire to throttle him. He was actually trying to call the shots while wearing handcuffs. She had no actual desire to arrest him, but she was far from done when it came to getting answers.

Turning, she allowed her eyes to connect with his. So much always passed between them in a simple glance. His jaws were clenched, his brows drawn together with a line of stress etched between them. The last thing she wanted was for him to shut down before she got the answers she needed.

"I want the truth, Ty. All of it."

...

Ty made no attempt to evade Jordan's questions. His gaze bore into her. "My chief and I decided a well-placed lie about a failed drug test made the most sense. We let the rumor leak to a few of the right people. I hoped Buck would find me more appealing if I'd run into a little drug trouble of my own.

"I turned in my badge, wrote a letter of resignation. Even told my family and friends I resigned. My chief and I are the only ones who know the truth. It had to be that way."

Still cuffed and sitting on the floor, he shifted, leaned against a padded chair, and stretched out his long legs. "Law enforcement in a small town is tricky. In bigger cities, it's more impersonal, more black and white. Around here, half the people are related in one way or another. I can't be sure who, but I'd bet my life Arlo Buck has local cops backing him. Hell, he has two cousins on the Titus police force."

"So you decide to simply dive into a dangerous undercover alone?" She sank to the floor, needing to be face-to-face with him. It was hard to sort out if what she felt while questioning someone was purely cop instinct or part of the perverse abilities she'd been stuck with, but she was sure she'd know if he was lying. "What possessed you to think you could go up against the Bucks without help?"

He glanced at her, then shifted his eyes away. Anger and sadness and something more passed across his face. It was there for only a moment, no longer than the brief click of a camera.

But she'd caught it. And she'd felt it. Devastation as crushing as the night her family was murdered. Breath clogged in her chest, and she shifted away from him to process what she'd just felt.

"It's a small town." He shrugged but refused to meet her eyes. "When you grow up somewhere like Titus, the lines blur, you know. Friends become family and vice versa."

Now he did look at her, his expression as open as a fresh wound. "It might be a case to you," he finally said. "And to the Feds, these kids are numbers, just statistics. But to me, they're family. I grew up here, Jordan. This is my home."

She felt his pain so brilliantly, so clearly. He couldn't possibly be this raw with grief if it was just a case. Something had turned it into a personal vendetta, of that she was sure. After all, she was the queen of personal vendettas.

"I'm well aware I don't always give the warmest, fuzziest first impression." Her voice sounded thick and hoarse. "But nobody who dies because of something as senseless as drugs is ever just a statistic to me. Especially the kids."

Still on her floor, he scooted closer and folded his legs. "Then maybe we understand each other better than either of us thought possible."

No, Jordan thought. Not really. Because she was having a hell of a time understanding any of it. Her emotions. His emotions. Both swirling together into a thick cloud of heartache. She squeezed her eyes shut, because if she looked at him, she was terrified of what would happen.

A couple of deep, steadying breaths and things would be better. She could do this. Determined to break through whatever tangled web the moment weaved around them, she opened her eyes.

But his gaze dipped to her lips.

Oh, God. That hungry shift of his eyes fueled a fire that already crackled through her blood. Memories of last night arrowed through her. His rough kiss, taking. His skilled hands, determined. His beautiful body, slick from the heat between them, slipping inside her.

She scooted away and stood. She needed distance. She needed time. Hell, she needed a drink. A strong one. But given the sorry state of her cabinets, ice water was going to have to do. Retreating to the kitchen, she let cool water run over her hands and splashed her face. Forgetting he was still cuffed, she returned and offered him a glass of water.

"I need a key first." He rattled the cuffs. "Unless you really think I'm a hardened criminal who needs to be restrained."

She nodded and moved to the desk. Any excuse to put some distance between them was a blessing. Lingering much longer than needed to pull out her key, she steered the conversation back to a professional one. "Even in Titus, there must be someone you trust. Why wouldn't you try to put a task force together?"

"We have three small towns that make up Titus County: Longdale, Cooper, and Titus. Each town has its own small PD with just a few guys. Do you know how many cops are on the Titus force?"

"Four," she answered. "Plus the chief. I've done my homework. I'm not an idiot, Ty."

"Then I guess you know that two are Buck's cousins. Plus, one of the other two cops, Troy, was married to Buck's sister about ten years back. They had a kid together. Now the kid and Bess live in a rental house owned by Buck. Rumor has it that Troy has to pay rent and/or housing costs for the child and mom until the kid turns eighteen."

"This is all terribly fascinating, but—"

"Just hold on." He sprang up off the floor and turned toward her. "The story is, Buck isn't making Troy pay him anything for the house Bess and the kid live in."

She shrugged. "So Buck isn't making his sister pay rent."

"It's more than helping a family member out of the goodness of his heart, Jordan. What do you think Buck expects in return for saving Troy about a thousand dollars a month? Don't you see? The reality of this is buried and complicated. In one way or the other, Buck owns just about everything around here, including the people. My chief and I made a decision. If we want the truth, we have to treat every person, even the cops, like suspects."

"Okay, I get what you're saying." He was good. Not nearly as half-assed as she'd wanted to first believe. He'd spent months single-handedly weaving a trap for the Bucks, and because he'd grown up here, he knew the people inside and out. "Your assessments of the local police are right on. We know some of the local cops are protecting Buck or at least looking the other way. I can appreciate what you're doing. It was brave." She smiled, attempting to lighten the mood. "And kind of stupid in that reckless, fuck-the-world, cowboy way you toss around. But you need to be reasonable now. We're talking big money and big players. Arlo Buck is only the bottom rung on a ladder to whoever is supplying these drugs.

"The guys in charge look for midlevel dealers, someone off the beaten path. Far enough away from a large city to keep from drawing the attention of the Feds or DEA, but close enough for there to be a good market. Right next door is Cooper, a college town, so that puts Buck's operation in an even sweeter spot. He's just over an hour from St. Louis, fifteen minutes from Lincoln University—both great drug markets. You said yourself that he owns most of Titus, even the cops. He figures he's golden."

She walked behind him to remove the cuffs. "I get this is personal to you, but there really is a bigger picture. Arresting Buck is all well and good, but if we get the guys supplying Buck, we're another rung up the ladder. We save more people, because we cut off the suppliers at their knees. You need to stop and let us handle it."

He spun toward her before she could open the second cuff. "I'm not an idiot, Jordan. I know how it works. But I don't work for the FBI or the DEA. I work for Longdale. I'm just a stupid country cop working in a town that won't even rate a dot on most maps, but I care. I care about the dead kids in my town. I care about their families and the loss. I'm investigating the Bucks, even if it's in my own backwoods, feeble way. If you want me to quit, then you might as well go ahead and lock me up. It's the only way I'll stop. You either let me into your investigation, or I'll continue with mine. Alone."

"Ty, I don't have the authority to invite you into this investigation. If anyone finds out you discovered I'm a cop, I'll be lucky to have the authority to write a traffic ticket."

She stepped close and gathered the courage to say what needed to be said. "Even if I did have the authority, this is too close to you. You could never be objective. It touches every part of your life. Not just the kids who have died, but cops you may have worked with. It puts you in a horrible position."

"I can handle myself. When you're a cop in a small town, everything is personal. I'm used to it."

"You. Can't. Continue. With. This. Investigation." There, she'd said it. Each word emphasized with a finger to his chest.

"You. Can't. Stop. Me." Instead of poking her chest, he lightly tapped his finger on her nose. "At least not without answering a lot of embarrassing questions from your superiors. They might want to know how we became close so quickly."

She almost growled. He was obviously trying to push her buttons. "You need to move on and trust that we'll take care of everything."

"Who the hell is we? Where is your backup, officer?" he asked.

"*Detective.*" She ground her teeth together. "Two local cops from Cooper approached my FBI contact several months ago. One of them had a nephew who overdosed on China White."

"Chief Dean?" he asked.

"Yeah."

"I knew his nephew. Owen. He was a good kid."

Jordan nodded. "Anyway, they're providing me with local backup until after Thanksgiving. Then my FBI team will be in place."

"Is that standard protocol? To dump a female undercover in a strip joint with no real surveillance in place? That doesn't sound right. Who's in charge of this—?"

"I've already told you more than you need to know," she lashed out. "Don't worry about me or my orders. I can take care of myself. You, on the other hand, are done at Buck's."

She hated it when he stepped so close and peered down at her like a Neanderthal.

"You're hiding something," he said. "Are you even wearing a wire?"

"Yes."

His eyes narrowed.

"Okay, not yet. But I will be. I needed to be sure I could secure the position at the nightclub before an entire surveillance operation rolls into town."

"Unbelievable," he growled. "And I'm the one who needs to walk away? You're a female inside a place like Buck's with almost no backup, and *I'm* the one doing something stupid. Not a chance in hell I'm walking away now."

"I've got power and resources that go far beyond Titus. I'll get this done, trust me."

"Trust you?" He choked out a humorless laugh. "Fine, do you trust me, Jordan? Do you trust me enough to work with me?"

She was silent.

"Great," he murmured. "You can have sex with me, but you can't work with me?"

"Yes, damn it. Okay, yes, I trust you." It was like balancing on an emotional jungle gym with him, trying to grab hold and navigate without falling. "I do, as stupid as that sounds, and let me tell you, it sounds ridiculous. That I would know someone—what, a week—and trust them goes against everything I know, everything I am. But put yourself in my place. Even if I believe your story, I don't believe you can stay objective."

A hard slap of guilt rose up out of her belly. She almost choked on the words. They were the same ones Bahan had thrown at her at least a dozen times. She rubbed her temples. Black-and-white crime scene photos sliced into her memory. Two undercover cops. Two friends beaten, burned, tortured, and sliced from neck to groin. Revenge. A warning. Handy work of the cartel believed to be supplying Buck. She pushed the images out of her mind. "Look, you just can't get involved with this. I'm sorry."

"Okay," he said, backing up and flopping down on her couch. "You made your choice. You continue with your investigation, I'll continue with mine."

"You can't do that." She walked to the table in front of him and sat. She'd almost forgotten he was still wearing a cuff on one of his hands.

"Okay, fine," he said when she tugged on his cuffed wrist to free it. "I just thought you might like to hear about the deliveries Buck told me were coming."

Chapter Nine

Jordan raised an eyebrow. "What deliveries? Where?"

"See, now that sounds like a question a partner would ask, but since you don't want to be my part—"

"You're screwing with a federal investigation, you ass." Instead of releasing the locked cuff, she reached for his free hand and slapped the open cuff back on it.

"Oh, for crying out loud." He rolled his eyes and slouched back into the couch. Fine. If she wanted to play hardball, he could do that. He had her attention *and* a little leverage. By the end of the night, he was going to be working with Jordan to take the Bucks down. She didn't know it yet, but there wasn't a chance in hell he was letting her do this alone.

Turning deaf ears on her colorful tirade, he decided a cocky grin would be his best defense.

"You know, I'm beginning to think you just like seeing me in handcuffs," he said. "If that's the case, sweetheart, all you had to do was ask." He flashed a slick smile and a wink that was ballsy even by his standards.

In mid-rant, she went silent. Judging by the glare in her eyes and the small jolt of her body, it was entirely possible she would now kill him. Probably would've been smarter to get rid of the cuffs before pushing her, but no one had ever accused him of being overly smart.

"Take these off, Jordan." He continued to bait her. "We both know you're not calling anyone to haul me away tonight."

He leaned forward, propping his elbows on his knees, letting his face settle just inches from hers. "If you do call, I'll suffer from a terrible case of amnesia. Probably won't even remember my name, much less when Buck said those deliveries were coming."

He took it as a bad sign when she didn't move. Even worse when she didn't speak. The wheels were turning behind those wild, green eyes. What she would do next was anyone's guess. He was, after all, essentially blackmailing her.

So why isn't she trying to rip my head off?

His muscles tensed. Practically holding his breath, he waited for her temper to kick in. Instead, she casually leaned back and offered up a small, sultry smile.

This is very bad.

Clearly posed for seduction, she crossed one long, smooth leg over the other, tugged on the zipper of her warm-up jacket, and pulled it lower and lower until it sprang open.

Or maybe it was very good.

Her sparkly pink bikini top peeked out from under the jacket. Hypnotized, he choked down the memory of last night's encounter when she'd been hot and willing under his hands. He would *not* allow himself to go there. Absolutely would *not* think about the perfect size or shape of her breasts.

Nope. Not going there.

In fact, he was pretty sure he was getting played. So when the spark of desire took off like a rocket, he tempered it with a good, healthy dose of caution.

She leaned toward him and traced one long, feminine finger seductively across his collarbone. Her slim hands with hot pink nails grabbed his shirt and tugged him close. Then her full lips—that could tempt the noblest of men—pressed against his and devoured not only his mouth but also most of his resolve.

Someone groaned. He prayed it wasn't him but was pretty sure it was.

His body didn't care whether he was getting played or not. It even had a few suggestions of its own. *Rip off her clothes. Take her—fast and hard.* Images of the previous night pierced his determination to stay strong. Vivid memories of pumping into her, seeing her eyes glaze, feeling her sleek body clamp down on him as she cried out, taunted him to do it all over again.

Is that what he wanted? A repeat of last night?

It surprised the hell out of him to realize the answer was no. His hands trembled on the silken skin of her waist as he teetered on the line between delirious fast and hard sex, and something more.

As good as last night's sex had been, the aftermath had almost killed him. They had come together like two cars in a head-on collision but left just as much devastation in their wake.

Vaguely aware of his shirt tearing and buttons flying, he

whispered her name while her tongue ravaged a line from ear to collarbone. Most men would never walk away from her. *Couldn't* walk away from her. On any other night, with anyone else, he'd already be inside her.

But this woman…this woman kept him circling back to the clawing feeling that something more was between them. A hell of a lot more than a quick fuck and being kicked to the door.

Kissing back and forth across his jaw line, she stopped only long enough to nip his chin. Returning to his mouth, she eased her tongue inside, driving the kiss deeper and harder.

Finally, she pulled back, and her lips curved in a satisfied gotcha smile. "Tell me what you know."

"Oh, that's low. You're kidding, right? You think you're going to use sex to get me to talk? I'm seriously attracted to you, Jordan, but I'm not desperate." Yeah, okay, he *was* desperate. Who was he kidding? He'd have sold his soul for another opportunity to be with her.

"Jordan, stop," he pleaded before she crushed her lips to his again and climbed into his lap, straddling him. Even if he could have hidden the way his muscles tightened, there was no hiding the tightening in his pants. He was so hard, he ached.

She lightly circled his lips with her tongue before diving into a kiss that left them both gasping for air. He groaned and his body quivered. Quivered, hell. Every inch of him shook with need. But Jordan was never going to be a simple, carefree tumble. He wasn't a stupid man; already, he felt too much.

"Baby, slow down." He'd be damned if they'd go zero to sixty in a heartbeat again and have the whole thing over before it started. And then what? Would she throw him out again?

His eyes opened, desperation humming loud and clear. "Take the cuffs off. *Now*."

"Tell me when the deliveries are coming," she said.

Barely containing his anger, he moved her back, pushed her off his lap and onto the coffee table. He wanted to scream. *Tell me this isn't a game to you.*

He stood and moved across the room, trying not to regret pushing away a woman he wanted more than his next breath. Hoping that his own handcuff key would work, he dug into his pocket and pulled out his key ring.

When the cuffs clicked open, he turned back to her and tossed them in her direction. "Would you really sleep with me to get information on Buck?"

Her hand shook as she brought her fingers to her lips. She looked stunned, hurt. "No. Yes. I don't know." She moved her hand away from her mouth. "What about last night? I thought you wanted this."

"You think I want handcuffs? Well, I don't. I hope this isn't your usual method to get information. This isn't a game, Jordan. At least, not for me." As soon as the words crossed his lips, bells went off in his head.

Did making it a game make it safer? Easier to walk away from? Maybe he'd stumbled upon the one woman in the world who was more scared of something real than most men.

Either she felt something for him, or she didn't. If it was only sex between them, there were a lot of women out there to fulfill that need without the ache this woman put in his chest. If he laid all his cards on the table, maybe she'd do the same.

He sat down next to her. "Buck is having a few big deliveries in mid-December. On Monday, while he's closed. That's what he told me. He wanted to make sure I had my weapon that day. Said some of the delivery guys are squirrely. My hunch is that there's more than food and alcohol coming."

"Oh." She was clearly shocked he'd shared the information. But then he watched as the cop in her started reasoning. "You think he'd be bold enough to have a truck drive up to his place of business and unload in front of all you guys?"

Ty shrugged. "I don't know. He's pretty bold, thinks the laws don't apply to him. I don't know if he's that stupid, but it's a possibility."

Silence sat between them like a canyon, wide and deep.

"Why did you tell me? I never agreed to let you into the investigation."

He turned his head to look at her. "You either want my help, or you don't. You either want me, or you don't. I think we'd be good together, but this case is important, and I'm done playing around. I've cooperated. I've told you everything I know." He stood, shrugged. "You know where to find me."

"You're leaving?"

The hurt in her voice clamped around his heart, but if he didn't hold his ground with her now, he didn't know if he ever could.

She stood, looking up at him. "Don't you think we have things to discuss?"

The hurt sounded angrier this time. She didn't want him to go, he could see it in her eyes, but she'd sooner choke on regret than admit she wanted him to stay. Her stubbornness infuriated him. If she only knew the restraint it was taking not to grab her and kiss some sense into her.

"That's up to you. I'm pretty well done discussing on my end. As far as I can see, I'm the only one giving around here. And I'm not talking just about the case."

She stepped back as if dodging a physical blow. "What is that supposed to mean? You came to my place last night. Remember? I didn't hunt *you* down. You wormed your way in here, and we ended up having sex. I'd say that's pretty damn giving on my part."

Ty watched her eyes well up with emotion.

"And tonight," she continued, "you broke into my apartment. You're damned lucky the only thing I did was slap cuffs on you."

Stepping closer, she jabbed a finger in his chest. "If I had any brains, I'd have called the FBI and let them haul you away. Let 'em work you over for a day or two. But did I? No. Just what the hell else do you want from me?"

Oh, that just ripped it.

The poking finger combined with fact that she was clueless about what he *wanted from her* pushed him right over the edge. Catching her wrist, he jerked her until they were nose to nose. "Not that I'm sure you're capable of it, but an emotion other than rage would be a nice damn start."

"Just go." She shook off his grip. "This is a mistake. What the hell was I thinking?"

"Well, it seems like you thought you could trade sex for information. Now, I'm standing here wondering how many times you've done it before." He knew damn well she didn't operate that way, but he wanted her to admit it, to at least acknowledge there was more going on between them than a case.

She charged like an angry bull, and she sure didn't fight like a female. It was all he could do to dodge left and shift right, avoiding contact with her fists. He grabbed her waist, hauled her flailing body into the air, and tossed her onto the couch.

Her lungs were heaving, and she scrambled to stand but didn't come out swinging again. "I've never used my body to get information."

"Yeah, I figured that," he said. "I'm fairly confident you'd disembowel a man before trading sexual favors for information."

Tears streaked down her cheeks.

He stepped closer, lowering his head to look at her. "Which leads me to wonder why you'd pull that crap with me."

She flicked the tears away.

He wanted to pull her close, ached with a need to touch her that had his hands shaking. But he wouldn't. Not this time.

Only one button dangled from his shirt. Fastening it, he grabbed his jacket and turned to leave. "When you decide what you want, get a hold of me. Having sex and getting kicked out five minutes later isn't cutting it for me."

Stopping with his hand on the door, he turned to her. "I'm not sure what this is, 'cause I don't think I've ever felt this way before. But I don't think I can keep it light and meaningless with you. I want more."

...

Everything inside Jordan crumbled. Normally, she craved being alone, but already she knew that tonight would be too dark and too lonely.

"I don't know how to do more, Ty." The weakness in her voice was frightening. "I've never had more with anyone."

His hand fell away from the door.

She had no idea if it was relief or panic that caused all the air to whoosh from her lungs. If he stayed, things would never be the same. *She'd* never be the same.

He walked toward her and stroked a knuckle down her cheek. "Maybe we should try to figure out *more* together."

She knew what he was asking, knew she couldn't deliver it, not long-term anyway. Forever would never be an option, but maybe one night was.

Face it, Jordan, you're a freak. Cut him loose before he shreds what's left of your heart.

Ty wasn't the kind of man to settle for anything less than complete honesty, and that was the one thing she could never give anyone.

"Do you want this? Do you want more with me?" he whispered against her cheek. "It'll be good. Let me show you."

Okay. For one night.

Speaking suddenly became too big a task. She merely nodded. Then the reality of what she'd just agreed to clamped around her heart. Would she really be able to have this man and then let him go, unscathed?

He cupped her face and softly kissed her, stirring to life emotions that she'd left for dead almost twenty years ago. But she couldn't help herself, couldn't keep her head from falling back as his lips grazed her neck. In all fairness, when he nuzzled her like that, she didn't stand a chance at rational thought.

He skimmed his tongue against her ear. Goose bumps flared across her skin, and she went boneless.

"See how good more can be." The amusement in his voice was loud and clear as his lips continued to torture her already sensitive lobe. "Now I know my tongue in your ear makes your knees collapse. Good to know in case we're making out on the edge of a cliff."

Smiling, she wrapped her arms around his neck. His lips returned to her mouth and desire, pure and brilliant, flashed through her system. She pushed his jacket to the floor, popped open the one dangling button on his shirt, and peeled it off him.

"Damn woman, you're hell on shirts."

She laughed but continued her assault. If she was going down, she was going down happy. Sliding her hands under his T-shirt, she ran her nails up his torso, stripping him in the process. The spectacular vision of Ty shirtless made her breath catch. His thick, wide chest and taut muscles never failed to take her breath away. God, she wanted his touch. No ulterior motives this time. Just need. Just make-love-to-me-until-I-scream-your-name need.

He popped open the button on her shorts and let them fall to the floor, leaving her in pink satin panties and her bikini top.

Stepping back, he scanned her nearly naked body from head to toe. He swallowed hard, and his nostrils flared. The look in his eyes reminded her of a wild animal someone had attempted to tame.

A punch of female power hit her full force. He was trying so very hard to slow things down, to make this special.

But she could tell by the way he closed his eyes and took a deep, shuddering breath that he was fighting against raw need. They both were. But for some reason she didn't fully understand, he was determined to batter her senses slowly.

He stepped close. His hands and lips continued their leisurely exploration of her body. Every tender, erogenous zone she possessed—her wrist, between her breasts, the sensitive skin under her navel—trembled with the need to feel more of him. He spun her, then caressed her breasts as his tongue danced a slow, tantalizing line down her spine. He missed nothing, teased every possible nerve ending to aching.

Breathless and impatient, she twisted in his arms, grabbed the waistband of his jeans, and ripped them open. "I appreciate the slow seduction, but—"

"Tonight's not going to be like last night, sweetheart." When she tugged on his zipper, he caught her hands and trapped them.

Through the almost blinding haze of lust, she began to understand. He was determined to take back the control that had so crudely been stripped from him last night. Their previous encounter had left them both reeling. Tonight, he was making up for his loss of control with deliberate, glorious torture.

Panting and on fire from his sultry burn, she discovered pride was no longer a factor. "I want you. No games this time, I promise. I just want you." She'd never begged for anything in her life, but she'd never had a half-naked Tyler McGee touching her before, either.

"Soon." He turned her again, pulled her backside tight against his chest. He cupped her breasts, and his coarse, masculine hair rubbed her back like an erotic lick against her skin. A large, hard erection pressed rigidly against her bottom. One hand circled her throat with quiet dominance and urged her head back against his shoulder.

"Now that we're on the same page, I intend to enjoy you," he murmured roughly against her ear, "and you damn well are going to enjoy me."

"Oh, God, I already am. It doesn't have to be like last night, but I can't take this. I need you inside me, Ty."

He laughed a low, throaty chuckle. "You are an impatient little thing, aren't you?"

Breathless, she murmured, "Patience has never been my strong point."

"I'd have never guessed."

In a move so smooth she never felt it happen, he opened the clasp on her bikini top. Moving a hand to her breast, he rolled the aching tip between his thumb and finger. Her back arched into the pressure, inviting a stronger, rougher touch.

"Better?" He spun her, ducked his head, and sucked her nipple deep into the heat of his mouth.

Yes, God. Finally.

The pleasure pierced her right down to her core. Surrendering to the sensations, she let go. Let go of the case, the dreams, the awareness that she shouldn't be doing this. He possessed her so completely that it was disturbingly easy to let the rest of the world simply fade away. Maybe tomorrow she'd regret her actions, but tonight there was only him. His hands. His body. His lips.

He picked her up. Her mind vaguely registered that they were both naked and she was now under him on the sofa.

Guiding her arms, he pushed them above her head and hooked them over the arm of the couch. "Don't move them," he ordered.

Her eyes blinked open. "What?" Desire muddled her brain. Comprehension was taking a minute.

"Be a good girl. No more hands tonight."

Raising her head off the couch, she arched an eyebrow. "Someone really does like to be in control."

That sexy, half-assed tilt of his lips made her feel as if her heart would beat right out of her chest.

"*Someone* would like to make a better impression than in our previous encounter. If your greedy, little hands enter the mix, I don't stand a prayer of a chance, baby."

Smiling, she let her head drop back to the couch, decided not to analyze why taking orders from him in this particular situation didn't bother her a bit.

"Oh, God." She groaned when he moved down her body and lightly nipped her breast.

"You are so damn beautiful, it messes with my mind. Sometimes, when I look at you, I can barely breathe."

Her eyes began to sting, and her throat felt thick. It wasn't the words—very likely there were more poetic phrases turned in the heat of the moment. But the tone in which the words were murmured, the raw way they tore from his heart, broke hers.

"Now, Ty. Now." She tugged on a handful of his thick hair, urging his lips closer to hers.

He fumbled for something on the floor next to them, pulled up the handcuffs he'd tossed at her earlier. "Don't make me use these."

She grabbed them and threw them to the other side of the room, afraid he just might. God only knew she was well past the ability to deny him anything, but she needed to be able to touch him.

Instead of being inspired to return to her lips, he headed farther down her body, anchored himself between her legs, and ran his tongue lightly across the inside of both thighs. Her muscles tightened. He'd yet to touch her, but she felt the moisture pouring from her body.

He opened her, eased a finger inside of her as he buried his tongue against her sensitive bud, and licked.

She jerked but didn't dare touch him, afraid he'd pause to scold her again. Anything that slowed the torturous pace wasn't an option. He continued to nuzzle and torture her, continued to stroke a spot deep inside that pushed her to the edge of delirious.

"Ty, I'm going to come if you keep it up."

Apparently, that was the intention. He groaned and moved faster, continued lashing his tongue against her aching flesh, and then slipped a second finger inside her. "Oh, God," she cried, and still, he didn't ease the pace. Her arms stayed locked against the sofa, but her lower half bucked wildly against him.

Sensations began to surge and splinter. She had no idea what kind of sound she made. A groan? A growl? Well beyond any kind of control, she gave him what he wanted—everything. Heart. Mind. Body. As long as he never stopped, he could have it all.

Her trembling moans vibrated louder as the force of her orgasm crashed around her. The air in her lungs rushed in and out.

Ty kissed his way up to her neck and then found her lips again. He was hard and ready, centered above her. The tip of his thick erection slid heavily against her slick folds, heating her again. Her hips arched to meet him.

His breath hissed between clenched teeth, and his body quaked.

"Protection?" he ground out.

"What?"

"Do you have protection, Jordan?"

She shook her head. Something told her it was going to take a lot more than a condom to protect herself from this man.

He got up, walked to his discarded jeans, and came back sheathed. In one hard, staggering burst of sensation, he buried himself deep inside her.

She gasped. Her body trembled. Every part of her shook, arms and legs vibrating against the deep, blissful pressure of his body inside hers. She hadn't expected this, hadn't known anything like it existed. She'd been touched before, in the most basic of ways, but not controlled like this, never destroyed like this.

He pulled back and then thrust again with a fierce groan. "Jordan," he growled, "open your eyes, baby. Look at me."

As she stared into his eyes, she felt him in the deepest marrow of her bones, felt the connection on a level so profoundly vulnerable it was terrifying. Tears streaked back into her hair. Her heart raced and thundered, trying to keep pace with her spiraling emotions. A blissful perfection and stunning fear warred inside her. She was coming undone in his arms and didn't have a clue how to stop it.

He kissed her and thrust again, soothing tears and stirring demons at the same time. Lacing his fingers with hers, he whispered her name. Her hands and body locked to his, and her heart tumbled in a free fall. She concentrated on his beautiful, beautiful eyes.

"I'm scared, Ty." The words slipped out even as she wrapped her legs tighter around him, urging his body deeper inside of hers.

Did he understand what he was doing to her? Did he realize he was destroying the protective armor she needed to live, that once it was gone, there was nothing but fear underneath?

"I know, baby, but I won't hurt you. I swear it," he whispered.

For the first time ever, she felt...*stripped* in every sense of the word. Crying out his name, surrendering to the moment, her body quivered and trembled as the orgasm clawed its way from the inside out.

Curling his fingers in her hair, burying his lips in the curve of her neck, he moaned her name, shuttered, and came inside her.

Deep breaths and lingering tremors gave way to soft kisses and the peaceful quiet of the early hours of the morning. Shifting to her side but still tangled with him, Jordan stroked fingernails through the sheen of moisture on Ty's back. He dozed, but her mind was too overwhelmed for sleep.

She tried to feel good about what just happened but couldn't quiet the little voice of reason.

Be afraid, the voice said, *because he'll hurt you*.

She could feel it as sharply as the dreams that haunted her nights. If he found out about the visions, there would be hurt.

What they shared was more than sex. He was more than a casual fling, and she was more than the shell she claimed to be. She understood that now. Her heart ached with the understanding that one night with him would never be enough.

That knowledge also clawed at her from the inside out.

Chapter Ten

Ty opened his eyes. Something had woken him.

A moan? A scream? Had it been Jordan?

A jab powered into his ribs. Grunting, he rolled to the edge of the bed and sat up. Damn, her elbow worked better than an alarm clock. Amused, he watched her toss around.

The woman slept like a cyclone, twisting and turning all over the bed. He considered waking her, but when he held down her flailing arm and kissed her shoulder, she rolled over and became quiet.

He chuckled.

A light from the parking lot glowed through the mini blinds, illuminating the bedroom. Jordan's bare, sleek back rose and fell as she took long, deep breaths. She was seductive even in sleep. His gaze traveled over her from the top of her blond hair down to the perfectly rounded bottom only half covered with the sheet.

A foreign pulse of emotion sizzled like a power surge.

Possession, need, and—if he was being honest—a good healthy dose of guilt, rose up out of nowhere.

She'd given herself to him when they'd made love, in ways he didn't expect. He knew she'd done it, seen the passion on her face, felt the surrender in the tears that almost choked her. He'd wanted more than sex, demanded it.

He closed his eyes, remembering how they'd reached for one another a second time in the darkness. The memory of her rising above him, taking him in, moving in a seductive rhythm while white slashes of light from the blinds fell across her naked body was a vision seared into his brain.

She'd given him what he'd asked for, a real piece of herself.

His eyes opened. And how had he repaid her? By hiding the truth. By hiding the real reason he wanted Buck behind bars.

He would tell her all of it, but not yet. Already she'd accused him of being too personally involved, and she didn't know the half of it. If he confessed, she'd never agree to work with him, and she was damn well going to work with him. He'd sooner open fire on the whole strip club than allow her to set foot in that dive without him. But that probably wasn't a smart thing to admit.

The clock read 6:17 a.m. A trip to the bathroom was in order, just in case her next jab was lower and more on point toward his bladder.

When he turned the water on to wash his hands, he heard the scream. Sprinting back to the bed, he found Jordan, apparently in the grip of a nightmare.

She sobbed and cried out. Most of the sounds were unintelligible half-words and sickly, terrified moans, but he thought he caught the name "Katy."

"Jordan? Jordan, wake up." His instinct was to grab her and hold her, but the last time he restrained her hadn't gone well. He picked up just one hand and squeezed. "Jordan?"

In one quick, sweeping motion, she woke, sat up, and scurried off the bed. Backing into a corner, she slumped to the floor like a cornered animal.

. . .

Jordan felt a dizzying flood of air fill her lungs. Folded on the floor with her head in her hands, she began to battle back the visions. Knees tucked under her, she rocked, desperate to break free of the faces.

Her mom's. Her sister's. And worst of all, the one face she'd fought against seeing for years…her father's.

Why did every dream have to end with his disappointed eyes staring her down? She sucked in more air to clear the burn in her lungs and erase the faces. A sob welled in her throat.

Maybe her dad was right. Even though his pathetic lifestyle had led a murderer to their home, she was the only one who'd really had the tools to stop what happened, yet she hadn't.

You could have saved them. You should have tried harder.

The vision she'd had the night before her family was killed had shown the gunman coming with absolute clarity. Still, she'd let everyone she loved die, let them silence her, treat her like a foolish ten-year-old. And it had cost her everything.

Her sister's death was the worst. She could still hear

Katy crying out.

Then the mystery girl with the long, dark hair cried out, too. The dreams had blended and twisted until she couldn't tell where one ended and another began. Both violent. Both deadly. Who *was* this girl? And why the hell did the vision of her death hurt as badly as Katy's?

Jordan kept her eyes closed tight as she continued to gulp in long, shuddering lungfuls of air. She couldn't shake the images this time. The terror. The pain. Katy's cold, empty stare after the sound of gunfire. Then the vacant gaze of the mystery girl as she slipped away, too. The boy put his hands around her neck and squeezed until her big, beautiful eyes, fierce and alive, drained to cold, hollow stones.

The boy hadn't planned a murder. He'd planned sex. Sex could be explained. Sex could be rationalized as mutual. Murder hadn't been on the agenda. He'd squeezed her neck, then let go. Squeezed and let go, unsure of what to do, where to turn. Finally, there were no more chances. The girl was gone.

Rein it in, Jordan. Take a deep breath.

Nausea, greasy and slick, roiled inside her.

She needed to get to the bathroom. She needed the shock of cold water on her skin.

Slow, deliberate steps came toward her. Oh, God. She wasn't alone. *Ty.*

She heard him kneel beside her.

"Are you okay?" He touched a cool rag to her cheek. "Do you know where you are? Can I help you?"

His voice was soft and kind and would have been extremely comforting if she hadn't felt so sick. She lifted her head to look at him. "Oh, God, I'm sorry—" She jumped up.

Not quick enough, she realized, with the cold rag or the shower. She dashed past him and into the bathroom. Experience told her that throwing up was best at this point. Get it over with quickly. Get coffee. Move on.

She dropped to her knees.

When he approached the bathroom, she slammed the door.

He opened it. "I'm coming in, okay?"

"No." The sickness tore through her a second time. "Don't you dare," she croaked, leaning against the toilet.

He stepped in with her robe.

She rubbed the cool cloth he'd given her across her face. "Don't you ever listen?"

"Not very well," he answered. "Come on, let's get you up." He tugged her to her feet and wrapped the thick, burgundy robe around her shoulders. "Are you sick? You're shivering. Should I turn up the heat?"

She shook her head. It wasn't cold in the apartment. It wasn't the flu. It wasn't food poisoning. It wasn't anything that could be explained logically. She shook her head a second time. Finally, he backed out of the bathroom and allowed her a minute.

Her knees trembled. The thought of what had happened made the nausea return; he'd witnessed another dream. What a mess. She stared at her ghostly complexion in the mirror. Splashing cold water on her face and brushing her teeth didn't give her nearly enough time to come up with a logical lie.

She walked out of the bathroom feeling caught and cornered. He deserved some explanation. He deserved a normal woman who could be truthful and honest, but her truth just wasn't an option. She'd never risk looking into his eyes and having him look back as if she were crazy. History told her that's exactly what would happen. It *had* happened.

After her family's murder, she'd trusted the people who claimed they only wanted to help. She'd told the police and the social workers about her dreams. Then she'd spent the next few years paying for it. Admitting to nightmares and conversations with the dead didn't get her help—it had gotten her labels. *PTSD, psychological trauma, severe anxiety, nightmares.*

It had also gotten her forced visits with a shrink who believed all of her sleep issues could be fixed in the form of a pill. As an adolescent, she may have been trapped in the system; as an adult, she had a choice.

That *choice* included happily eating a bullet from her own gun before spending a single second of her adult life in the same antidepressant haze she'd spent a good portion of her childhood.

Ty was a good man, but it didn't mean he'd understand her dreams.

"I started a pot of coffee," he said. "Come sit down."

When she didn't move, he stepped closer and slipped his hands around her waist. His lips brushed her forehead, and the hot jolt of need was nearly painful. Melting against him, she trembled at the feel of his warm body holding her.

"Oh, God." The plea ripped from her throat. She'd made it almost thirty years without getting into this kind of mess. Her entire adult life, she'd avoided this kind of intimacy to escape this exact moment. She'd done the one thing she promised herself she'd never do: let a lover in. Now she had to push him away.

"I can't do this, Ty. I'm sorry." Looking at him wasn't an option. Turning away, she stepped toward the one small window in the apartment.

He walked up behind her and settled his hands on her hips. "You seemed to do fine last night."

"It's not a joke. I'm not ready for what this feels like it's turning into."

His hands dropped. In the silence, his breathing went faster, deeper, and, she was quite sure, angrier.

Forcing herself to face him, she prepared for the fight. "I tried to tell you from the beginning, I don't do this. My job, my life, it's just too…" Her throat swelled, and she blinked, determined to hold back the tears attempting to form.

"You're trying to push me away because of a couple of nightmares? That's ridiculous. You think I don't understand the stress you're under because of this case? You think I haven't driven myself crazy worrying about the best way to take the Bucks down?"

"It's not just this case. There's more." *A hell of a lot more.* "My life…It's just…I can't, Ty. Please just leave it at that."

The thoughts were there, but she couldn't get the words out. In the past, kicking a lover to the curb had filled her with relief. Now, her knees were ready to buckle under the weight of the regret. "I'm sorry." She turned away again, knowing she could never look in his eyes and end it with dignity. "I've messed up, and I don't know the best way to fix it—"

He spun her back around. "Then I'll tell you. You're going to continue with this case, and you're going to continue being with me. We'll work together, and when we're done, the Bucks won't be seeing the light of day for a very long time."

The delivery of his words was as confident as ever, but she saw the glimmer of uncertainty in his expression.

"Then things will get better. The stress will get better," he said. "The nightmares will get better."

"They won't. You're not *listening*. They're not going away. I'm trying to be honest—"

"Then try being honest with yourself first. After last night, can you really push me away and be done with me? I don't think so."

Habit made her want to lash out, verbally shred him with some flip remark, but his eyes held enough heat to silence her.

His grip tightened on her shoulders. "There's no way you can pretend last night didn't mean something. Is that *really* what you want? For me to walk away and not look back?"

She wanted him to stay, maybe more than she'd ever wanted anything. But it wasn't realistic, and the longer she let him stick around, the more it would hurt in the end. "If you have any brains, you *will* walk away, and you *won't* look back. I've been lying to you since I met you. My family didn't die in a car accident…They were murdered."

...

Ty wasn't entirely sure he'd heard her right. "Your family was murdered?"

Jordan nodded.

"But you said there was a car accident."

She knuckled the tears away. "People understand car accidents. Since it wouldn't be polite, they don't ask questions." She exhaled on a bark of hysterical laughter, but her chin quivered. "Murder, on the other hand…No one understands murder."

The words sliced through him. He understood murder. Enough to know it cut you off at the knees, leaving a big, gaping hole forever. He sucked in a breath and swallowed back his own memories, trying to focus on what had happened to Jordan. "How?"

Her teary gaze locked onto his. "A gunman broke in to my home when I was ten. He shot my family on Thanksgiving night. I only survived because I cowered in a closet." The words spewed out, full of anger and self-loathing. "I did nothing, absolutely nothing, while some crazy son of a bitch killed everyone I loved. I have nightmares. All the time. They never go away, Ty. Never."

Of all the things he expected her to say, it hadn't been that. He eased closer, but her eyes opened wide.

She backed around the small dining table, putting a very clear barrier between them. "The nightmares don't come every night." Her face blanched, her words barely a whisper now. "But often enough."

His mind raced as he tried to figure out what to do for her, what to say. But experience told him that no words were going to make it any better. He swallowed, working up the nerve to ask, "Who's Katy?"

Her gaze shifted restlessly around the room, as if searching for an escape. He wondered if he hadn't been standing between her and the door, if she may have just bolted. Finally, she exhaled a long, defeated breath and allowed her eyes to settle on him. "Katy was my sister. She was eight when she was murdered."

Her admission powered into his gut like a physical blow.

The image of a little girl hiding in a closet, listening to her family being killed, stalled in his mind. Momentarily frozen, he forced himself to breathe and absorb the enormity of her words. Honestly, he wasn't sure whether to push for more details or insist she stop. "Do you want to tell me what happened?" he asked softly.

She shook her head as if she couldn't bear it, but spoke anyway. "Katy and I spent the whole day cooking with Mom. My dad had been gone for weeks." She shrugged. "He was always gone, but Mom said he was coming home for the holiday, and she was like a different person when he was there, so happy and…"

Ty tried to piece together the details. "Your dad traveled? Like a salesman?"

"Oh, he was a salesman all right. Just not the kind you're thinking of. My mom said his job kept him away, but even at ten, I knew things didn't add up. Katy and I would listen to her cry at night, sometimes until she passed out. We were little, but we knew it wasn't right.

"After Thanksgiving dinner, Mom told Katy and me to take a bath. On holidays, it was kind of a tradition for the four of us to snuggle in Mom and Dad's bed and watch movies." She absently swiped at her tears. "We were all curled up together watching a movie when it started. Out of nowhere, there was a vicious pounding and a horrible, angry voice. My dad jumped up and sprinted toward the front of the house and…"

She stopped. Even her full, pink lips drained to a pale, sickly gray. "He killed my dad," she finally said. "We were in the bedroom, but we heard the gun go off. Mom screamed and started crying. She scooted Katy under the bed. At the last second, Mom grabbed me and pushed me in the bottom of her closet.

"The guy busted through the bedroom door. My mom begged and begged. I heard her plead with him. She said we didn't have his money." Jordan's quiet gaze held his for a long moment. "Or his drugs."

"Oh, Jordan," Ty said. "It was drug related? You think your dad was dealing?" His heartbeat raced with the implications.

Jordan nodded. "I don't think it, I know it. I have an uncle in Kansas City that I stayed with for about a week after it happened." Shrugging like it was no big deal, she said, "When the cops came to talk to him, I listened in. They said my dad made a horrible decision, and it cost his family their lives. My uncle told them they had to find a different place for me to stay. He said he wasn't risking his family because my dad had been involved in a huge drug war."

So many things began to make sense. The way she attempted to kept him at arm's length. Working narcotics. The stupid damn risks she took. All the cryptic answers she'd given him fell into place and completed a large part of the puzzle. "I'm sorry that you had to hear that, baby," he murmured.

"I'm not. Asking why over and over is almost as hard as living through it the first time."

Unable to stop himself, he took a step closer, but she jerked a chair between them and held up one shaky hand. "When you're ten, no one wants to break you with the truth. But for me, the truth was better. I knew exactly why it happened, and I knew exactly who to hate."

Ty watched her eyes drift shut and her body stiffen. He eased a little closer, thinking she might pass out or something.

"I lost my mom and sister because of my father. He led

a crazy, high drug addict straight to our door. My mom tried so hard to talk to the gunman. She begged to go to the autoteller with him, promised him an insane amount of money just to get him out of there and save Katy and me. But he shot her anyway."

He decided she wasn't passing out, just trapped in a flashback.

"Katy whimpered when the gun went off. Soft at first. I thought maybe he didn't hear her, but he looked under the bed and grabbed her by the leg of her pajamas. I had about an inch of space under the door that I was looking through. He dragged her across the floor. Tossed her on the bed. She rolled off, trying to get to the closet. To me. She kicked and screamed and…and he pulled the trigger."

Jordan opened her eyes and stared at him. "If I'd have just opened the closet. If I'd have done something…She was trying to get to me, her older sister, for protection. But I did nothing. I could've jumped from the closet or startled him."

"No," he said sternly. "You'd be dead now, too. You know that, right? You can't blame yourself for something like that, baby. Sometimes it just…" He opened his eyes wide, blinking away the burn. "You were a kid, Jordan. You had no idea what was happening on the other side of the door."

"I wish that were true," she whispered, then swayed.

Ty moved around the table, decided to hell with her barriers.

"Ty, no!" she yelled when he pushed past the chair. "Don't. I don't want you to touch me." She backed further into the corner and tried to steady herself against the wall but wilted toward the floor instead. "God, please go. Please just go."

"Stop it," he growled, swooping her up. He couldn't—wouldn't—do it anymore. Stand on the other side of the room and watch her drown in misery. "I'm not going anywhere. If you don't like it, that's too damn bad."

There was no fight left in her. She sagged in his arms.

"Ty. Oh, God." Breaking, she buried her face against his neck and sobbed.

His chest hurt. His heart pounded with a painful, wretched throb. Still cradling her, he fell back onto the sofa. He had no idea what to do, so he simply held her, let her cry it out. He wondered if the tears were helping or just sucking her farther into the past.

Finally, she collapsed, limp and exhausted across his lap. Her voice was weak, barely audible when she spoke. "I think I've pushed it down for so long that when I sleep, it just swallows me whole. The dreams about that night, they get worse at stressful times, especially when I'm undercover. But they never go away, not totally."

She tilted her head back and looked at him. "I'm messed up, Ty. I'm broken when it comes to caring for someone. Not even what happened between us last night can fix me."

He picked up her hand and laced his fingers with hers. "Have you ever told anyone what you just told me?"

She shook her head.

"Then why did you tell me? Why trust me with something you've never told anyone?"

She sat up straighter on his lap. Shrugged. "Because I think you want something I'm not capable of giving. You deserve more. You're handsome and kind." Her mouth curved in the hint of a smile. "And brave in a totally warped kind of way. You should be with someone who can give you everything, a life, a family, a—" Her brows drew together. "What?"

He knew his smile confused her. Her mood shifted ever so slightly from wrecked to mild irritation. For that little spark, he was grateful.

Her eyes narrowed. "You could be a little more broken up that I'm ending this, cowboy," she said. "Are you even listening to me?"

"Yeah," he tossed back smugly. "Are *you* listening to you? Because you sound an awful lot like someone who cares to me. Enough to risk a secret you've never shared with anyone. Enough to warn me you're a pain in the ass. But lucky for you"—he tapped her nose with his finger—"I'd already figured out the pain-in-the-ass part."

Her eyes brimmed with tears again. "This isn't a joke."

"No, nothing about any of this is funny. But your past doesn't matter to me. The dreams don't matter." He tipped her chin up and sealed his mouth over hers, figuring he was a whole lot better at kissing than he ever would be with words. His tongue stroked between her lips, and that sizzle of connection that could bind them whether they were making love or standing on opposite ends of the room ignited, bright and brilliant.

"*That's* what matters," he said breathlessly when he pulled his lips from hers. "It's the only thing that matters. I'm not asking for marriage or forever. We've both got a lot of issues to work through. I'm just asking for a chance. I want to get to know you better, and I want to help with this case."

He touched her cheek, forcing her eyes toward his. "So for once in your damn life, can you just mutter a simple okay?"

She dropped her head back to his chest and nodded. "Okay," she said. "Okay."

Chapter Eleven

Thanksgiving Day officially sucked sideways in Jordan's book. And this one was looking less promising than the last nineteen. In fact, this year she was going to have to endure it sober and awake. Drinking wasn't Jordan's normal style, but once a year, she made an exception, although she'd yet to find the magic bullet that could put her in a coma from about noon on Wednesday straight through black Friday. But in past years, the most promising results had come in the form of cheap red wine.

Unfortunately, today would be spent without the numbing effect of alcohol. She was on her way to the Bucks' family home, and if all the stars aligned just right, she'd figure out a way to get inside Arlo's home office long enough to riffle through some of his documents. One small break—a scribbled phone number, a date on a calendar—was all she needed to tie the Bucks to the Delago Cartel and possibly confirm whether Ty's suspected delivery date was correct or not.

But something about the raw ache that began when she kissed Ty good-bye continued to churn in her chest. The lingering unease of it baffled her. The whole thing with Ty baffled her. The last week had been unlike any she'd ever experienced. Her evenings at Buck's had been spent ignoring Ty with frigid disregard, only for them to discreetly meet at her place after work and make love until the early hours of the morning.

She craved him like an addict craved the next fix. How ironic for a narc cop to develop a dependency. And not just any dependency. It took a special kind of Jordan Delany dysfunction to let a man be her drug of choice.

He'd shocked her with his support and understanding when she confessed about her family's murder. Then he'd carved a path for her she'd never thought to travel down by herself.

"Wouldn't it be stupid to push me away now," he had said, "after you've told me all your secrets, and I've told you none of it matters?"

She'd spent every day since then turning his words over in her mind. He knew what happened to her family. He knew she dreamed. She told him the dreams never went away. She warned him she wasn't good with relationships. The only thing she hadn't confessed was that the dreams sometimes held visions from the dead.

But did he ever need to know that? Why would he need to know that?

If he witnessed another nightmare, wouldn't he think she'd dreamed of her family? She often did. Perhaps it was selfish, but he'd offered her a chance. A chance that might never come again. The insanity of her life made falling into a relationship feel wrong, but thinking about pushing Ty away was nearly unbearable.

She glanced into the rearview mirror. A stranger with big, blond hair, thick eyeliner, and glossy pink lips stared back. As an undercover look, it wasn't all that unusual, but the unease that accompanied it certainly was. Trepidation had gnawed at her since she'd accepted the invitation to Thanksgiving at the Bucks, and this year, she knew it was more than the normal stress the holiday usually carried for her.

Working with little backup and no wire while at the nightclub was one thing. Walking straight into the lion's den with no way to defend herself was stupidity on a whole different level. It was obvious Warren wanted more than a friendship. And while flirting with him had once seemed like a sensible plan, she was now rethinking it. How was he going to react when she finally put her foot down and said no? She'd survived a lot of crazy stunts in the name of justice, but sleeping with Warren Buck wasn't going to be one of them.

She turned on the little gravel road leading to the Buck family home and blew out a huge breath. What a mess. Thank God Bahan and her surveillance team would be in place by tomorrow, most likely before her shift began. That knowledge alone made her breathe easier.

It was just before one p.m. when she pulled in front of the old, two-story farmhouse. It could have used a fresh coat of paint, but it was pretty and surrounded by its own personal forest of trees. She stepped onto a huge porch decorated with festive holiday pumpkins and corn stalks. A large swing swayed from the overhang. It was better, homier, than any place she pictured Arlo and Warren living.

"Hey, baby, glad you could make it." Warren took her coat and gloves, and then kissed her. Not in a friendly, welcoming sort of way, but with a much darker undertone. She'd definitely pushed the flirting thing a little too far, but how else would she have gotten an invitation to their home?

Warren introduced her to his grandparents and a gathering of aunts, uncles, and cousins. Then he pulled her into the kitchen to meet his mother.

The scent of turkey clogged the air. The sickly smell of pumpkin pie bombarded her. Sage. Onion. Celery. The smells, one on top of the other, grabbed her around the throat and squeezed.

One of the children flew through the kitchen door, and the loud crack of wood smacking wood made her whirl around in defense. Her gaze flittered to the table lined with bowls of stuffing, mashed potatoes, cranberries, and rolls piled high on a platter.

Her heart raced, thundering in her ears. No air seemed to pass in or out of her lungs. Then Warren's mom touched her shoulder, and the spell broke.

"I'm sorry, honey, that door is louder than a firecracker when the kids run in and out. Anyway, I'm glad you could join us."

"Thank you for having me." Jordan said. "Is there a restroom where I can wash up?"

Warren led her past the large group watching football. The restroom on the main floor was occupied, so he guided her to a bathroom on the second level. "What's wrong? You okay? You looked like you were gonna pass out."

"Yeah, I'm sorry. I've had a bad headache all morning, but I'll be fine. I'll just take a couple aspirin, wash up, and be down in a minute."

Warren tapped her bottom as she turned from him.

Jordan stepped into the bathroom, locked the door, and sank to the floor. She scrubbed her hands up and down her face. Her ears were still ringing, but her heart rate had dropped from wildly rapid to just moderately fast. She could breathe now.

"I'm so stupid." She hadn't participated in a real Thanksgiving since her family had been gone. Why had she thought she could manage it today? Ty had been furious when she'd admitted where she was going, and he was right, she should have stayed with him. He would have understood. He would have made it better.

Turning the water to its coldest setting, she let it run over her hands and splashed her face. "Rein it in, Jordan," she whispered. There was a job to do.

She dried off, straightened her clothes, and opened the bathroom door. When she stepped out, she looked around.

Arlo Buck's home office sat directly across the hall. She made it to the threshold before she heard footsteps on the stairs.

"Hurry up, Jordan," Warren said as he peeked the top of the stairs. "Everyone's sitting down to eat."

As the day progressed, Jordan had to admit the Bucks seemed like any other family sitting down to a holiday dinner. Not that she had much to base the experience on, but it all felt relatively normal. Enough food to feed a small country. Men debating football strategies. Grandpa telling stories.

Warren pulled her to her feet after dinner. "I could use a little fresh air." He grabbed a blanket and two glasses of wine and led her out to the swing on the front porch. He shoved off the two pre-teens who'd been giggling over something. They giggled even more when they caught Jordan's eye.

Anything that moved her away from the overwhelming Thanksgiving gathering was a blessing, so she didn't argue. But she did say, "Jeez, Warren, it's like thirty degrees out here. We'll freeze to death."

"Trust me, I'll keep you warm." He pulled her down onto the swing and threw a blanket over them both.

They swayed with gentle movements, chatted, and sipped wine. Warren pulled her legs onto his lap, slipped off her shoes, and began rubbing her feet. Thank God she'd opted for no clutch piece today.

"Something tells me you've had more than one girl out on this porch swing." Jordan smiled at him, but all the while she contemplated how to get upstairs to his dad's office and how much time she needed to put in before she could leave.

Warren took her wine, shifted their positions, and put his arm around her.

You're walking a dangerous line, Ty had said. *I don't like it.*

Warren brushed her hair back from her cheek. "A few of us from the club are going to lunch and a movie tomorrow. I want you to come."

"I have to work. I start at four. You probably won't be back by then, so I better not. Your dad said the day after Thanksgiving is always packed."

"Tell you what, I know both of your bosses, and they're pretty nice guys. I'll take care of everything, and you meet us at the bar about noon."

Since undercover work was second nature, something

better than *okay* should have come to her mind. But it didn't.

"So how many girls have you seduced out here on this swing?"

"One or two." He smiled. "But nobody I wanted to be with more than you." He pulled her close and dove headfirst into a kiss. A dark, greedy, take-all kiss. She tried to ease back, but his arm clutched tight around her waist. He tasted like whiskey and desperation. His other hand found the hem of her sweater and slid underneath to grope her skin.

Automatically, her back stiffened. She wedged an arm across her stomach to create a barrier and gently pushed at his chest with the other hand.

A dark, ominous cloud of warning invaded her senses just as quickly as Warren's hands. She hadn't been with Ty long, but guilt and betrayal weighed heavily on her. So did knowing that if Ty ever caught sight of her with Warren, like this, the end result would be disastrous for all of them.

Warren had quick hands and a quicker tongue. Harsh, greedy lips nipped and sucked at her neck. With several drinks under his belt, he certainly wasn't comprehending the subtle cues to back off.

The front door rattled, and Arlo cleared his throat as he stepped out onto the porch. He flashed a slight smile at both of them. "Sorry to interrupt. The security company called, said the alarm is going off at the club. I have to go check it out. Warren, you need to come with me. Sorry, Jordan. We should be right back."

"Oh, I should be going anyway. I hope everything's okay." Jordan couldn't remember ever being relieved to hear about a break-in, but she was damned relieved about this one.

Warren grabbed the nape of her neck and pulled her close. "Why don't you stay? I promise I'll hurry."

"It's been a long day for everyone, and I'd feel a little strange without you or your dad here."

"Tomorrow then?" Warren asked.

"Tomorrow," she said.

Back inside the house, she approached Warren's mom. "Mrs. Buck, thank you for having me. The food was wonderful. I need to get going, but tell the guys I said goodnight."

"One second, darlin', and I'll get your coat as soon as I finish scrubbing this pan."

"I can probably find it myself if you point me in the right direction." Bingo. *Buy some time, Jordan. Buy some time.* "I need to use the restroom before I leave anyway."

"Sweetie, I think Warren took all the coats upstairs to his room. There's a restroom in the hallway up there. Help yourself, if you don't mind."

"No problem. I'm sure I'll find my way." Straight to Buck's office.

She hustled up the stairs.

Time was critical. In and out, she told herself as she slipped inside the office door. She grabbed her cell phone and started snapping pictures of every document she could get her hands on.

No book of contacts sitting around, not in this day and age. Everything would be in his phone. Maybe. But maybe not, if he was smart.

There was a calendar. She flipped through the last year, snapped a picture of each month. Opened a couple of drawers, looked up and saw a picture of Warren on the beach with some buddies.

Nothing, damn it. Nothing she could take to Bahan. Maybe Buck was a little smarter than she'd given him credit for. She didn't expect a list of drug contacts lying around for the taking, but Christ, there had to be something. What about financials? Accounts? Where would they be?

"Jordan?" The voice echoed up the stairs. Warren's mom. Damn. "Did you find your coat, hon?"

Something about the picture of Warren on the beach bothered her. She snapped a picture of it and blazed into the bedroom and grabbed her coat.

"Yes, thank you," she said, meeting Warren's mom in the hallway. "I was looking at all the family pictures. There must be hundreds here."

"Taking pictures is kind of a hobby. I've always loved it, and Warren is so photogenic." She smiled.

"Thank you again, Mrs. Buck." Jordan headed down the stairs. "Good night."

. . .

She'd survived.

That was the good news. The bad news—she had another date with Warren tomorrow.

But hopefully it would present an opportunity to talk with Warren, as adults, and set the record straight.

If he got angry and fired her, well, she'd need to cross that bridge when it collapsed. Tolerating the hands and comments had been one thing, and even Warren's kiss she could shrug off. But no one, especially Bahan, would expect her to sacrifice anything more for a case.

Working undercover was often tricky for females. Doors

opened a little more easily than for the men, but often there was a price to pay for that ease of entry. Even without Ty's insistent warnings, Jordan knew enough to back off when the situation got heated, and Warren had been very heated tonight.

She pulled into the parking lot of her apartment complex with Ty on her mind. Big shock, since that's where it had been since the first night she'd met him. She'd become one of those women she hated, obsessing over a man rather than focusing on the task at hand. Of course this particular man had done things to her body she hadn't understood were possible, but still, he was a distraction nonetheless.

And she couldn't wait to get inside and call him, let him know she made it home okay.

Jesus, what the hell is wrong with me?

She stepped out of the car and headed for her building. The wind kicked up. She tugged the collar of her coat tighter around her neck and realized she'd left her scarf and gloves at the Buck's. Well, she'd just have to do without, because she sure wasn't going back after them tonight.

She clipped through the parking lot and was halfway to the stairwell when someone fell in step behind her and closed his hands around her waist. In a move that was pure instinct, she threw her head back, slammed her skull hard into the face of the idiot behind her and stomped on his instep. A satisfying grunt erupted as she spun around and crouched, lowering her center of gravity in preparation for a fight.

"What *the* fuck?" he said.

Shit. She straightened her stance. It was Ty. Of course it was Ty. Who else would it have been?

"Damn it, woman," he said bending over, putting his hands on his knees. He spit some blood from his mouth and stood back up.

She'd split his lip good. "I'm sorry, but you should know better than to sneak up on another cop."

"I wasn't sneaking up on another cop. I was walking up behind my girlfriend to kiss her. And I said your name. Didn't you hear me?"

The girlfriend comment momentarily threw her but she didn't comment on it. Or run in the other direction. "No, I didn't hear you…I…"

Ty turned his head and spit a little more blood. She felt bad. Really bad. Nothing about it was funny, really. His lip was puffing up and still dribbling blood. Yet she was fighting a grin. She looked down at the purse that had tumbled out of her hand. She grabbed it, stuck her hand in, and rooted around for a tissue. Glancing left and right to make sure no one was near, she shifted her Glock out of the way and tugged the tissue free.

"You gonna shoot me now? The head butt wasn't enough?" He stared at her as she stepped closer and dabbed at his lip. "You think this is funny, don't you?"

"Shut up, you big baby," she said around a smile. "I'm pretty sure you're going to make it."

His lip had mostly stopped bleeding, but she gently smoothed a finger back and forth across the tiny cut anyway. She was dying to do the same thing with her tongue. Everything about Ty was big and rugged, from his masculine jaw with just enough growth to make him look badass to his firm and fine backside. But he had the softest damn lips she'd ever tasted. And he certainly knew how to—

"You're not listening to anything I say, are you?" he asked.

Nope. "Of course I am. We just need to get inside," she said, nodding to the speeding cars racing by on the road next to them. "Someone could see us."

"Hey, you're the one who pulled a Jackie Chan on a poor, unsuspecting soul in the middle of a parking lot."

"Come on." She rolled her eyes and tugged on his hand, but he didn't move.

"For someone who was paying attention, you don't seem to have any idea what I just asked you." He fisted her coat in his hands and pulled her close, kissing his way up her neck to her ear. "I asked you to come home with me. I thought since we couldn't spend today together, maybe we could spend tonight. Thanksgiving dessert, so to speak."

The deep timbre of his voice murmuring in her ear caused heat to radiate through her veins like a good shot of tequila. She barely had the brainpower to tilt her head back and eye him suspiciously, but she finally managed to pull it off. "Will there be actual dessert? Or by dessert, do you just mean sex?"

"Real sugar and real whipped cream." He wiggled his eyebrows.

"Well then, looks like tonight we'll be going to your place."

Chapter Twelve

They stepped up to the door outside Ty's apartment. He pulled the scarf from his neck and tied it around her eyes.

"What in the world are you doing?"

"No questions and no peeking." He guided her inside and left her near the door.

He started some soft, romantic music and fumbled around for several minutes. Finally, he walked back to her and pulled the scarf from her eyes.

No lights, just candles. Everywhere. And flowers. Four huge vases were placed around the room, with a mountain of roses in each.

"Why, Tyler McGee, I believe you have a romantic side." Her eyes started to sting. She fought the foolish sensation as she walked to the roses and took a deep, appreciative sniff. The man certainly knew how to set a scene. Realizing that no one had ever given her roses or cared enough to create any kind of romance made her breath catch. She pivoted slowly, taking it all in. There must have been a month's rent tied up in flowers and candles.

He walked up behind her, slid her coat off her shoulders, and wrapped his hands around her waist. "Happy Thanksgiving." He trailed soft kisses behind her ear.

She turned in his arms and honestly was a little embarrassed at how his thoughtfulness affected her.

"Hey, hey, I'm sorry. It was supposed to make you happy, not make you cry." He pulled her close and kissed the top of her head.

She squeezed her arms around him. "I am happy, Ty. It's just that no one has ever done anything like this."

"I told you I could be downright romantic if you give me a chance, city girl. I realize this isn't a hot night out on the town or anything, but my options were limited considering you're undercover, and we can't be seen together."

"Ha." She laughed and pulled her head from his shoulder long enough to smile up at him. "Cowboy, your options were limited, because we're in a town the size of a peanut, and the most interesting thing here is a strip club."

He chuckled. "Perhaps, but what any self-respecting small-town boy knows," he whispered, moving them both to the music, "is that it's not where you take your dates that'll rock their world. It's what you do to them once you get 'em there that's important."

She stopped moving and stroked his cheek. "Thank you. Everything is beautiful."

He stood silent and still for several moments. Too many emotions passed across his face for Jordan to figure out what he was thinking. His soulful stare never wavered from her, but he didn't kiss her, didn't pull her closer.

"You are, by far, the most beautiful thing in this room. I've pictured you here, like this. Candlelight. Flowers. Music."

"Well then, I guess this just went from being my fantasy to yours. Because however you pictured me, I'm happy to oblige." She lifted her sweater up and over her head, then tossed it aside, exposing a black camisole and bra. He wasn't the only one who'd done a little shopping. After popping open all the buttons on his shirt, she wrapped her arms around him and nuzzled into his neck.

"Damn, woman. Way to play hard to get."

"Mmmm, can't help it," she murmured while trailing kisses across his chest. "You're smooth, McGee. Swept me right off my feet."

They began swaying to the music again. The motion was too intimate to call dancing, but they were moving, caressing, and touching light, gentle kisses over one another.

"Wanting you here was mostly selfish," Ty said, nuzzling her neck. "Didn't think I could endure one more night on that horrible bag of springs you call a mattress."

She laughed. "Bahan and his people picked out the apartment. I intend to pay him back for sticking me there. I guess he was able to find a furnished apartment in a good location, so he snatched it up."

God, it felt good and right and natural to be in his arms. The comfort and peace of swaying to the music and resting her head against his chest was like stepping into a third dimension. A calming quiet she never realized existed.

"So you're not responsible for any of the decorations inside the place?" he asked.

"Are you kidding? Everything is like a hundred years old. Supposedly, a ninety-two-year-old woman died, left all her stuff." She rambled peacefully with her eyes closed. "I have no idea why they didn't sell off everything, but there you go."

"Thank God. I was seriously worried about your taste in interior furnishings. Plus, those roosters are just scary."

She could hear the smile in his voice. "Oh, those are mine. I brought 'em with me."

He tugged on her hair and pulled her head back. "Smartass."

"But I had you scared there for a second, didn't I? By the way, I'm more than happy to participate in any fantasy you've got, but if you want to do anything but this," she said, tucking her head back against his chest, "you're going to have to make the first move, because I could stay like this for days. Being here in your arms, with the candles and music, it's like a little slice of heaven I never knew existed."

...

She'd muttered the words without thought, without realizing how they'd power through him. He'd battled her reluctance long enough to know surrender. Little by little, she had opened up. When it happened, he couldn't pinpoint, but somewhere along the way, they'd turned a corner. And her words were the proof.

Tilting her head back, eyes closed, she lifted her mouth in invitation.

God, how he loved those lips—covering his own, trailing across his skin, sliding up and down his...

"Are you gonna kiss me, cowboy? I'm feeling a little neglected." Her eyes opened while his were fixated on her mouth. She smiled knowingly and like a little devil, leaned in and ran her tongue slowly up the length of his neck. Then she whispered, "Warm and moist, just how you like it."

His control snapped. He took her mouth in a move much more urgent than seductive. Ravaging her hadn't been in tonight's game plan, but it was exactly what he was doing, and there wasn't a chance in hell he could stop himself.

A smooth, sensual temptation was originally what he had in mind. Tonight was supposed to be about romance, about seduction, about driving her to the edge of madness with a slow, torturing flame. Now the only image he could summon was one of clawing her clothes off and dragging her to the floor. Her needy little growl did him in.

"Oh, God, that's good," she purred when he ripped her camisole and bra over her head and cupped both breasts. "So where is this mattress you claim to be so fond—hey!" she shrieked when he swooped her up and all but ran into the bedroom. He tossed her onto the bed and stripped while she watched.

Her head fell back with a low, sexy laugh. *Damn*, even that evil, teasing cackle stirred his blood.

She smiled like the cat who clearly had the canary dead center in her cross hairs. "Someone seems to be in a hurry tonight, and for once, I don't think it's me."

He elicited another shriek when he grabbed her ankle and pulled her to the edge of the bed.

"Ty-ler," she squealed as he pulled her up, tore open her jeans, and slid them—along with her panties—down to the floor in one seamless motion. Her breath caught as he captured her breast in his mouth.

Jordan was beautiful from across a room. With her long, blonde hair and slender figure, she turned heads. But the sight of her breasts staggered him like nothing else ever had. Touching her, making her shudder, hearing her moan as he worked her nipple into a long, hard peak nearly undid him. Every. Damn. Time.

"Oh, Ty. *Mmm,*" she purred, as her whole body vibrated against his mouth.

Pure male determination had him silently swearing he was going to make her come like this. Some day. When the ache to get inside of her wasn't clawing a hole clean through him. Right now, he decided her other breast deserved the same careful attention, so he released the first nipple and began to lick a path across her chest.

But she flipped their positions and urged him up onto the bed. "Scoot up. Right here." She patted the center of the pillow as she arranged it against the headboard.

He wasn't a fool. He moved exactly where she directed him.

Tucking a knee on either side of his hips, she straddled his lap.

The warm, moist heat of her slid against his dick. Oh, yeah, he liked that. *A lot.* It was enough to make him growl. He wrapped his hands around her waist to position her more to his liking.

She giggled and shifted slightly off center. "Forgetting something?" she asked and reached into his nightstand for a condom. "I thought you were the master of patience, king of seduction, Mr. In-Control."

"I have every intention of controlling you." Which was just a damn joke. He barely had enough control to keep from coming as she rolled on the condom. But to be fair, Jordan never just *rolled* on a condom. Not without a significant amount of teasing...tasting...torture.

"You think so?" She moved back into position, slid against his length again, but pulled back before he could arch into her.

Taking a deep, sexually frustrated gulp of air, he dropped his head back against the headboard.

She laughed again, then pierced herself in one quick thrust, burying him to the hilt.

His breath exhaled on a hiss. "God*damn* it, woman, you're gonna kill me."

Her lips curled into a wicked grin. "No way. You've become irreplaceable. Some parts more than others, of course."

She rocked against him, one hand braced for leverage against his leg, the other stroking her nipples, teasing and taunting as she watched his face.

He didn't stand a chance of taking his eyes off of her. But as he watched, he knew the exact moment her mood shifted from carefree and playful to one of uncontrolled need. Her eyes drifted closed, and her head tilted back. Lost to pleasure, she rode him with single-minded focus.

Sitting up straighter, he pulled her close so that they were chest to chest. Her breasts flattened against him, and he moved his hands down to the globes of her ass, digging in, holding her firm so he could thrust deep enough to make her moan.

He kissed her neck, her chin, her ear. "Jordan" rolled from his lips in a whisper over and over. Dipping his head to her breast, he closed his teeth around her nipple.

Sliding his fingers between them, he stroked her where their bodies were joined.

He couldn't have said who trembled more at that hot, thrilling slide of his fingers against her sensitized flesh. When she jerked and cried out, control was just a distant memory. He roughly anchored her hips and drove as deeply as possible with several quick, frenzied thrusts.

Her core pulsed. She moaned, and her body trembled viciously as she clung to him. "What the hell, cowboy?" She cried out, and jerked him just as brutally over the edge. "Holy shit," she managed as her breathing shuddered in and out. "Do our bodies fit together like puzzle pieces or what?"

Her words said it all. It had become better, hotter, and more intense every single time. But he hoped Jordan didn't analyze it too deeply. Because if she figured out what he had—that it had nothing to do with their bodies, and everything to do with their hearts—he had no clue how she'd react.

...

They stayed quietly tangled for more than an hour. Jordan drifted on a contented high, although she sensed reality was going to bite her in the ass soon. She rolled over to face Ty. His eyes remained closed, and his breathing stayed deep. She took the opportunity to study his handsome profile.

His dark hair had grown long enough to look well tumbled after a healthy round of sex. *Thank you very much.* And the whiskers she affectionately called scruff looked more like a full-blown beard than a couple days of overgrowth. She'd teased him about shaving and offered up her razor, but the truth was, she'd come to crave the coarseness of his whiskers against the tender skin of her breasts. Who knew that a sensation she'd never ever contemplated could be so powerful? It was one of those erotic little surprises you just never thought about until you were in a...Her breath escaped on a rush. *Shit.* Was she in a relationship?

She watched his chest rise and fall, and another unexplainable sensation waved through her. A warm, twisting rush that momentarily turned her insides to liquid.

"If you take a picture, it'll last longer," Ty murmured with his eyes still closed.

She damn near jumped out of her skin.

"What are you thinking about?" he grumbled again. "How good-lookin' I am?"

Since he wasn't that far off base, her face scorched hot for a quick second before she decided how to best play it off. Not a snowball's chance in hell she was going with the truth. She reached over and pinched a few chest hairs between her fingers and yanked.

"Ouch. What was that for?" His eyes popped open, and he rubbed a hand across the spot missing a few hairs.

"Because you're a liar," she answered, poking him hard in the chest.

He sprang up on an elbow and grabbed her when she moved to roll off the bed. "What? I'm sorry. What did I do?"

"You promised dessert. I knew that was just your sneaky way of getting me here for sex."

He fell back on the bed. "Christ, woman, you scared me. I thought you were really pissed about something."

"I *am* really pissed about something," she teased, pulling on his shirt. "You don't promise a girl sugar and then fail to deliver."

"I never fail." He chuckled.

Lightning fast, he sprang forward and tugged her down on top of him. "I delivered something a hell of a lot more enjoyable than dessert." Rolling them, he pinned her beneath his body. "Didn't I?"

Damn, the weight of him felt good, both arousing and comforting. "That depends. Was this fictional dessert just a little generic ice cream or something really great like...well, say...Antonio's cheesecake?"

"What? There's a sliding scale or something? Now you're really starting to hack me off." He slammed her hands above her head. "I'm better than ice cream but not as good as cheesecake?"

"Exactly. But you do rank high. I'd put you at the very top of the scale. Somewhere between German chocolate cake and cheesecake."

"You *will* pay for that, you know." He lowered his head, grazed her ear with his lips. "And I don't remember the cheesecake making you come and tremble like you were having a seizure."

"Get off me, you idiot." She laughed, pushed him aside, and scrambled into the bathroom before he could grab her again.

She washed up and opened the bathroom door. Ty streaked past, back into the bedroom, with champagne in his hand. He flopped onto the bed, panting and out of breath but trying to give the appearance of calm and casual.

She narrowed her eyes but didn't question him. "Okay, you win. Your apartment kicks my rooster apartment's butt. And you're very tidy for a guy. I like that."

A person's home spoke volumes about them. As a female, she liked that he was neat, nothing out of place, no junk piles. As a detective, she was equally satisfied. He liked his things in order, organized. The effect was simple, but with a strong masculine essence. His living space reflected him.

She stopped next to his dresser, and her eyes were immediately drawn to a small female class ring. How odd that a grown man would have a girl's high school ring on his dresser. She picked it up, slipping it on her pinky. "Care to explain this? Going steady with someone?"

He leaped from the bed, took the ring off her finger, and tossed it into a drawer. "It was someone from my past, someone I used to be close with. Come on." He took her hand and tried to pull her toward the bed.

"Wait, wait, wait." She jerked out of his grip. "That's it? That's the only explanation I get? Aren't you a little old to be exchanging high school rings?"

"Aren't you a little nosy?" he countered.

"I'm a cop; deal with it. Why do you have that ring? Does it have something to do with this case?"

"No, Jordan," he said, clearly aggravated. "It's a ring from…" He sighed, did the hair thing, "…a girl. We grew up together."

Jordan felt that odd shock wave of pain that radiated off him from time to time. She couldn't keep from asking about it any longer. If he had unresolved feelings for someone else, she wanted to know. "Someone you loved? Still love?"

"No. Not how you're thinking. She was…a kid. Just a kid. But she's dead. Killed not long ago. We were close when we were younger, so her mom gave me the ring to remember her by. Okay?"

She nodded. "Okay." He clearly didn't want to talk about it. Ty was a lot of things—a little intimidating, bullheaded maybe—but he wasn't a liar. She'd always felt his goodness, his honesty. So she let it drop. Tonight had been too beautiful to spoil. She pushed him backwards until he fell onto the bed, then crawled on top of him. "Your apartment is really nice, cowboy. It suits you."

He rolled them both and adjusted positions until they were relaxed against the pillows. "Well," he said, reaching for the champagne glasses, "if somewhere in the future, we end up living together, I'll do the decorating."

"Hey, take it back." She pinched his nipple, knowing he was defenseless with two glasses of champagne in his hands. "I told you I didn't have anything to do with the way my place looks. You should see my apartment in St. Louis. I think you'd approve."

"Is that an invitation? You know, I've given some thought to what happens after we arrest the Bucks. Just because this case ends, I don't want us to. You ever given any thought to moving here when this is over?"

She grabbed one of the champagne glasses and took a long sip. "About as much thought as I give to driving painful little stakes underneath my fingernails."

He laughed. "Man, you're cold. This is my hometown. Born and raised."

She poured a tiny bit of champagne on his chest, admiring how it looked on his skin. Then she bent down and licked. "Well," she murmured, pouring more below his belly button and proceeding to kiss and slurp her way down him. "It's time you branched out."

He sat up, snagged her glass, and set it on the nightstand with his. Tumbling her to the bed, he tickled her ribs until she squealed like a girl.

"Ty-ler, stop it." She squirmed and laughed. "You have something against champagne? I was just getting to the good part."

"I have every intention of letting you pick up exactly where you left off, but first, you owe me an apology."

"For?"

"First, for knocking my hometown, but second…" He reached beside the bed to pick up the bakery box. "Second for doubting me. I am a man of my word. Ah, ah, ah," he said, pulling the box away when she sat up and made a grab for it.

"Jordan, I know Thanksgiving stirs hard memories for you, but I don't want you to feel that way forever. I hoped we could start a new tradition. Together."

The sting in her eyes started immediately. She knew it, didn't she? Knew that the one person who would understand her, who could help her break through the awfulness of this day, was Ty. She wasn't good at breaking down in front of people, never did it, but this man could honestly reduce her to a little puddle of goo with the snap of his fingers. It was incredibly frightening, at the same time, it touched her like crazy.

"I'm sorry. I didn't mean to hurt you." He dropped the box to the bed and picked up her hand, running his fingers over hers. "This was a mistake." Hurt etched in the tiny lines around his eyes. "There are just some things you can never move past, aren't there?" He looked into her eyes and thumbed away her tears.

The question bothered her. She got the distinct impression it wasn't rhetorical, but she didn't understand what he was asking. And she wasn't sure she wanted to know. Not now. She picked up the bakery box and opened the lid. Antonio's sinfully delicious cheesecake stared back with a big, whipped-cream smiley face. "You're right; it's time."

"I never wanted to make you cry, just...I don't know." He swallowed hard. "I just wanted you to be able to enjoy Thanksgiving and the holidays again."

This big strong man with the heart of an angel sat in front of her with glistening eyes. She was pretty sure he'd gouge his eyeballs out before he'd let a tear fall, but she could feel how much he cared.

"You won't forget them," he said. "I know you'll never forget them, but given enough time and no other choice, maybe you just have to move on. I'm—"

She pressed her fingers over his lips. "It's the most beautiful, thoughtful thing anyone has ever done for me."

Words weren't what either of them needed, neither was the cheesecake. Not now. He pulled her into a long, deep kiss. Then another. He pushed her back, moved against her, eased between her legs. Stroking her hair away from her face, he grazed down her neck, then quickly jerked away.

Lost in his touch, finally, she blinked her eyes open.

His face was hard, his body rigid. A blind woman could have seen the fury that was ready to erupt.

The sexual haze vanished.

"What happened to your neck?" he asked, his voice flat.

The angel-like apparition of a few seconds ago had disintegrated. His nostrils flared, and Jordan got the impression he was barely hanging on to restraint.

She moved her head from side to side. Everything appeared in working order. "What do you mean? What's wrong?"

"Your neck. It looks like a hickey."

Shrugging, she said, "Okay, not your smartest move considering the Warren situation, but my hair will cover it." She fingered her skin. His expression never changed.

Silence echoed.

Then her mental fog lifted, and the memory of Warren and his determined lips sliding down her neck surfaced. Oh, shit! This was going to get very ugly, very quickly. She recognized the dangerous shade of red riding his face.

"I. Did not. Do that."

"Sure you did. Things got pretty heated there for a while." She doubted whether he was going to buy that approach, but she was going to sell it and sell it hard. "Remember when we—"

"Can it, Jordan. You and I both know I didn't do that." He jumped out of the bed and threw on a pair of shorts. "You let Warren Buck touch you, didn't you? A hickey? A damned hickey? I asked you what happened tonight. Funny, I don't remember you mentioning making out with Warren."

No, she hadn't told him, hadn't felt either of them had anything to gain by it. "Look, he did try to kiss me, b—"

"Try? Sure as hell looks like he succeeded. You let him put his hands on you, his lips on you. Have you lost your fucking mind?" His voice rose. Hot rage blanketed the room. "Are you getting some sort of twisted kick out of stringing him along?"

"Don't be an idiot." Jordan scooted out of the bed and walked toward him. At odds with herself, she struggled between fighting back and trying to keep a cooler head. "You know better than that. After all that's happened between us, do you honestly believe I've got some side thing with Warren?"

"You tell me. How far are you willing to go to crack this case?" He thrust his hands through his hair and turned away. "In order to keep some level of sanity right now, I won't let myself believe you'd do what I'm visualizing in my head. But what am I supposed to think when I see his mark on your neck?" He turned back and stabbed a finger at her. "No more, Jordan. It's over. You will *not* see him again. I mean it."

Being given orders by Ty should have offended her on every level. As a cop, as a woman, she should have been fighting the rage, but there was none. She couldn't explain why, but the fact that he had become so completely irrational touched her in a way she didn't understand.

Still, she was in Titus for a reason and had a job to do. "Ty, you know I can't do that." For good measure, she said it with more anger in her voice than she actually felt. "I may look like backwoods Betty Jo in those ridiculous clothes and disastrous hair and make-up, but I'm a cop the same as you. I'm in the middle of an undercover investigation. How am I supposed to stay away from Warren?"

"What you did tonight crosses a line. A dangerous line. I want it to stop, and I want the truth. All of it this time."

"Okay, here's the truth: you're letting something insignificant mess you up."

"This," he said, touching her neck, "is anything but insignificant. In fact, it's the last straw. You don't get it, do you? Titus was a great place to grow up. Safe. Everybody knew everybody else. I loved this town. But you're right. It's a pit now because the Bucks have turned it into one. They ruin lives; they destroy everything good. And if you think I'm going to sit back and let them take one more thing from me that I love, you're wrong."

She stepped back, her mouth gaped open. Emotions she couldn't even name swam in her head, but the most prominent one felt a lot like fear.

He propped his hands on his hips and dropped his head. "Damn it. I guess that wasn't the most romantic way to say that, huh?" He took a few deep breaths before lifting his head again. He stepped toward her, pinched her chin, and forced her gaze to meet his. "I am in love with you, Jordan. And I'll see Warren Buck dead before he touches you again."

Chapter Thirteen

Spending Thanksgiving night with Ty brought to the surface more emotions than Jordan was ready to deal with. He actually had the nerve to let the L word loose on her. The man just didn't play fair.

The attraction had seized them both before they even knew each other's name. And the sex… Jesus, the power of the sex was mind-boggling. The rest of the world simply didn't exist when Ty was inside her. Nothing had prepared her for the intensity. That reality alone scared the hell out of her.

The man had twisted her inside out, upside down, and every other unnatural direction until she honestly felt her head could spin off the top of her shoulders.

Good God, what next?

For starters, she was going to brush Warren off as gently as possible. She'd play the let's-just-be-friends card. How he'd react would be anyone's guess.

Jordan pulled into Buck's expecting to see more than one car in the parking lot. Her head buzzed with questions. Had there been a real burglary last night? Where was the group of people meeting for lunch today? Why was Warren's red Mustang sitting alone?

Ty had damn near lost his mind when she got out of his bed this morning and admitted that she was going to see Warren again today. He'd stood like a barricade in front of the door and threatened to handcuff her to the headboard until she came to her senses.

She'd put up a good show of outrage at his demands. She had more undercover experience in her pinky than most cops ever saw in an entire career, so the last thing she needed was a man dictating how she should do her job.

And yet the truth was obvious. To Ty. To Bahan. She'd jumped too fast and too hard on this one. China White had begun to spiral in her St. Louis jurisdiction a couple of years ago, but in recent months, it had spread like the flu in high season. Law enforcement had a war on their hands.

But two officers from her unit had lost their lives while in deep cover. Maybe that shouldn't have made a difference in her sense of urgency to nail the Bucks, but it had. She'd gotten in way over her head with Warren Buck, and now she had to fix things.

Go to lunch. Go to the movie. But set Warren straight.

She turned off the ignition and opened her purse to drop the keys inside. They rapped against the grip of her gun. After scoping out the parking lot and side street to make sure she was alone, she slipped the Glock from her purse and laid it in her lap.

Her gun was so familiar, so comforting. Now, every time

she locked it in the glove box before entering Buck's, a little wave of sickness shot through her. Today the sickness felt more like full-on nausea.

Again, she contemplated taking her clutch piece. If she'd been wearing it last night, Warren would have found it when they were together on the swing. Nothing screamed *cop* quite as loudly as a Glock in a handbag or a gun strapped fashionably to an ankle.

She'd heard it said—on Oprah, if she remembered correctly—that instinct was the whisper in your head that told you something didn't feel right.

Many ignored the whisper.

Despite the training, despite all the undercover years, even despite her perverse flirtation with a world of spirits and energies she didn't fully understand, she ignored the gnawing sensation that something was off and walked through the door of Buck's.

Warren sat at the bar with his back to her. She approached him and smelled booze and sweat filtering through the air. And was he wearing the same clothes from yesterday?

He swiveled around, and his wild, bloodshot eyes met hers.

As the whisper in her head did indeed become a full-blown surly voice, she wondered for half a second how Oprah was always right. She also wondered why the hell she'd left her gun in the car.

"You forgot your gloves and scarf at my house last night." Anger dripped from every drunken syllable. "I thought you might need them today. Supposed to be cold." He threw them at her, hard, like a major league pitcher in the bottom of the ninth.

"Okay, thanks." The scarf and gloves had bounced off her body. She bent and picked them up. Maybe she'd downplayed the first few subtle warnings, but the danger in the room had her full attention now.

He'd figured it out. Made her as a cop.

He slid off the barstool and stalked toward her. "See, the thing was, I decided to bring them to you last night. I had your address on file from your work application."

The pieces of the puzzle shifted and clicked. Last night ran through her mind like a silent horror flick.

The scuffle.

The kiss.

The cars passing by.

He hadn't made her as a cop. He'd seen her in the parking lot with Ty. The whole encounter had lasted maybe a couple minutes. But that was apparently long enough. It was a careless, dangerous mistake, and she was pretty sure she was about to pay for it. She took a few defensive steps backwards.

"How long you been screwing McGee?" He stabbed the words at her.

Stupid.

She never made mistakes. Never allowed a distraction.

Ridiculously stupid.

"I don't know what you're talking about. I'm not—"

"Save it. Does he know I felt you up about an hour before you banged him?" In one swift movement, he backhanded her across the cheekbone.

She could take a blow, had done it before, but the alcohol and the giant ex-football-playing hand made a hell of a combination. The sharp, brittle snap sent a searing pain straight into her eye socket. Blood swam in her eye and blurred her vision. It was going to make landing a good punch of her own more challenging.

The only encouraging thought: he was drunk, stupid, and most importantly—slow.

"Did you have a good laugh at my expense, you fucking, little whore?" He snatched up a beer bottle and swung it at her head. But this time, even with one eye, she saw it coming and blocked with her wrist. The bottle shattered and sprayed, sending glass, blood, and her keys to the floor in a chaotic explosion.

She aimed a kick to his groin, made him grunt, but knew she'd missed the bull's-eye. She bent and grabbed for her keys.

He kicked up, snapping her jaw shut and sending a fierce tremor through her head.

She fell back. The room twisted and spun. Black dots danced in her vision, and she was pretty sure he'd cracked a couple of her teeth.

Warren came at her, but she rolled and managed to get to her feet. Her only hope was her keys. Her car held her weapon and her escape. She grabbed a chair and hurled it at him.

Maybe it was adrenaline. Maybe it was drugs. But his huge body barely registered the blow.

A few seconds—a few minutes—she had no idea how long she dodged and countered his fists. Training and hand-to-hand techniques flipped through her mind like pages in a magazine. Groin, throat, nose, eyes. She struck all the vulnerable spots a 137-pound female was trained to target against a man three times larger, but her vision sucked. Blood and beer stung her eyes and rendered her damn near blind. Still, she landed a vicious kick to his knee.

His blurry image went down.

Of all the thoughts that could have entered her mind, it was with stunning clarity that she realized how precious a few seconds could be. No longer was the issue success or failure of a case, but life and death.

She made one last effort to locate her keys, and she did find them. But the search took too long. When she grabbed them and turned to run, Warren landed a fist across her jaw that knocked her on her back. She slid across the floor a good four or five feet. Blood erupted from her mouth. Pain and a wave of sickness gave way to a cloudy tunnel vision.

The trained cop began to crumble under pure female desperation.

He fell on top of her and ripped at her clothes. "You want to play games, you little bitch? You like it rough? Cause that's exactly how it's going to be."

Someone pulled Warren off of her. She could swear she heard Arlo's voice, but she couldn't see through the blood and tears. Rolling to her side, she curled into a fetal position and vomited.

Soft gray edges dulled what little vision she had left. As everything faded to black, she could only think that Ty was right. Balancing on a tightrope of trouble could only happen for so long. Eventually, some son of a bitch was going to tumble you into a slick spot on the street.

Chapter Fourteen

Ty paced like a caged animal as he pretended not to be half out of his mind.

Where was she?

He couldn't keep his head from turning toward Jordan's usual station. He'd been at Buck's for almost two hours, and she still hadn't showed. Quarter to six. She was never late. Warren wasn't there yet, either.

No way was she still somewhere with Warren.

She'd given her word. Promised she was going to put some space between herself and Buck's idiot son, no matter how it affected the case.

"Hey, Casey, you heard from Jordan?" Ty tried to act casual while teetering on the edge of a meltdown.

"No, but she better get her sweet ass here before too long, or I'm going to kick it. This is one of our busiest nights of the year. I can't cover both of our stations alone."

He nodded and walked away. He'd questioned every

person in the place. No one had heard from her. Christ, where could she be?

She wasn't answering her phone. Her car was nowhere in the parking lot. A person didn't just disappear. She wouldn't do that. Something was wrong. They'd agreed to touch base as soon as she talked to Warren.

What if the asshole got crazy with her?

Time crept along like snarled traffic in rush hour. Seconds passed like minutes, minutes like hours. Every damn pulse of the music pushed the likeliness of seeing her walk through the door, safe and unharmed, further and further away.

He checked his watch. Eight thirty. Still no sign of Jordan. No calls. No nothing.

Where the hell was she?

His heart thrummed all the way to his eardrums. It wasn't worry anymore; he'd passed worry two hours back. Keeping himself from raging through the place was taking super-human control. He desperately wanted to topple tables and aim his gun at a few select targets.

He'd had enough. Weaving through the sea of customers, he walked up behind Buck. "Casey needs help covering Jordan's section. She says Jordan never showed up."

"Haven't seen her," Buck grumbled. "Might be sick, but she should've called in."

"Warren said he was going to sign some paperwork for me tonight. What about him?"

"Warren's with his mother in Kansas City. They left late last night to take his grandma back home. Anything that needs to be signed, you can bring to me."

Warren wasn't in Kansas City. He was gone. Missing. And so was Jordan. But Buck had just provided his son with an airtight alibi for the whole night and day.

Ty's gut twisted into a sick, desperate knot. He had to start looking for her. The Fed she talked about was named Bahan, and he worked out of the St. Louis field office. Jordan said he'd be in Titus by nightfall, so he had to be somewhere close. It couldn't be that hard to find him.

...

Only one eye managed to open. Jordan blinked, trying to regain a small amount of sight. A twilight sky freckled with clouds told her she faced the last few moments of daylight. Dried, dead weeds and the tall, brown grass of winter surrounded her.

She was outside. In a field.

Being beaten unconscious and dreaming felt strangely similar; the line that separated reality from violent, painful visions blurred. She'd never ridden in a dark trunk before, but she was certain that was how she'd gotten here.

Cold. It was unbearably cold. At the same time, she couldn't stop sweating.

Curled on her side, she tasted blood and dirt as she licked her dry lips and struggled to suck air in against the searing pain in her lungs.

She rose on an elbow and vomited into the sticky pool of blood that had formed under her head.

And she thought of the girl with the beautiful eyes and the long dark hair. The girl was with her now; that's why the dreams about her had felt so different. That's why they had a connection. The beautiful girl was preparing her for her own similar fate. Beaten, broken, bloody, and very much left for dead in the middle of nowhere.

Her life couldn't end like this, could it? After everything she'd survived, had her destiny been decided by the likes of Warren Buck?

Determined not to follow the girl quietly into death, she struggled to a sitting position. Barren winter fields spread as far as her eye could see. A tiny structure in the distance came into focus. Real or a hallucination? She couldn't be sure, but false hope was better than none. Without something to cut the bitter night wind, she'd be dead by sunrise.

Before attempting to move toward the building, she inventoried her injuries.

Her chest ached as if someone had sliced her open and plucked out several ribs with pliers. With every breath, every movement, nausea roiled. One ankle had swollen to twice its normal size, and one shoe was missing.

Who was she kidding? Even with shelter, she'd likely be dead by morning. Warm tears rolled against her frigid skin, but the earnest realization that maybe this was it gave her a final jolt of adrenaline.

She hobbled, crawled, struggled. Rested after every few painful feet. The structure ended up being a tiny, dilapidated old shed, the only sign that life had once been anywhere near. It was pitch black by the time she inched her way there. When she made it, she collapsed against an outside wall and fell into a dream.

"Shhh, it's going to be okay, baby girl," her dad whispered, tucking her hair behind her ear.

"Dad?"

"I'm here to help you," he said. *"I'll keep you warm until he finds you. I love you, baby girl. Always have."*

Jordan struggled awake and upright. She'd take death, wasn't scared of it. But she damn sure wasn't taking help from the man who had cost her everything. Why did he keep coming back? Night after night. Dream after dream. *Go away*, she thought. *Please just go, and don't come back.* She tried to scream the words, cry them out, but her lungs wouldn't allow it. Pain sliced through her chest, trapping her breath.

When the air surged back, she drank it in, swallowed it, wanted to stockpile it for the next suffocating moment.

Bitter coldness pierced her.

Dizzy now, so very dizzy, she lay back and inched as close to the broken-down shed as she could get. Its dilapidated walls eased the strength of the wind. Inside would be better, but she couldn't move any more. She closed her eyes and tumbled in and out of the abyss of her mind.

Years of police work and snapshots of her personal life flickered like old silent movies.

Katy's giggle. Her mom baking in the kitchen.

Peaceful.

Soothing.

That's what she needed. Good things. Good thoughts. Precious memories to hold on to. Ty.

Always Ty. Forever it would be Ty.

His beautiful cocky face. Eyes that shimmered with humor and seduction. The strong jaw that clenched when he was angry. Nothing bad could ever touch her when his arms wrapped her up.

Oh, God, Ty. Where are you? I need you.

It wasn't Ty who came to her. It was the beautiful girl. She was back, swinging behind her house, and the boy was with her. He pushed her swing. Handed her a beer. Threw his jacket and football gear in his trunk.

"Tara."

He called her Tara. Her name was Tara. The jacket, the football gear. It looped again and again and again. It meant something. But the pain and the sickness and the blood kept interfering.

Jordan fought herself awake, but her eyelids were unbearably heavy. Truth be told, the vision was no longer more frightening than reality. For the first time, she wanted to escape back into a dream instead of away from it. She felt herself drift again, to find Tara and tell her that she was sorry.

Sorry because she hadn't found the boy. Sorry for leaving Ty behind. Sorry because of the decisions she'd made.

She closed her eyes. She was done.

"I'm ready. Mom. Katy. Somebody please come. I just want to be with you again."

"Not tonight, baby."

Jordan used her last bit of strength to blink her eyes open.

Her dad was the one that appeared. "You're not ready. Not yet." He kneeled beside her, stroking her hair. "Your life won't end tonight, I won't let it. You have too many people to help."

Her eyes fell closed. She would have laughed had there been any air in her lungs. "I can't even help myself right now."

Her dad chuckled. "Then you're lucky you don't have to. I know of a young man who's perfectly willing to walk across fire to help you. All you have to do is let him." The humor in his voice turned somber. "Let someone help, Jordan. Let someone in your life."

Anger burned like vicious little fires surrounding her heart. She hated that she didn't even have the strength to raise her eyelids and level him with a nasty look. "Is that why you haunt me year after year? Dream after dream? To offer me your words of wisdom? Just a little hypocritical coming from you, isn't it? The one person who ensured I was left completely alone."

"That's why I'm here. I don't haunt you, I try to guide you. To keep you from making the same mistakes I did."

How dare he? She was nothing—nothing—like him. "Newsflash, Daddy. I'm not a drug dealer. Mission accomplished. I'm nothing like you."

"You are me." *The soothing cadence of his voice turned harsh.* "The mistakes I'm talking about are not the ones you think. Yes, I messed up, Jordan. Horribly. My mistakes cost our family everything, and the one's I'm sorriest for are the ones I made with you. Secrets destroy much more powerfully than the truth ever will. I lost everything learning that. If you don't change, you'll learn it, too.

"Baby girl," *his voice cracked with emotion now.* "Be better than me. Be stronger. Let people love you. All of you. They will if you let them."

He slid next to her and pulled her onto his lap. He held her, kissed her, rocked her. And she let him. Because in his arms, she didn't hurt anymore. Surprisingly, not her body or her heart. Opening her eyes hurt and made her sick.

"Are you leaving now?"

"I'm never leaving, not as long as you need me."

If he let go, it would be the end. Even so, she let the hostile words roll from her tongue. "I don't need anyone."

"You've got to stop this," *he demanded, even as he softly*

touched her cheek. "It's been long enough. You've shut down so completely no one can get through, living or dead. Whether you like it or not, you have to make connections. Spirits need you to help those left behind. The living need you to bring them closure. What you have is a gift to help and to heal. If you're not going to use it, you might as well join us."

Finally, she broke. "I let my whole family die," she sobbed. "What if I screw up again?"

The soft comfort of his embrace turned fierce and rigid. "If you hear nothing else tonight, hear this—nothing that happened the night of the murder was your fault. It was all mine."

Stunned at his harsh tone, Jordan managed to open her eyes and not just look, but really see him, all of him. The sadness, the sorrow, even the hope. She nodded, took a breath, and realized the struggle for air was a bit easier now. "I'm so cold."

"I'll keep you warm until he comes. Now shush and go to sleep." He kissed her forehead again and wrapped his arms tighter around her. "Ty loves you, and he's already searching."

Chapter Fifteen

Ty found Theodore K. Bahan through the St. Louis field office.

He'd been patched through to the special agent's cellphone. If he stood any chance of saving Jordan, Bahan was the only logical choice to help him. They arranged a meeting in the parking lot of Jed's Gas Mart for thirty minutes later. In fifteen, he was sandwiched between two scruffy Neanderthals in the back seat of a sedan. If these guys were FBI, they'd missed the memo about the standard dark suit and tie.

Jordan told him Bahan was arriving the day after Thanksgiving. Apparently, he'd already been in Titus when Ty placed the call.

After two goons searched him, cuffed him, and threw him in a backseat, a third guy behind the wheel peeled out of Jed's and punched it. "I'm Bahan," he said. "Talk. Now."

They'd purposely been intimidating and rough, but every

second was critical. Ty already figured he wasn't going to get a warm welcome, so he gave a clear, concise report. Most of it was true. He tweaked the personal part a bit, basically omitting it. He had a feeling the Fed was smart enough to read between the lines.

Bahan wheeled into an empty parking lot and did a one-eighty before screeching to a stop. He looked in the rearview mirror and said, "Tommy, find her. Start by tracing her phone." Then he twisted around to the other guy. "When he finds her location, get 'em there. Ground, air, K-9. No sirens. Step out, please."

The two guys on either side of Ty opened the doors, got out, and continued working from the parking lot.

"You slept with her."

It didn't sound like a question, so Ty didn't answer. It wasn't relevant. "Does it matter?"

"I've known the woman ten years. Never known her to screw up, not like this. You've known her ten minutes, and she's missing." Bahan leveled a look at him in the mirror. "Or she's dead. Trust me, it's going to matter."

"You're wasting time," Ty argued. "Time she may not have."

"I don't think you want to screw with me right now. If I'm going to find her, I need to know exact—"

"Yes. All right, yes. We're working together and…yes." It was Bahan's ballgame. Ty would have confessed to anything to get one step closer to Jordan. "Is that what you needed to hear to hang me? You want to charge me with something? Lock me up? Blame me for everything, I don't give a fuck. Just do it after you find her."

"I don't like you, and I don't trust you." Bahan turned

this time to look Ty in the eyes. "But I trust Jordan. I don't know what it is, but her instincts are never wrong. If she told you things, worked with you, there was a reason for it. But you're on a very short leash with me, and make no mistake, if you get in my way or at any moment hinder instead of help, I'll put a bullet in you and won't even pause as I step over you."

Given the circumstances, Ty figured that was as close to bonding as they were going to get, so he dove headfirst into an exact account of Jordan's days. At least as much as he knew and as far as he could remember. Bahan stopped him when he mentioned Thanksgiving.

"Wait a minute. She went to their house on Thanksgiving?"

"I wasn't happy about it, but I couldn't change her mind," Ty said. "And trust me, I tried. She told me she was working with the FBI. I assumed someone knew what she was doing."

"Unbelievable." Bahan scrubbed his hands up and down his face. "I mean seriously, what in the name of God was she thinking?"

Fury bubbled as Ty remembered the mark Warren had put on her neck. "Warren Buck had a thing for her, and she was using it to get closer to both him and Buck."

Bahan shook his head.

"We argued this morning." Ty closed his eyes and remembered their words, remembered touching her. Prayed it hadn't been for the last time. "She promised me she'd set him straight today. Tell him she wasn't interested that way."

"Guess he didn't take it well," Bahan murmured.

"That'd be my guess. I don't think he figured her for a cop. I'm not sure I'd have figured it out except for the way she reacted when I startled her one night. I — " He met Bahan's eyes and began to remember the couple of times he had grabbed her and pulled her close. Including Thanksgiving night.

The other two Feds opened the doors. "We got her phone. Location's about an hour from here."

"Get in." Bahan's words and the movement of the car barely registered in Ty's mind. He thought back to Thanksgiving night. He'd kissed her in the parking lot of her apartment. Could someone have seen? He remembered the cars flying by on the road next to the parking lot and how nervous Jordan had been because of it. If one of those cars had been Warren's, and he'd seen them...

"Oh, God." Ty dropped his head in his hands. "This *is* all my fault."

...

"We're close. If she's anywhere near her phone, we'll find her." Bahan picked up the police radio and contacted the K-9 unit again. "Her phone has led us about nine miles east, off Highway P. It's a gravel and dirt road about a hundred yards past P and Klondike. Don't blink or you'll miss it, and hurry up." Bahan wound his way through the trees, and they traveled slowly down the narrow, dusty road.

Ty rolled down the back window and looked for a sign that someone had recently been in the area. He also blinked and sucked in as much of the cold night air as his lungs could absorb. Every minute that she was missing chipped away at his ability to hold it together.

"Stop," he yelled. "Over there." A spot of weeds and

brush next to the road had been flattened with obvious tire marks.

Bahan stopped, they got out and started searching. It took less than twenty minutes to find Jordan's purse, phone, and scraps of clothing. It looked as if someone had tossed them as an afterthought. But Jordan was nowhere near her things.

Bahan moved the car into a clearing at the end of the gravel road and made a makeshift headquarters for the search. "It's almost one. The darkness is going to complicate things, but we're still going to have search parties briefed and ready to roll within the hour."

Ty grabbed a flashlight and started to walk off.

"McGee," Bahan called. "We do this in teams with radios and K-9 units."

Ty stopped. Bahan may have been a Fed with a fair amount of contacts, but none of them were familiar with this area. "I want to call my people in. Cops from around here will know this land. I can get twenty guys here in half an hour."

"No. The last thing I need is twenty local yokels stomping through my crime scene. This is Jordan's investigation and mine. If she's here, I'll find her. But if I can't or she's—" Bahan paused, tossed some equipment from his trunk on the ground. "If she's dead, I'm going back to that little backwoods town of yours and taking out every single one of those motherfuckers, one bloody painful kill at a time."

"So…what? We don't get the people we need out here to help, because you're more interested in preserving the scene than finding her? How many units do you have coming? If she's hurt, we have to find her. Fast."

Bahan exploded. "How stupid are you? Do you think he dumped her here, in the middle of nowhere, alive?"

Ty lunged. He plowed into Bahan, knocked him flat, and started throwing wild, uncontrolled punches.

A police cruiser skidded to a stop. "Break it up," the cop yelled out his window.

Ty looked toward the K-9 unit. It was just enough of a distraction to allow Bahan to land a punch and throw Ty off. But Bahan apparently had a quick change of heart. He got up, swiped at the blood rolling down his lip, and then bent to Ty and extended a hand. "I shouldn't have said that. Sorry. I'm not giving up on her."

Things started moving quickly once the two K-9 units started to track. They scented the dogs from the scraps of Jordan's clothing and split into two teams. Bahan went with one team and sent Ty with the other. It was only minutes before one of the dogs found the spot where she'd been dumped.

"Team two is on scent," Bahan said across the radio.

"Please let her be alive." Ty repeated it over and over in a chant. Maybe if he said it enough times, it would be true.

Ty saw two more cop cars and an ambulance pull down the gravel road as he raced to where Linx, the German shepherd, was tracking. Nose down, ears back, the dog barreled forward. Shining his flashlight ahead for Linx, Ty saw it—the small shed and the figure on the ground next to it.

Relief and horror simultaneously gripped him. He ran to the shed and fell to his knees.

Her face was black and blue and swollen. Her clothes were in tatters. Her hair was bloody and matted. She had no color, and if Ty hadn't known her body so well, he may have been able to convince himself it wasn't Jordan.

"We need paramedics," Bahan ordered, running up to them.

Ty dropped the flashlight and bent over her, swept her hair back from her face, and gently touched his cheek against hers. Chaos buzzed in the dark night, but for Ty, the world shrank to a small bubble around the two of them. Her skin was frigid. Emotions swamped him. He couldn't be sure if she was alive or not, and he was terrified to put his finger up to her freezing neck to feel for a pulse.

"Ty." She whispered so quietly he didn't know if he had actually heard her or just imagined that he did.

He pulled back to study her. One eye barely opened, but it was enough to know she was in there. And enough to know he needed to let the paramedics get her somewhere quickly.

"Don't. Please don't let go." She made a horrible, almost inhuman screech as he tried to ease back enough for the paramedics to start working on her. "Keep holding me. Daddy said you'd hold me now."

"Give her something," he yelled. "She's in pain."

Everything limped by in a slow, devastating blur, but at least she was alive. He didn't understand the medical jargon, but he picked up a few key words like broken ribs and head trauma. The vicious punch that broke him was the call for the helicopter that was needed to get her airlifted back to St. Louis *in time*.

"In time for what?" Ty fisted his hands in Bahan's jacket and shook him hard, slamming him up against a large tree next to the shed.

Ted Bahan never laid a hand on him and even waved off the two cops stepping forward to intervene.

Ty took a deep breath, looked around at everyone staring at him. He'd lost it. And it was pity he saw on every one of their faces. He'd seen it before. He'd been here before.

Déjà vu slammed into him. Rage and pain and sickness all over again. Standing in the middle of nowhere watching someone he loved being carried away, hurt and lifeless because of Warren and Arlo Buck.

It'd end different this time, though. Jordan wouldn't leave him. He didn't know how he was so certain, but she'd hang on, because she'd know, understand, he didn't have a life without her. It would end differently this time.

He repeated the words, fighting for sanity. Then he blinked. Ted Bahan was still pinned against the tree, with Ty's hands clutching his jacket. Even more cops and Feds surrounded them. Still, Bahan held them off.

"We're airlifting her to St. Louis," Bahan said. He talked slow and clear, as though he were speaking to a child unable to comprehend. "They'll probably only let one of us go with her. I need to do it, McGee. I have all her medical information, and I know how to contact the right people."

Bahan squinted and leaned his head against the tree, as if preparing for a blow. Ty dropped his hands and stepped back.

"Are we good?" Bahan asked.

Ty swallowed and eventually nodded.

The Fed waved off his goons, and Ty reached past his own grief and studied Bahan. The guy obviously cared for Jordan. "You'll stay with her, all the way? And keep in contact with me?"

"All the way," Bahan agreed.

"Fine," Ty said, holding out his hand. "But I'll need your keys."

Bahan reached into his pocket but turned a hard stare on Ty. "You can't go after him, McGee."

"Your keys, please. I have to get to St. Louis somehow."

"You can ride with Peterson and Linx. They can put the lights on and get you there almost as quick as the chopper."

"Give me the damned keys," Ty shouted at Bahan. "Warren Buck may have just killed her, and you know it. You're supposed to be her friend. Are we all just going to stand here and let him roam free? Maybe you can do that, but it's not gonna work for me."

Ty was raging now. He could feel it, hear it in his own words.

"We need time to figure out how to handle this," Bahan challenged him. "I'm not ready to put her in a grave yet, and I sure as hell am not lying to her when she wakes up asking for you. So either you'll get your sorry ass in that police car willingly, or I'll cuff you and throw you in the back of it. Either way is fine by me."

"Great. Just great. Jordan may die. Do you get that? She may die. I lose her. You lose her. But you want to let the asshole who did this walk away?"

Bahan snapped. His face turned red and a vein on his forehead bulged. It pulsed larger with the rising intensity of his voice. "Warren Buck will pay for what he's done. His freedom is on countdown, I promise you that, McGee. You want to charge out of here? Go after him? Blow the very case that may cost Jordan her life? Be my guest," he said, throwing the keys at Ty. "But if you ask me, there's someone who needs your attention *right this damn minute* a hell of a lot more than Warren Buck does."

Ty turned and closed his eyes against the burn that was threatening tears if he wasn't careful. He wanted to scream until the pieces of his heart fused together again. He wanted to kill Warren Buck. He wanted to make Jordan magically well. But he couldn't do any of those things.

So he did the only thing that he could. He tossed Bahan's keys back, walked over to the police cruiser, and opened the door. Then he slid next to Linx and buried his face in the fur of the dog that had found the woman he loved.

Chapter Sixteen

"I want your word you're not going to fly out of here half-cocked, or I'll cuff you to the closest coma patient." Bahan said.

Ty didn't answer. He was making no such promises. As far as he was concerned, the earth would rotate much more smoothly without the stink of Arlo and Warren Buck polluting the surface. If anything happened to Jordan, he was going to do his part to clean up the environment before sundown.

But the Fed's threat to cuff him may not have been an idle one, so he kept quiet. He figured he could take Bahan, but there were twelve other cops huddled around, and all of them seemed to be kissing Bahan's ass. The odds weren't in his favor.

Ty straightened, lunging forward when a doctor walked into the waiting room. "Are any of you Detective Delany's next of kin?"

"She's a cop, we're all cops, so yeah, we're family," Bahan answered.

"I need to contact her legal family. Does she have—"

"No husband, her parents are dead, no living relatives. I have her power of attorney, so spill it."

The doctor looked around at the large huddle of cops with a skeptical glance, then must have concluded the odds weren't in his favor, either. "She's doing remarkably well under the circumstances. She's had some head trauma and comes in and out of consciousness. She has four cracked ribs. That's what we're dealing with first.

"A more minor concern is an injury to her eye. We'll have a specialist look at it, but she's quite a fighter and doing quite well, I'd say. We'll know more in an hour or so."

Those were much needed words. Ty inhaled deeply, feeling like it was his first real breath since they'd found her. Gauging by the collective sigh that shot through the waiting room, he wasn't the only one that had been holding his breath. As the doctor left, Ty said to Bahan, "I want to see her, but then I'm taking off for a little while."

Bahan nodded toward the hallway. Ty followed him out of the waiting room and into a deserted hospital room.

"You want to be in this investigation, hotshot, you're in," Bahan said. "What's your plan? Who's your backup? We just learned the hard way that everybody needs backup."

Ty had a Colt 1911 with seven in the clip and one in the chamber holstered to his chest. He didn't figure he needed any other kind of backup, but he kept quiet.

"You're pissed and not thinking it through, I can see it all over your face. You think I don't want payback. Jordan and I have worked together for ten years. She's a good friend and great cop. But if you go kill him, you spend the rest of your life in jail. You try to arrest him without lab reports and a statement from Jordan, his daddy will have him out and on an airplane to God knows where within the hour. Then we really *might* never see him again."

Ty walked over to the window and stared out. It was the very last thing he wanted to admit—but the Fed was right. Ty understood better that anyone what was at stake. "So you want me to do nothing?"

"That's exactly what I want you to do," Bahan answered. "Think about it. Why did Warren do this?"

Ty jammed his hands in his pockets and turned to Bahan. "I think he did it because I screwed up." He shrugged a shoulder. Guilt cut as sharply as a knife blade. "Either he figured out she was a cop, which I doubt. Or Warren beat the hell out of her because he saw me kiss her in the parking lot last night. My money's on the second reason."

"And now you're the only connection we have on the inside."

Ty let out a humorless laugh. "Some connection. You don't honestly think Buck will let me step foot in his place now, do you?"

"Well, let's think about this for a minute." Bahan paced the length of the tiny room. "Whether it was Arlo or Warren who dumped her, they took her over an hour away from town and left her in the middle of nowhere. See, they thought she was just a worthless cocktail waitress with no family, because that's how she played it. They never intended for anyone to find her. Hell, they probably figured it would be quite a while before anyone even bothered to report her missing. So we work with that. Get her to a safe house. For all intents and purposes, she's dead."

"But they know my connection with her. I'd lay money on it."

"Good," Bahan said. "Go back in there. Be distraught. Ask if anyone's seen her."

Ty tossed it around in his mind. "That might actually work." It wasn't a bad plan. In fact, he liked it better with every lap Bahan made across the room. "I could tell him we'd only been together a few times, but I thought we might have really had something. Cry on his shoulder a little, confess to him how worried I am because she hasn't returned my calls."

Bahan grinned. "I have a feeling Buck won't be at all angry about the fact you were with her. He'll be relieved. He may still hope no one finds her body, but if they do, he'll pray that it's your DNA, instead of Warren's, that's all over her. He'll think he's found a nail for your coffin and Warren's ticket to freedom. Oh, I think Big Daddy Buck is going to want to keep you—his son's get-out-of-jail-free card—very, very close."

Chapter Seventeen

Jordan suspected she was at Ty's boyhood home. Of course, she had no idea where that was. Nor did she care. An exorbitant amount of pain did that to a person, reduced curiosity to nil.

After four nights in the hospital, she'd been stable enough to leave. The following four days whirled by in a blur of exhaustion, discomfort, and Vicodin, all accompanied by Ty's placating answers when she did work up enough energy to ask a question.

But when she woke this morning, the fog had lifted. Likely because she refused the handful of pills Ty attempted to poke down her last night. Oh, yeah, her aches were starting to spike a little, but she was coherent for the first time in over a week. And the perpetual stomach grinding from all the medicine was easing. That alone was worth tolerating some discomfort.

A shower sounded like heaven. Had she dreamed of Ty

washing her off with a wet rag and feeding her milkshakes through a straw, or was the man really that much of a saint?

The clock read 8:58 a.m. Where was he?

She remembered periods of time when he'd been gone. An older woman had sat by her bedside. His mother? Grandmother? She couldn't remember. The days and nights and details ran together.

She gingerly scooted to the edge of the bed. There was pain and stiffness, but moving felt good. Today, Ty was *not* going to dodge her. Once and for all, she intended to get answers.

She walked out of the bedroom, stopping at the top of the stairs. Never before had one flight looked so daunting. But she took them slow and easy and made it to the first floor without incident.

"What are you doing down here?" Ty grabbed a rolling chair and scooted it under her legs when she staggered into the kitchen. "I think you're pale, but it's hard to tell for sure through the bruises." He pushed her to the table and shook his head.

The crooked tilt of his lips made her heart skip a beat.

"You know that scene in *Rocky*," he said, "where he was getting beat up, and his trainer had to cut his eyelids open so he could see?"

Not at all amused, she narrowed her one good eye at him. "I'm a disaster. I get it."

"Yo, Adrienne. You want I should make you some eggs and bacon," he said with a pathetic Rocky imitation.

"You're a real comedian." She continued to glare. "Don't give up your day job."

He pulled up a chair facing her. "You didn't take any

pain meds last night. How do you feel?"

"Better. Everything's better." She moved a hand to his cheek. "I don't know how to thank you for taking care of me."

"I've got a few ideas about that. See if you feel good enough to start with this." He kissed her, as light as a feather, then leaned his forehead against hers. Fatigue and worry weaved noticeably through his long sigh. "It's so good to have you back. You just don't know—"

"Shhh." She stroked his face and kissed him. "I do know. You've been through hell, too, and I'm sorry." She picked up his hand. "But I need you to talk to me. For real this time. No beating around the bush."

Her words were met with silence. He stood, walked to the stove, and cracked a couple of eggs. "What do you want to know?"

"Start with something easy. Who's the little gray-haired woman who's sometimes in the bedroom when I wake up?"

He glanced over his shoulder as he whipped the eggs.

"My nana."

Jordan couldn't help the bark of laughter that escaped. Couldn't help the ache that punched through her ribs, either.

Ty turned, fisted his hands on his hips. "What?"

"Big, bad, stud-muffin Tyler McGee has a nana." She laughed again, gentler this time.

"A nana who was a nurse for forty-one years, thank you very much." He turned back to the stove.

"Does she bake you cookies and pinch your cheeks?"

"No, smartass." He poured the eggs in the pan. "She makes rockin' pies and teaches ballroom dancing at the high school every Thursday night." He slipped back into his

Rocky imitation. "You got a problem with that?"

"Not at all," she said. "No problem at all." She watched him cook, noticing he looked pretty much at home in front of a frying pan. "I can see how much you love her. I'm grateful, and I'll want to thank her, but I don't want her coming here anymore. She'll be in danger. I don't want that kind of responsibility." She looked around the room. "Why are we here anyway? And where exactly *is* here?"

He scooped the eggs onto a plate and slid them in front of her. "This is my parents' house, a farm in Longdale. It's private—no close neighbors. Good security system I personally installed. Mom and Dad spend winters in Florida, and I keep things running around here. They won't mind."

"And it's close enough so you can still work at Buck's, right?" His quiet hesitation answered her question. Her heart hammered against already painful ribs. "How the hell can you still be working inside Buck's?"

He sat next to her. "I told Buck about us."

She dropped her fork and pushed the eggs away. Her throat squeezed so tight, she could barely speak. "You did what?"

"Told him I was worried and didn't know what happened. Didn't understand why you'd just take off." With two fingers, Ty tapped a thudding beat into the table. "It was Bahan's call, and he called it exactly right. Buck was downright warm. Offered me sympathies about irrational women and assured me you'd show up. Said you probably just took off with a friend for a week or so."

Jordan didn't look at him, didn't want to hear what he was saying.

"Buck wants me close so he can point the finger at me if

and when your body is found."

"Oh, God, they still think I'm dead?"

Ty nodded.

Of course they did. She had to admit, it was a good plan. Ty was still inside Buck's, still the best chance they had to nail Arlo and Warren, and the thought of him under the same roof as the Bucks made her absolutely sick to her stomach.

She picked up his hand, twined her fingers though his. "Look, I'm a cop, so I understand the job. I understand the risks. I'm not a neurotic, panicked female asking you to give up a career or anything." She looked him in the eye, hoping it was enough. "But please don't go back there. I really don't want you inside that nightclub, or anywhere inside Buck's organization."

His jaw clenched, and she recognized the stubborn set of his eyes.

"And *I* really need to finish this."

"Why?" she asked. "Revenge? You don't need to prove anything because of me."

"It's not because of you, Jordan."

That's a lie, she thought, cocking her head as she eyed him.

"Okay, it's not *only* because of you. All the things we talked about before, they still apply."

"I understand, I really do. How could I not? But for the first time in my life…" She looked away, deciding she really needed to shut up and get a handle on her emotions.

He touched her face, gently turned her head until she looked at him. "What? For the first time in your life, what?"

She waved him off, then stood to get away, but pain shot through her chest and froze her in place. She eased back into the chair, attempted to bend forward and bury her face in her hands. But the tenderness in her ribs wouldn't allow that, either.

"Damn it," she growled, leaning back and realizing she couldn't move fast enough to hide her emotions. She gave in and peeked at him. He was clearly fighting a smile.

"It's not funny," she said through the tears. "I hate being weak."

He scooted his chair closer and took her hands. "No, baby, I know. It's not funny. And it's damned hard to make a dramatic exit with so many boo-boos, isn't it?"

She socked him in the shoulder. "You're such a jerk sometimes." But he'd broken the tension. Which she supposed was his plan.

He leaned forward and kissed her lightly.

It felt like years had passed since they'd been together. She raised both hands to his face and parted his lips with a gentle lick. He fell deeply, quickly, into the kiss, and she sucked at his tongue, desperate to have some part of him, any part of him, inside her.

The lingering rough edges of pain began to smooth and numb. She gasped as his lips traveled across her cheek and down her neck. The way the real world and all of its darkness faded under his touch was nothing short of miraculous.

His hand smoothed around her ribs. At her slight wince, he jerked away, breathing heavily. "Baby, I'm sorry."

She smiled. "I'm not. If fact, I was just working out the logistics—"

"No." He scooted back but still held her hands. "You'd never survive that today." He smiled, but then his gray eyes narrowed in suspicion. "You were trying to distract me," he accused.

"You kissed me first."

"Quit avoiding my question. Spill it, detective. For the first time in your life, what?"

Pausing for a long moment, she finally said, "For the first time in my life, there is something besides the job." She looked into his eyes and swallowed hard. "I didn't think I'd ever find that. Being a cop has given me sanity in a lot of ways, ways I can't explain. But without you…" Damn it, she *had* become a neurotic, panicked female.

"Let me ask you something." He held her head in place so she had no choice but to look at him. Softly, he brushed her tears away with his thumbs. "And answer me honestly. If Warren had beaten me almost to death, and you had a chance to shut him and Buck down, would you walk away? Could you walk away?"

It was an unfair question, because they both knew the answer was no.

"Warren doesn't need to figure out you're still a cop to kill you. He hates you because of me. Any moment you let your guard down, he could hurt you."

"If we don't stop Warren and Arlo, they continue to hurt all of us. You, me, this town, the whole damn Midwest. Their drugs are going everywhere, Jordan." Obviously frustrated, he stood, pacing away and back again. "Bahan retrieved your phone and all the photos you snapped in Buck's office. There was a picture of Warren on a beach with a couple other guys. One of those guys was identified as Fredrick Lopez. Lopez is a suspected drug runner for Julio Delago. Solid proof of the connection between the Bucks and the Delago Cartel."

Jordan exhaled a shaky breath. She *knew* something

about that picture was off.

Ty tilted her head up. "You've spent your whole career fighting against this kind of thing." He leveled her with a pointed look. "And unlike someone else I know, I'm wearing a wire and carrying a gun. You know I'll be careful. I know you understand this."

What she understood was that he would continue with or without her blessing, and that guilt was a dangerous distraction he couldn't afford. She'd already put him through hell. So she nodded and choked back the horrible images of how the last two officers she'd worked with ended up after crossing the Delago Cartel.

Chapter Eighteen

Ty left early for Buck's, and Jordan missed him already. She'd promised to stay in bed and rest, but seriously, how much TV could one person possibly take? Plus his scent on the sheets was driving her crazy. His pillow was a poor substitute for that warm groove on his shoulder where her head fit like a key in a keyhole.

Yeah, it was corny, but he'd reduced her to that. Would she ever have the strength to tell him that his touch, his arms wrapped around her, had been the only place she'd ever felt at peace? Probably not. Putting such sappy feeling into words would make her feel like an idiot, so she'd keep it her little secret, just like the visions.

But really, *secret* was too strong of a word. She'd told Ty that she dreamed, and many of her dreams were about the night her family died. So technically, there was no lie to feel guilty about.

Now that she'd locked her conscience in a box and wrapped

it up neatly, she was going to scavenge through the kitchen for some ice cream. Ice cream could smooth the jagged edges off any guilt. And there would be no calories in the ice cream, because she wouldn't read the label. If she didn't know about the calories, they wouldn't exist any more than the visions did.

Okay, that theory was a work in progress, but she thought she could make it fly.

It was only the second time she would venture down the stairs, the first without Ty in the house, but she felt pretty steady on her feet.

Taking a good look around Ty's boyhood home could be entertaining. Didn't parents always have a few embarrassing pictures hanging around, the kind that highlighted those awkward teenage years of bad hair and ugly braces? Although, if she had to lay money on it, she'd wager that Tyler McGee never had an awkward day in his life. Nature had dealt him a royal flush in the looks department.

It was aggravating how one measly flight of stairs had her panting by the time she walked into the kitchen. She leaned against the countertop to catch her breath and studied the room. The walls were a bright and cheery yellow. White antiqued cabinets filled the space. Photos and magnets hung on the fridge, and plants lined the windowsill. The small touches of a home were everywhere.

A giant oak table sat as the centerpiece, and she wondered how many meals Ty and his family had shared there. Then she wondered if she would have had a home like this and a large table full of memories if her family had survived. She ran a now-shaking hand across the counter, absentmindedly opening a drawer and then closing it. Ice cream suddenly lost its appeal.

She strolled into the family room. It was furnished with overstuffed furniture, a large-screen TV, a fireplace. Homey, cozy, safe—everything her life hadn't been. That was how he'd grown up, she thought, and that was what he brought to her.

Love.

Her heart burst into a thousand terrifying pieces at the notion of being in love. She stumbled around the couch and sat. Broken ribs were nothing compared to the ache of realizing, beyond any doubt, that she was in love with Ty.

Oh, God, she loved him. Deeply. Irrationally. Stupidly.

Why was the thought so terrifying?

Because the last time you had people in your life to love, you let them all die.

The reality was a painful one. It wasn't being in love with Ty that was hard. It was the possibility of seeing him hurt or killed in a vision and being as powerless to stop it as she had been with her own family. She'd never survive that kind of pain again, wasn't entirely sure how she had survived it once.

She'd been running from any real connections since she'd been ten.

Falling in love was never supposed to happen, not to her, but now that it had, the thought of life without him was unbearable. If she could keep the past where it belonged and the visions under control, maybe she could have a real future with Ty. The kind of life that normal people had.

She took a steadying breath and stood. Enough adventure and soul-searching for one day. Her restless energy was draining quickly, and if she moved fast enough, she might just make it back to bed.

Heading toward the stairs, she passed a small space off

the family room that looked like a home office. It held a large desk, computer, and hundreds of pictures on bookshelves and the walls. This is where she would find it, the one embarrassing picture of Ty, if such a thing existed.

Surely there was one goofy shot in the bunch. She'd just have to put her detective skills to work. Then she'd prop it up on his pillow so that when he came home, she could thoroughly tease him.

Geesh, she was bored.

The pictures—a whole lot of pictures—were aligned along the bookshelves in an almost perfect timeline progression. Even if her mother had lived, Jordan doubted that they'd have had this many photos.

Ty as a little baby. Ty as a toddler.

She was right. He'd had the face of an angel from the day he was born. There he was scampering around in a diaper and adult slippers, then naked in the bathtub. At seven or eight, a mischievous silver-eyed cutie posing with a tinier version of himself. Must be his baby brother. They looked identical. Too cute.

And there they both were with a baby girl sitting between them.

Ty had talked about his brother, Trevor, but she couldn't recall him mentioning a sister. Surely he must have, 'cause there she was. Same hair, same eyes on all three of them. Each one as picture-perfect and adorable as the next.

Tyler McGee was not only handsome in the flesh, he was downright photogenic. He looked better in the pictures than he did in real life, and that she wouldn't have believed possible.

Trailing along the bookshelves, Jordan enjoyed the age

progression of Ty and his siblings over the years. Good-looking kids. Good-looking parents. The all-American dream. It was nice to know someone had lived it.

The last bookshelf held professional, posed, eight by ten portraits. As Jordan took in just how attractive all three kids were, a cold, clammy dew broke out on her skin.

Oh, my God.

Her eyes shifted back and forth as she tried to make sense of what she saw. No, no, no! There was some horrible, cruel mistake.

"Tara."

She managed to whisper the name through the choking ache that had seeped from one injured lung into her whole chest. The cute little girl with no front teeth and pigtails had turned into Tara, the dark-haired, beautiful teen who haunted Jordan's dreams.

She took a deliberate step back and forced herself to focus, gasping in enough air to keep herself upright.

Tara. Beautiful Tara. Tara who had been raped and murdered over and over in Jordan's dreams.

It wasn't true. It couldn't be true. She could be crazy, and *that* she could live with. She could be unconscious and all of this one big, fat, ugly hallucination—like the one she'd had of her father. *Let it be anything, anything other than what it looked like. Please don't let the dark-haired beauty be Tyler's sister.*

One after another, questions whirled through her mind. Why would Ty hide this from her? He knew about her family. How could he think she wouldn't have understood? Did he know what had happened to his sister? Had they found the guy that had done it?

A devastated certainty claimed the last bit of hope: Tara wouldn't have come to her in a dream if Ty didn't still need answers.

She gazed toward the back of the house. Sickness and dread tore through her, but she needed to know, had to see for herself. Stumbling down the hall, she reached the back of the house, turned the lock, and swung the door open.

There it was, perfectly centered in the yard like an evil picture—Tara's swing and the giant old oak tree. The thick, fringed rope and the worn, wooden seat swayed helplessly in the wind, waiting for the girl who'd once perched there like an angel.

Jordan stumbled barefoot and in shorts across the cold, dead grass. She couldn't have said what made her do it, but she picked up the wooden plank swing and turned it over to look at the bottom.

Happy seventh birthday, Angel—Love Daddy.

Jordan looked up at the house. Tara's bedroom window loomed back down at her. Her heart beat with a sick, sick ache. She blinked through the tears, attempting to clear the images from her eyes, the implications in her mind, and the injury to her heart.

Still, her gaze kept returning to a barren garden filled with small stones. She walked closer, dragged her toe through the pebbles. These were the rocks the boy had thrown at Tara's window. Bile lurched into her throat. Clamping a hand over her mouth, she dashed into the house and up the stairs.

Cold and trembling, she paused at the threshold of Tara's door. Breathing roughly, she pressed one hand to her chest, but forced the other to turn the knob. She stepped into the room and walked straight into her dream. Baby blue walls closed in around her. Nothing had been touched since the night of Tara's murder.

The walls were just as she'd seen them, lined with trophies and medals for running track. Pennants. Cheerleading pictures. Tara's world shifted and came to life. More vivid now, with more detail, but the dream had been eerily on target.

Tara's presence invaded the room. Jordan trembled, sensed Tara's spirit spurring her on, pushing her to think.

"I've tried," Jordan cried out. "I really have." She *had* been thinking, really *had* tried to see his face…but…maybe she…

"Oh, hell." Jordan stopped, thought for a second. Then stepped toward Tara's pennant, the blue and white pennant. "It's the colors," she whispered running her fingers over the soft triangle of cloth. She glanced at the cheerleading picture. Tara's uniform was blue and white. The pompoms on the floor next to the dresser, blue and white.

Jordan closed her eyes, trying to recall the details of her dreams. She still couldn't see the boy, nothing about his face, but she could see his football gear. And his jacket. The answers had been in the jacket the whole time. She hadn't see any colors or numbers before, but now, in Tara's room, she saw them all.

The boy's jacket, maroon and gold.

His graduation year, sewn on the sleeve.

Even his car, white.

Tara's presence in the room was still bold and certain, as if the girl stood before her in flesh and bone. But nothing about her was threatening. Tara was filled only with sweet innocence and a desire for Ty to know it all. So Jordan would tell him. And when he deemed her to be the freak that she was, she would lose him.

Stumbling to the bed, she picked up a doll. Tara's favorite. How did she know? Who the hell cared how she knew any of the crap that raced around in her head?

Too much. Too much. Too much.

She collapsed against a wall and slid to the floor, clutching Tara's doll.

...

Ty barreled down the long, gravel driveway leading to his parents' house. The alarm company had notified him there was a breach of security, and Warren had been oddly absent from the club tonight. They'd been so careful, but the fear of Warren figuring out Jordan was alive never strayed far from Ty's mind. His tires ground to a stop as he hit the brakes, threw his truck in park, and plowed through the front door.

"Jordan?" he yelled. "Damn it, Jordan, where are you?"

She didn't answer. Adrenaline flooding his body, he flew up the steps. Why the hell had he left her by herself?

The door to Tara's bedroom was open. Why would that door be open? Terrifying thoughts pushed him through the threshold of his baby sister's room.

Jordan was on the floor, pale and shaking.

His heart raced as he knelt in front of her. "Christ, what happened?"

Her eyes were glazed. No awareness that he'd entered the room passed across her face. He looked for signs of a struggle, but the room looked exactly as it always did. Except that Tara's doll was not on the bed, but in Jordan's hands.

He lightly stroked her cheek. He'd seen her stunned before, confused and terrified after a nightmare. Her face had the same look now, her body the same rigid tremble.

"Did you have a dream, baby?"

"You didn't tell me you had a sister, did you?" she asked.

He slid a hand around her arm. *Fuck*. His mother had kept every newspaper article that had been printed about Tara's murder. Apparently, Jordan had found them. "I...I don't. She died. Come on, let's get you up."

"Don't touch me." She jerked out of his grip. Her gaze, lined with betrayal and hurt, finally met his. "You should have *told* me she'd been murdered."

He broke out in a cold sweat as fear flooded his body. She was right; she'd deserved the truth a long time ago. Now he had to make her understand. "I'm sorry. I wanted to tell you a million different times in a million different ways."

"Did you find her body? Do you know who did it?"

Without answering, he pulled her to her feet, lifted the doll out of her hands, and scooted her out of Tara's bedroom. He guided her across the hall to the room he'd grown up in and sat her down onto the bed.

"Did you catch her killer?" She demanded again.

He shook his head, searching for the best way to begin. "A buddy of mine called me the morning her body was found." A painful lump swelled in his throat. "But, no, there hasn't been an arrest yet. I was going to tell you. About everything. I swear I was, but..."

She nailed him with an icy glare. "But having sex with me was a much easier way to get what you wanted?"

It took a second for him to get it, to really grasp what she was saying. He understood her anger about the deception, but it never occurred to him that she'd think their whole relationship had been a lie.

"Nice work, McGee." She was trying to remain distant and unemotional, but he saw tears begin to swim in her eyes. "Much easier to get what you want, to talk me into letting you in on the investigation, when you leave out the most important details and twist me up with sex. Well played."

"Are you fucking kidding me?" Fury shot up his spine with enough intensity that he thought his head might explode. He grabbed her arms and hauled her close. "After everything, after every goddamned thing we've been through, how could you think I'm sleeping with you to use you? Tell me that's not what you really believe."

She pushed at his chest, shrugging out of his grip. "Then tell me the real reason you're so hell-bent on staying inside Buck's. It's not because of me. It's not to shut down a drug ring. It's because of Tara. You think Buck is responsible for her death, and you want revenge."

"Of course I want revenge. For my sister, for every kid around here who's died because of the drugs he's selling. You're damn straight I want revenge. Every night, I pray to God that Arlo and Warren die slow, painful deaths. *After* suffering long, torturous, jail sentences.

"I always believed the best way to get that revenge was by destroying them slowly, beating them at their own game, working inside the law." He glared at her. "Until Warren hurt you. Now all I think about is walking into that dirty, damned bar and killing both of them with my bare hands." He moved to her and held her face so that she had no choice but to listen. "Don't you dare stand there and say my feelings for you have been a lie, because you damn well know better. I may be guilty of hiding the truth about Tara, but I've never lied about loving you."

Some of the rigid anger rushed from her body on a shuddering exhale. Tears spilled over and down her cheeks. He'd never been so grateful for tears. Tears he could work with. The frigid indifference scared the hell out of him.

"Then why?" she cried. "I told you about my family, about Katy. Trusted you with memories, pain, and secrets I've never told anyone. Did you really think I wouldn't understand? Didn't you trust me enough to tell me about Tara?"

"It had nothing to do with trust, Jordan. I just couldn't." He knew how badly he'd screwed up, but it hurt like hell to even mention Tara. He simply didn't have the words. Not then. Not now. "Look, it was wrong not to tell you, but you kept saying the investigation was too personal for me. I was afraid you'd push me out of it. Would you have ever let me work this case knowing about Tara?"

"No," she shot back. "Because you *shouldn't* be working this case. Are you even trying to bust Arlo and Warren for drugs, or are you looking for your sister's killer? Because I can tell you, he's not connected to the Bucks."

"She was drugged. Had been at a party with drugs, maybe killed by some high dumbass. You know Arlo Buck is making drugs available to every kid in town. I'd say that's pretty fucking connected."

The bedroom got quiet, quiet enough for him to hear what she'd said just a moment earlier. Her words, sharp and clear, penetrated the thick fog of guilt.

Confused, he stepped away from her. "How do you know the killer isn't connected to the Bucks? Do you know who killed my sister?"

...

Jordan shook her head. She could feel Ty's confusion radiate through the confines of the small bedroom. "I don't have a name, but I can help you find him."

"What could you possibly know about Tara's murder?"

His pained expression pierced her heart like a rusty knife. She knew it all—knew everything about Tara's murder, more information than she'd ever burden him with. But now there was no choice. If she didn't tell him enough to bring Tara's killer to justice, she'd never be able to live with herself. And she suspected Tara would never let her have another peaceful moment, either.

"My dreams..." She tried to push the words out, but they wouldn't come. Swallowing, she choked back the shards of fear and began again.

"The dreams didn't start after my family was murdered; they started before. I dreamed about a gunman coming into my house and killing my family. The next night, it happened just the way I dreamed it."

Twenty years later, she still hadn't worked out what spirit had been responsible for that god-awful dream, but the direction of her life had done a sharp one-eighty that night. Nothing had been the same since. "It was the first vision I remember playing out in such vivid detail. I've had a lot of visions since then."

Breathing deeper and faster, Ty blinked, but he didn't move, didn't say anything. He was trying to make sense of her words, she could tell. From the look on his face, he wasn't even close to understanding.

She took a deep breath. "I dream, Ty. I dream or have visions or whatever you want to call it. And I saw Tara." Her voice cracked. "I saw what happened to her."

Stumbling back, he crashed into the chair behind him. His chest began to heave as if the air had thinned, and he struggled for oxygen. "You were there? You saw Tara get murdered?"

The simple answer was yes, but even to *her* ears that sounded insane. How could she expect him to understand? And yet, she knew he needed this closure.

"What the hell are you saying, Jordan?" Anger began to mix with his confusion.

A thick, greasy fear tumbled in her stomach as she stepped in front of him and sank to her knees. She took his hands. "Tara came to me. In a dream. In several dreams. I think she wants you to know what happened."

He frowned, his jaw flexing. "And you're going to tell me? Because you had a dream about her murder?"

She nodded, feeling sick and foolish, but stopping now clearly wasn't an option. "Tara came home after a graduation party. This boy—man, whatever you choose to call him—he threw rocks at her window, motioned for her to come outside."

Jordan closed her eyes, took in as much air as her lungs would allow, and let the vision take over. "She went outside to her swing. To talk to him. He gave her a beer laced with something. He didn't intend to kill her, but I don't think he gave her enough of the drug, because she came around and fought him. It got out of hand, and he got scared, strangled her." Jordan opened her eyes. "I'm so sorry, Ty."

Ty jerked his hands from hers. Rising slowly, he moved away from her. "This is crazy. *You're crazy*." He turned on her. "What the hell would make you think it's okay to make up something about my sister's murder?"

"I would never, *never* lie about Tara. I know it's a lot to take in, but I saw what happened to her." Desperate and wanting so badly for him to understand, she stood and went to him again, curling her fingers in his shirt. "You have to believe me."

"The hell I do."

He grabbed her wrists and pushed her hands away. "Enough. Just stop. Cut the crap, Jordan. *Fuck*." He stepped back, rubbing his temples. "Is it the medicine? The head injury? Help me out here. Give me some reason for this to make sense. I want just a tiny bit of hope that the woman I love is not completely insane."

And there it was.

His words arrowed through her. If possible, she'd underestimated the pain that ricocheted through her body.

He turned his back, propped his arms against the dresser.

Maybe he was processing, trying to understand. Maybe...

With a violent slash of his hand, he cleared the dresser of everything on it. Even the small flat-screen TV dropped to the floor with a crash.

Jordan jumped, realizing he wasn't processing or understanding at all. Sensing his fury and his need for space, she eased back. But he swung around and came at her. "Don't screw with me, Jordan. This is a deal-breaker. You need to start again, with the truth this time."

"I'm telling you the truth."

"You've gotten a hold of her files," he accused. "You and

your FBI pal read the police reports."

"What?" She shook her head. "No, I'm trying to help you."

"Help me? By telling me you're what, a psychic or something? By making up crazy details about something as painful as my sister's murder? That's supposed to help me? Because I think a real psychic would have told me all this before my sister was killed, been able to prevent it. Now *that* would have helped me."

"Really?" She fired back. Twenty years of living with that precise guilt shredded her composure. "Because it didn't help Katy. It didn't help my mom or dad. I *did* see what happened to them. I *tried* to tell my mom. She thought I was as crazy as you do."

Fury, brilliant and blinding, flashed through her. "You want the truth? I have visions. I dream. All the time. All the fucking time. But especially when I'm undercover. I don't know why, and I hate it. The dreams aren't just about my family; they're about the cases I work, too.

"I wake up sick and screaming. If there was *anything* I could do to stop it, stop them, I would. I've tried drugs, doctors, alcohol, you name it, and still they're here," she said, jabbing a finger against her head. "So, yes, if that makes me insane, I am. But I can't change it."

The throbbing in her chest suddenly roared back, and she had to fight for even the shallowest breath. Everything hurt, and she couldn't tell if the pain was from the broken ribs or just from being broken.

Ty stood silent for several long moments, then shook his head but wouldn't quite meet her eyes. "When I left Buck's tonight, I told Big Tom to take over for a while, that I was taking a break to grab a bite and run an errand. But we're so close to breaking this case open, I need to go back and finish the night."

In his voice, she heard the mixed tones of anger and suspicion. His beautiful eyes, eyes that had never held anything but warmth and seduction toward her, were now filled with resentment and contempt.

She nodded. "Yeah, you should."

He stepped toward her, started to touch her cheek as he so often did, but then he dropped his hand to his side. The rejection in that one simple movement spoke volumes. The man who couldn't keep his hands off of her just a few hours before now couldn't stand to touch her.

"Maybe this is more than I can deal with right now; just give me some time. I need to get back to Buck's. We'll talk later tonight when I get home."

No, we won't. Because she knew she wouldn't be there, but she nodded anyway.

He went out the door and stepped down the porch stairs.

She followed him out into the cold night air, needing to be absolutely sure where she stood. "You don't believe me." It was more statement that question, so that's how she phrased it.

He turned toward her, but still didn't look her in the eye. "I'm not sure why you told me all this." He shrugged. "I already knew she was drugged. I knew she was strangled." This time he did look at her. "Anyone who poked into her files would know that, too."

"So that's it? You think I abused my FBI connections to get information about Tara's murder and then made up a fake dream? Why would I do that?"

"That's what I'm trying to figure out," he muttered. "If you're so damn psychic, how about a name or description?"

"I don't know his name." She went down the stairs, too, and stood on the last step so they were eye to eye. "But you're looking for a young man who played football in high school and had a jacket, like a letterman jacket with the year sewn on the sleeve. I think he graduated last year and that his school colors were maroon and gold. I'm also thinking he drove a white car."

Determined to end this with some dignity intact and the last word, she blinked away her tears and watched a stunned Tyler McGee try to assimilate the facts she'd just thrown at him.

"You should have his DNA from her body. You'll be able to narrow it down and connect the boy with the evidence based on what I've just told you."

She turned and headed back inside while her chest heaved and struggled against injury and shock and the sick, sick feeling of knowing that she'd seen Ty for the last time.

Chapter Nineteen

Jordan had no intention of discussing why she was leaving, but wanted to be long gone by the time Ty made it home from Buck's. She needed a ride. Bahan was still in charge, and after the angry dressing down she'd gotten from him while still in the hospital, she didn't dare make another move without informing him.

When Bahan made it to McGee's house, she had a few personal things in a grocery bag and was sitting on the front step.

"Jordan, it's freezing out here. Why didn't you wait inside? I would have been here sooner but…"

He stopped talking when she refused to meet his eyes.

"Jordan?" he said again.

If she looked at him or spoke, she was afraid of what might happen. Bahan was plenty smart enough to put two and two together just by looking at her.

"Well, shit." He sat next to her, put an arm around her

shoulder. "What happened?"

She broke, fucking cried in front of another cop. Now she wanted to shoot herself for that fact alone. But Bahan wouldn't push. He'd be as happy to pretend it wasn't happening as she was. That's why they got along so well, both of them too dysfunctional to admit to any real emotion.

Finally he said one simple word. "McGee?"

She nodded.

"Is it over?"

She nodded again.

"You want to talk about it?" he asked.

The fact that he was kind enough to offer when she was certain he'd prefer for the earth to open up and swallow him whole almost made her grin. "What do you think?" she finally muttered.

"All right. Then let's get out of here."

They were almost back to St. Louis before she dared to speak. "He's going to keep going inside Buck's. He'll need you and the team. You guys can finish this off together. He'll outsmart Buck. Promise me you'll be there when he does."

"Or I could just let one of the Bucks put a bullet in him for hurting you," he said.

Jordan knew it was a joke, but her chin quivered. Warren Buck was a drunk and a hothead. The very real possibility that he just might put a bullet hole in Ty before this was over made tears streak down her face again.

"Come on, Jordan, I'm just kidding. He's the only one we have on the inside now. I've been working with him. I'll keep helping the bastard. I'll even keep you in the loop if you want."

"No, I'm done. Way done with this case." She swiped her

hands across her cheeks. "Can you take me to storage to get my car?"

Bahan glanced at her, hesitated a moment before he spoke. "You're not going to like this, but…You can't go home, use your bank accounts, or drive your car until we break this case open. We're gambling on the fact the Bucks had no idea you were a cop. But we've learned the hard way to never underestimate these drug assholes. People think you're dead, so you're going to stay dead."

"I wasn't planning to go home anyway." She didn't think Ty would come after her given the way they'd left things, but there was no sense in taking a chance. She'd never survive coming face-to-face with him. Seeing the angry disappointment in his eyes once had been quite enough. "I'm going to need some money and a vehicle then. You have my word I'll lay low."

"You'll stay with me. Stop." He cut her off when she started to object. "I'm barely there anyway. I'm lucky if I get to come home long enough to shower and grab a few hours' sleep. You'll have the run of the place. I don't have a TV in the guest bedroom, but you can share mine." He winked.

She managed a faint smile. "Your TV or your room?"

"Either. Both."

She rolled her eyes at him without crying, and that, she supposed, was progress.

...

Ty returned to Buck's and finished out the night. Barely. Physically, he'd been there. Mentally, he'd checked out the moment Jordan had told him about her dreams. Being forced to return to the nightclub for a few hours had given him time to think. But now he needed answers. He needed to understand exactly what Jordan meant when she said she had visions. And why she'd been having them about Tara.

It was almost two a.m. when he pulled in front of his parent's house again. All the lights were out, but he doubted Jordan was asleep. She seemed to sleep less than any human he'd ever known, now he was starting to have an inkling why.

As soon as he unlocked the door, he noticed she hadn't reset the alarm. They'd talked about this, about how important it was. Usually, she left a lamp on for him. Tonight, the place was black. The farther he walked, the more real the dread became. "Tell me you wouldn't do this, baby. Tell me you didn't leave."

He hit the stairs two at a time, searched every room, and looked for a note. He checked his texts, then his voicemail. But he already knew, probably should have known the moment he'd walked away from her.

Jordan was gone.

If you didn't count the boulder sitting on his chest, she'd left no sign that she'd been anywhere inside the house. The couple items she'd worn, her handbag, the few toiletries he'd bought for her—all of it—gone. He dialed her and got her voicemail, probably her way of saying that she wasn't speaking to him.

So he texted her:

I'm sorry. Let me know you're safe. Call me.

What the fuck was he supposed to do now? *Damn it.* How could she just leave? He stood paralyzed in his old bedroom at his parents' house. His mother seriously needed to learn to move forward. Trophies and sports equipment still lined the walls as if he'd been away at camp instead of on his own for nearly a decade. His high school and college diplomas that she kept in frames on his dresser were now in a heap next to the broken TV on the floor.

He picked them up, and his chest tightened another notch as his thoughts turned to Tara. His little sister would never reach such basic milestones. She'd been robbed of growing up. Not by an accident. Not by an illness. But if Jordan was correct, by a selfish, little bastard who hadn't even gotten his hand slapped for killing her. His family's lives had been turned to shit. But the guy who killed Tara might very well be partying or pledging a fraternity at college right now.

The urge to hurt someone—anyone—broke loose inside him. He slung the high school diploma against the wall first, then winged the college one quickly in its wake.

How many hours had he spent trying to get answers, or at least some closure? He was no closer now than he had been six months ago, but the one person who'd stepped up with possible information, he'd pushed away.

He stomped down the stairs and grabbed a legal pad out of his parents den, purposely avoiding the sight of all the family pictures. No wonder his mom and dad spent the winter in Florida. Everything in the house was a reminder of Tara. It was a damn miracle his parents were still sane.

He moved to the kitchen, tossed the note pad on the table, and grabbed a pen. What he was about to do made no sense. But he sat, closed his eyes, and concentrated on Jordan's exact words.

A kid that played football, he scribbled. *Maroon and*

gold colors.

Maroon and gold were North Cooper colors. The football connection made sense. North Cooper always had a good football team. They'd won the playoffs more often than not.

Could Jordan have really seen that information somehow? Even if she was right, they'd have a hard time arresting someone based on a dream. Still, it was a lead he didn't have before.

All of Tara's friends were interviewed about her murder, and they all claimed she'd left the party alone. It made sense—Tara wasn't the kind of girl to leave with a guy she didn't know. The other theory was that she had returned home but made plans to sneak out and meet up with a guy. A guy she hadn't mentioned, even to her closest girlfriends. Ty had never bought it.

If Tara didn't leave the party with someone, and she hadn't made a middle of the night date…

Jordan's story makes more sense than any other theory ever has.

If there had been a guy at the party, and he'd followed Tara home and then threw rocks at her window. Yeah, he could see her going outside to talk to him.

He rubbed the wetness away from his eyes. God, he was tired. And not the kind of tired that could be solved with a good night's sleep. Part of him wanted to drop his head on the table and cry like a baby. Another part wanted to load every gun in his arsenal and blast anyone stupid enough to cross him.

He looked down at the note pad, picked up the pen, and wrote: *Senior. White car.*

Had he missed anything Jordan had mentioned? He looked at the list again.

A kid that played football
Maroon and gold colors. North Cooper
Senior
White car
No fucking way.

After all the walls he'd banged his head against for six months, there was no way it could be this easy. Only a handful of guys would fit that exact criteria. Guilt settled in nicely with all his other whirling emotions. It was going to be Jordan's information that finally pointed him toward a finish line he'd never been able to find on his own.

He picked up his phone, debated, and set it down again. Should he call his buddy from the Cooper Police Department? Ty had known Officer Benjamin Blake since he'd been labeled Benji B. back in kindergarten. Blake was the investigating officer of Tara's case. He'd been thorough, tolerant, and compassionate to Ty and his family. And probably because they'd grown up together, Blake had shared a lot more information than he'd been obligated to, but how willing he'd be to hand over an actual list of names, Ty wasn't sure.

He picked up the phone to dial Blake, but desperation had him texting Jordan again:

Are you okay? Please call me!

Christ, he wished she were here, wished to God he could hear her voice, talk to her, and ask her questions. "Stubborn-ass woman," he muttered, dialing her number for what felt like the hundredth time.

"This is Jordan. Leave a message at the tone, and I'll call you."

"I doubt it," he muttered to himself. He'd screwed up in a big way, which sucked, because the only thing he did know with absolute clarity was that he wanted Jordan back. With dreams. Without dreams. Right now, he didn't care. Even if she claimed to be the black witch of death, he was pretty certain he'd take his chances.

His Longdale cop shop was less than ten minutes from where he sat. Thirty minutes inside and a few key strokes later, he'd have the names of all the senior boys at North Cooper who had a white vehicle registered to their families. The temptation to head there was powerful, but Buck had eyes everywhere, maybe even inside Ty's own precinct.

Blake was still the safest way to get the information he needed. He grabbed the pad of paper, his phone, and his coat. He was heading to St. Louis to find Jordan, but on the way, he was going to bargain with his buddy Blake.

Chapter Twenty

Ty was trying—Really. Fucking. Hard.—to sound patient and coherent. But it was after six a.m. and he'd spent three hours driving to Jordan's condo in St. Louis and back. He'd yet to make contact with her. He figured if anyone knew where she'd gone, it would be Bahan. When he called, Bahan confirmed that Jordan was safe but refused to tell him where to find her.

If he could have reached through the phone and strangled Bahan with the man's own dick, he would have.

The sun was coming up, and he was almost back in Titus, but his patience had bottomed out about five miles back. Blake promised to call back with the information Ty had asked for, but now he was playing twenty questions before handing it over.

"I have the list of names, but I'm not giving it to you until you tell me why I'm giving it to you," Blake said.

"Look," Ty said. "I received a tip. It's probably nothing.

I'm just dotting i's and crossing t's. Do you want to go down a million dead ends? Or can you trust that since I was a cop, too, I might have enough sense to weed through the bullshit?"

"You don't get to decide what's bullshit. This isn't your investigation, Ty."

"Of course not. You never fail to remind me of that. But it was my sister." Ty stopped and took a breath before everything else he'd been holding back came raging through his voice. "I'm sorry, Blake. You've done everything I've asked you to. If you give me the list of names, you have my word I'll come to your office and tell you everything I know."

Blake laughed. "My face may be ugly, but it ain't stupid, McGee. I think we'll do it my way. You come to my office. Tell me what you know. Then we'll talk about this list of names I'm holding."

Ty sighed and dug deep for his most sincere-sounding voice. "You know as well as I do, that I could have called in a favor with one of my Longdale buddies. Just because I'm not a cop anymore doesn't mean I don't have friends. Why call you if I'm trying to hide something? I'm just trying to figure out if this is even a lead worth looking into. You've known me since kindergarten, Blake. Trust me."

Two hours later, Ty had already crossed off two of the four names Blake had given him. *Trust me.* Famous last words. Blake was going to kick his ass, but with every minute that ticked by, he was closer to getting the asshole who'd killed Tara. Call it instinct, but he could feel it. Jordan's dream had whittled his suspect list down to four kids.

The first suspect had been on a graduation trip in Florida with six other kids during the time of Tara's murder. That's what he had learned from the kid's mom.

The second guy had joined the military. He'd left for basic training three days before Tara's death. Of all the alibis in the world, basic training was a pretty solid one.

If Jordan's information proved correct, two suspects were left. Only one had a white car. The other a white pickup.

Not that he had a clue how a dream worked, but he was going with his gut. His gut told him that Jordan had some sort of gift that scared the shit out of him. On top of it, she was a cop with a trained eye. She'd likely gut him if he doubted her ability to tell the difference between a car and a pickup. He hadn't eliminated the kid with a pickup, but it's not where his instincts had taken him next.

He pulled down a grassy lane, stopped in front of a tall, skinny two-story that nearly had its first level swallowed by the bushes and overgrowth. Ty walked to the door, raised his hand to knock, then dropped it back to his side. His entire being felt crushed under the weight of something he couldn't see, couldn't touch, and had no fucking clue how to fight against. But he needed to get his shit together, because he really believed he was closer now than he'd ever been to getting justice for Tara.

He combed his fingers back through his hair, taking a minute to organize his exhausted mind. Flipping open the borrowed yearbook, he looked down at the kid who smiled just like every other high school senior on the page. Arron Thomas.

But if the information Jordan gave him was correct, this kid was likely Tara's murderer.

He looked at the flaking paint on the house, briefly wondering what kind of life Arron Thomas had lived. Then wondered if Arron would live to see another day if he happened to be unfortunate enough to open the door.

Ty raised his hand again, but before he could knock, the door swung open.

"Yeah?" An older, stocky man looked up. "Can I help you?"

"Tyler McGee, sir. I'm from the Longdale PD. I need to speak with Arron Thomas."

The older guy sighed. "What now?" he asked, waving Ty in.

He stepped inside and looked around. Place seemed nice enough. But what was a house that raised a murderer supposed to look like?

"Linda, come here, honey," the older guy said.

Ty turned when a woman walked in from another room. Her lips drew together, her face rigid.

"This is an officer from Longdale. He's looking for Arron."

By the look on her face, chances were good Arron had been in trouble before. Ty extended his hand. "Hi, ma'am. Are you Arron's mom?"

"Yes. And this is his grandpa. What's happened?" she asked. "Is he okay?"

"Oh, I'm sure he's fine. Nothing's happened. I didn't mean to alarm you. I'm following up on an old case from months ago. There was a graduation party, some property damage, the owners are angry. That sort of thing. We're talking to some kids that were at the party, double checking that nobody saw anything." Ty put on his most charming grin. "Is Arron home? May I speak with him?"

She paled and stood silent for a long moment before

she answered. "Arron doesn't live here anymore. He's got his own place."

"Oh, okay." Ty glanced at Arron's grandpa then back at his mom. "This is the address his vehicle is registered to. Is he away at school?"

The woman sighed and shook her head. "He should be, but no, he's not in college. Apparently, flipping burgers at The Burger Shack offered a better future than a football scholarship to Lincoln U."

The real answer was always in the tone, the eyes, the body language—disappointment was written all over Arron's mom. Ty decided he wasn't the only one looking for answers.

"One minute he was dreaming of playing in the NFL, the next…" she shrugged, never taking her eyes off of Ty. "After graduation, it was like someone flipped a switch in him. I tried to get answers, but he got angry and moved out." Her eyes flooded with emotion. "This isn't about property damage, is it? What really happened at that party?"

Ty swallowed, drew in a steadying breath. "I honestly don't know. But if you tell me where he is, you have my word I'll find out."

...

As soon as the waitress pointed to the back corner booth of The Burger Shack, a dirty-haired kid smoking a cigarette looked up. The kid's eyes did a double take. He dropped the cigarette and straightened in the booth. The air thinned and became much too toxic to breathe. A laser of awareness fused one deadly gaze to the other.

Officer Blake was on the way. Ty had held true to his word and called him. An arrest would never stick in court if made by the victim's brother. But as he looked at the punk who'd killed Tara, he wondered if an arrest was enough.

He'd promised his family justice. After what Tara had been through, handcuffs and bail felt damn short of justice.

Ty rooted himself to the spot, terrified one step forward would snap his control. Envisioning killing another human just for the sake of needing to see them die wasn't something a cop should do. Clinging to that thin, little thread of reason, he pushed the image of Tara's body out of his mind and told himself he needed to—no, *had to*—wait for Blake.

But the kid had the actual balls to spring from the booth, jackrabbit over the counter, and fly through the back door of the diner.

"You little fuck," Ty yelled, trailing closely behind. He could have pulled his gun, could have issued a formal warning to freeze and drop as any cop would have. But in that moment, he knew he hadn't come to the diner as a cop. He'd come as a brother. One that needed to sense some sort of remorse from a guy who'd raped and killed his sister.

The kid flew down the alleyway behind The Burger Shack. For a football player, he wasn't nearly fast enough. Ty was gaining with lightning speed and actually eased off some because if he caught the kid…*fuck*… If he caught the kid, things were going to get very ugly for both of them.

The little shit rounded a corner at a cross street. And like a mouse who'd dead-ended in maze, he stopped and turned frantically when a tall fence blocked his path. His eyes met Ty's again. His breath was wild and heaving. There may have been sweat, but Ty decided most of the wetness running down the kid's face was tears.

Without much enthusiasm this time, the kid attempted to lunge and run again.

Ty grabbed him, took him down, and pinned the bastard's head against the pavement. He flipped the kid over, straddled his body, and slid his fingers around the kid's neck.

The moment of truth rained down, a rush of blood thrummed in Ty's eardrums and beat wildly against his skull. His heart squeezed to bursting, crushed under the weight of a war he could never win.

"I'm sorry," the kid sobbed. "So fucking sorry. I was scared and high. I couldn't think. I never wanted to kill her." He looked up at Ty and his body collapsed, as if he accepted, almost welcomed, his fate. "I'm so fucking sorry," he whispered.

Ty squeezed his eyes, trying to clear his tears and avoid the voices echoing in his head. It would be so easy. His hands shook against the sweat-slicked neck of a murderer. Ironically, the bastard's heartbeat pulsed against the pad of his finger. Had the murdering little fuck felt Tara's heartbeat in the same way? Tara deserved justice, deserved this. His parents deserved this. *He* fucking deserved this. What kind of brother ended up here and didn't have the balls to finish it?

A brother I worshipped my whole life because of his goodness and strength. A brother who'd never devastate an already broken family with another tragedy.

"Tara?" Ty cried.

His breath roared in and out. He dropped his head and pulled his fingers away from the kid's throat but kept his shoulders pinned against the ground. "You little fuck. You have no idea, just no idea what you've done to my family."

"Freeze. Hands in the air. Both of you." Blake's voice echoed off the building behind them.

Ty heard it but couldn't move.

"Come on, McGee. Get off him. I've got it from here, buddy."

Ty slid off of the kid's body. A quick end would have been too easy for the little prick, anyway. He fell back against the cool pavement and stayed there. Minutes later, he struggled to sit and vaguely took in the scene carrying on around him. The arrest, Blake shouting orders, a couple other cops hauling the kid away.

Finally, Blake squatted next to him, put a hand on his shoulder. "You did good. I know what you're thinking, but the person who would have suffered the most if you'd killed him would have been you."

For the most part, Ty had managed to come back into his body and bring down the rage to a bearable level. Actually, bearable was a bit optimistic, but he felt himself begin to function more normally. He looked at Blake and shook his head. "I was trying to figure out the fair thing to do. But nothing will ever make it fair. My sister's gone, and he's still breathing."

Blake stood and held out his hand to help Ty up. "He may still be breathing, but for years and years and years, he's going to do it behind bars. And he's got that young, skinny, fresh meat look about him." Blake turned to Ty and winked. "Trust me, McGee, you did the right thing."

They started back toward the restaurant's parking lot. "I've got to bring you in, you know. Let you explain how

I figured all this out, then we need to make sure it sticks in court." Blake glanced at him again. "But you look like shit. You want me to call an ambulance? You could develop some sudden chest pain. It'll buy you some time to get your head on straight."

Ty let a defeated chuckle escape. "Thanks but getting my head on straight is going to take a lot more than a bogus trip to the ER." The sooner he could get this over with, the sooner he could get to the only person he wanted to see. He owed her a thank you, an apology, and probably a substantial amount of groveling, too. If he stood any chance of ever having his life straight again, it would only be after he fixed things with Jordan.

Chapter Twenty-one

Jordan despised drugs. She was even wary of the kind doctors prescribed. But a nerve pill wasn't sounding half-bad at the moment. Today was delivery day at Buck's. With any luck, Warren and Arlo would be sharing a cell by tonight.

She turned on the TV, turned it off. Opened a magazine, flipped it shut. Made lunch, fed it to Bahan's cat. Lay down, got back up. Her mind was in overdrive, and she couldn't explain it.

Who was she trying to kid? Of course she could explain it.

In the last few weeks, she'd been beaten, had failed to close an undercover case for the first time in her career, and had lost the man she…loved. It was a bitter pill to swallow, but she didn't think the unrelenting ache would hurt quite so badly if she hadn't really loved him.

All that was probably enough to make a person edgy. But that wasn't it. Her mind was in Titus.

Determined to put some space between herself and Ty,

she'd stubbornly stayed in St. Louis when Bahan left this morning. She'd regretted every moment since. She needed to be in Titus. What if something happened to Ty? She'd refused every one of his phone calls over the last several days, and now the terror of never hearing his voice again was about to bring her to her knees.

But their relationship had ended. When a relationship went wrong, weren't you supposed to walk away and not look back? Guess she hadn't made it to that point, because she'd done nothing *but* look back and think of him.

She could still see Ty's expression when she'd given him the details of his sister's murder. The dark skepticism in his eyes, the sharp blade of anger thinning his lips—like the information didn't quite compute, but he'd decided to kill the messenger all the same.

Her body was at war with itself. She couldn't sit still but barely had the strength to cross the room. She had no desire to work but resented the hell out of the fact she was sitting on Bahan's couch, completely useless. And the one talent she'd honed to complete perfection—shutting off emotions—had been in epic fail mode since the night she'd left Ty. The beating Warren Buck had given her was nothing compared to the damage Ty had left.

She was losing it. Seriously losing it.

The seconds crawled like minutes, minutes like hours. She didn't know if it was the need for sleep so much as her brain shorting out that made her finally drift off on the sofa.

When Bahan came home, she heard the door open and sprang up. "You didn't call me."

"I did call you. Where's your phone?"

She felt up and down her hips. "Oh, I don't have pockets

in these pants. I must have laid it down somewhere. What happened? You're back early." Now she was awake enough to see his frustration as he flopped down into a chair.

"Not a damned thing. Buck had a ton of booze and food delivered. We had McGee wired the whole time. He was in the middle of all of it—hauling boxes, working with the delivery guys, filling out paperwork. We ID'd every delivery truck that came near. One junker pulled in, and two sleazy-looking guys hopped out. The plates were stolen, and we knew it was something illegal, but it turned out to be fifteen cases of moonshine—no drugs. I was so pissed."

"Is Ty okay?" she asked quietly.

Bahan rubbed at his eyes. "Well, he wasn't happy. None of us were, but yeah, he's okay."

"So what now?"

"I don't know. I told McGee to just keep on working until we make a decision."

She squeezed her eyes tight. "Ty's going to stay there?" She thought it would be over today. Why couldn't it have been over today?

"He'll be fine, Jordan." Bahan moved next to her on the couch and slung an arm around her shoulders. "We've got him wired, and good people are keeping an eye on him."

His head fell back against the cushion. "It was frustrating as shit, though, thinking that every truck pulling into the lot was the one. I tied up over twenty guys between the FBI, DEA, and police. For moonshine. The asshole probably wouldn't even get a slap on the wrist for fucking moonshine," he added. "Screw it. We're having alcohol and pizza."

The very thought of food made her want to heave, much less images of the greasy pizza from Bahan's favorite hole in the wall.

"Don't look at me like you're going to bail. I'm in a foul mood, and you owe me at least one night of food and drinks. I'll have it delivered." He sulked off to his room to take a shower.

"Why not?" she said to the empty room. It wasn't like she was going to rest peacefully tonight anyway.

The pizza and alcohol didn't end up calming her nerves. She broke a glass, knocked the pizza box on the floor, and damn near killed Bahan's cat when she tripped over it.

She decided to go to bed before she really hurt someone. At least the amount of damage she could do in the spare bedroom would be minimal. After flipping through the same magazine over and over and not comprehending a single word, she turned out the light.

. . .

Cool fingers gripped Jordan's arm. She turned her head and saw Tara in a halo of light. Why wouldn't this girl go away? Jordan had done all that she could. Enough that it had cost her Ty.

Jordan studied the girl's face, the brilliant, silver eyes and long, black lashes were the reason Tara felt so familiar. She was the feminine image of her brother, both of them blessedly beautiful.

Tara pulled her hand back toward herself, motioning for Jordan to follow.

No way. Where would Tara take her? Heaven? Hell?

Jordan tried to resist following, but the pull was too strong. Christ, they were in hell. She recognized the streets of Titus, the restaurants, the bank, the gas station. Even Buck's sleazy nightclub.

The Main Street Diner sparkled with Christmas lights, and Tara stopped in front of it. Why would Tara take her here?

The door opened. A large banner featuring Santa in a sleigh heaped with eight-dollar pizzas hung on the wall as the Tuesday special. The neon clock next to it read 2:10.

Arlo and Warren Buck were seated at a table with two other men, strangers to Jordan.

A Longdale cop with buzzed, blond hair sat drinking coffee at the counter. He was a regular at Buck's. Ty had been friendly with him, because they'd worked together as cops.

Ty sat at a table behind Arlo and Warren. Two other bouncers from the nightclub were with him.

Tara glided around Ty, looking every bit the angel Jordan believed her to be. Suddenly, Tara stopped moving and focused on Warren. Jordan followed her lead and saw what had Tara's attention.

Warren was using his foot to push a duffel bag from between his legs to the man across from him.

Here it was, the payoff. The drug exchange. Anyone in the place would miss it if they weren't watching. A casual nodding of heads and the two strangers were up and carrying the duffel out the door.

Ty pulled his gun and aimed it at the two suspects. They were halfway to the door and kept going.

The Longdale cop pulled his gun, too, but not on the suspects. He aimed at Ty. Shot Ty. Once…twice…three times.

Tara stood like a shield in front of her brother. The vision was silent. No voices. No sounds of gunfire. But in that one instant, Jordan could see the plea in Tara's eyes.

Save my brother.

Chapter Twenty-two

"Please God, no! Please, no!" Jordan heard the words, felt them pouring, over and over from her mouth, but she couldn't quiet them.

"Jordan, it's okay. I'm here."

"Ty."

"No, it's Bahan."

Disoriented, she struggled to remember where she was. Tara and the diner were still front and center in her mind. "That's why Tara took me to the diner," she whispered.

"What? Damn it, Jordan. What are you saying?"

She turned her head and looked at Bahan. "The drugs," she said. "It's going to happen tomorrow. At the Titus Diner. Ty's going to get shot unless we help him."

Bahan wasn't an easy guy to shake up, but Jordan knew she'd managed to do it. His eyes were huge, and he was holding his gun. "Jordan, you had a dream. A bad one, apparently. You scared the shit out of me screaming like that." He sat his gun on the nightstand. "Wait here."

Bahan left the room and returned with two glasses. "Drink this." He pushed one into her hand and tossed back the other.

Coughing, she choked down the vodka. "Are you trying to kill me? I thought that was water."

"You need something stronger than water after that dream. So do I. Damn it, you scared the crap out of me, Jordan."

Searching the room, she located her jeans and then pulled them on. "It wasn't just a dream. I mean, it was but… Look, I can't explain right now, but the drug exchange is going to happen in the diner on Main Street in Titus. I think tomorrow around two. We have to go. We have to be there."

He pulled her to the bed and sat beside her. "I know sometimes dreams seem very real. But I think—"

"No buts, Bahan. You have to call your people, tell them to be ready." She took his hands and squeezed tight. "We have enough time to set up everything." She was familiar with the look he was giving her, the are-you-crazy one. "I know we don't have much to go on, but I swear this is for real."

"Are you listening to yourself? I mean, really listening? You want me to gather DEA, FBI agents, and police officers for the second day in a row, waste all that man power again, because you had a dream? I can't do that. You know I can't do that."

"I'm not some crazy off the street, Bahan." She grabbed the sweatshirt she had on earlier. "Don't treat me like I've lost my mind."

"Jordan, come on. If McGee suspected something else

was going to happen, don't you think he would have said something?"

"He doesn't suspect anything." Damn. She didn't have time for this. Ty's life was in danger, and Bahan was giving her the third degree. Telling him about the dreams could end their friendship, not to mention their working relationship, if he decided she was nuts.

She covered her eyes with her hand. Was she really going to do this again? Hell, yes. If it was the only way to get backup for Ty, she'd risk anything.

Bahan was still sitting on the bed. She eased down next to him and looked him in the eyes. "I've never told you this before, I hoped I'd never have to tell anyone, but sometimes I have dreams. In the dreams are visions. Most of the time, it's visions of a case I'm working on. I can't explain it, I don't know why or how it happens, so don't ask.

"It's how I knew to look for traces of blood in the garage on the last case. It's how I tracked down that old warehouse the Angelo brothers killed that girl in, and it's how I know the drugs are coming into Titus tomorrow. I've never asked you to go out on a limb for me like this, but I need your trust. I'm not making it up. I swear to you, I'm not."

"I need another drink." He walked out of the room and returned a few seconds later with the entire bottle of vodka. "So...you're telling me you're like, what? A witch? Voodoo? Psychic?" He leaned against the doorframe.

"No. I don't stick pins in dolls and put curses on my enemies. See, this is why I don't tell people."

"Relax, Broomhilda, I'm just trying to figure out what you're saying."

"Ha ha, you're hysterical. Just forget it." She pulled her

hair back and slipped a rubber band around it. She felt like an idiot. Should have known better than to say anything to him. "Can you at least take me home? I have things I need to do."

"No. You can't drop a bomb like 'I have visions, I have dreams', and then get angry because I need a little explanation. Things are fairly black and white to me."

He grabbed her wrist as she attempted to push past him. "Are you saying you're so good at what you do because you're a psychic?"

"No." On a flash of anger, she jerked away, but then had second thoughts about letting anger get in the way of Ty's safety. If Bahan didn't understand and wouldn't help her, no one would.

"I don't know," she said. "I've never put a label on it. I think I'd be considered more a medium than a psychic. I can't read minds or anything, but I see a lot of dead people. It's not something I do on purpose; it just happens."

He paced away and ran a hand down the back of his neck. "There are a couple of psychics that contact the bureau from time to time. Some of the guys claim they've gotten a pretty good lead from them once or twice. I know people say it happens, but I—"

"Always thought those people were full of it. Yeah, me, too. I guess I still figure a good portion of people who claim some kind of sixth sense are liars. I've done my best to suppress it, make it go away. During the day, I've pretty much got it licked. But at night, when I'm sleeping, sometimes it comes back with a vengeance.

"This has been happening your whole life?"

"Pretty much."

"And you've never told anyone? Why?"

"Are you serious? You just called me Broomhilda, you idiot. Nothing good has ever come out of me telling anyone about this. Ty was the first person I've told in years and only because I had no choice."

He held up both hands. "Back up. What's McGee have to do with your dreams?"

This was getting complicated. She hesitated, but coming clean with Bahan was the only chance she had, that Ty had. "While I was in Titus, I kept having dreams about a teenage girl. I had no idea who she was, but I kept seeing her murder over and over. Ty had never told me he even had a sister, but when I was at his parents' house, I saw her picture."

Bahan stepped back and squeezed his eyes shut like his head was swimming. "McGee had a sister that was murdered?"

"Yes. Her name was Tara," Jordan said.

"Let me see if I got this straight. You saw a girl get killed in one of your dreams, but had no idea who the victim was?"

She nodded.

"And McGee had a sister who was murdered, but never mentioned it, even after you two had slept together?"

She nodded again. "It's hard to explain—"

Bahan held up one finger to stop her. "You really need to work on your communication skills." He grabbed the vodka bottle and took a healthy swig. "So you saw the guy who killed McGee's sister? Were you able to arrest him?"

"I don't know." Jordan shrugged. She was trying to ignore the lump welling in her throat. "Ty didn't believe me when I explained how to track the guy down. In fact, he was brutally honest in his reaction. Asked me if I was crazy."

She blinked back the tears, simply refused to cry in front of Bahan. "I haven't taken any of his calls or returned his texts since."

"Unbelievable. He's called me a million times, you know that? I told him to back off. I figured he did some stupid asshole man thing that all of us do, but…Did you give him time to absorb this bombshell?"

She wouldn't admit it to Bahan, but the answer was no. She was too hurt to give him any time to understand. Now she wondered if maybe it would have made a difference.

Bahan sat her down on the bed. Stared at her as if she were in the interrogation room. "Are you in love with him?"

The tears did come now. She shook her head, refusing to answer because she'd never been good at lying to Bahan. "It doesn't matter. Loving someone doesn't mean you can accept who they are."

"I don't want to play devil's advocate," he said, "but I've known you for years. We've got a long history, so whatever you're telling me isn't going to keep me from caring. But it is big. Huge, in fact. Did you give McGee a fair shake?"

"I don't know. I tried to hide the truth and pretend I was normal. But I'm not normal, and I never will be."

"No arguments here."

She glared at him.

"Based on the number of times he's tried to get me to spill information about you, I'm thinking if you asked McGee if he wants normal or he wants you, you'd probably be surprised how quickly he'd jump on a little insanity in his life."

Jordan tugged on her shoes. "I can't waste any more time. I've got to go. It's okay if you can't come with me."

"Yeah, I'm going to let you go back to Titus alone and play renegade again, since it worked so well for you last time." He shook his head, then whistled. "We're really talking about a dream here? How do you know it hasn't already happened? Or maybe it's going to happen next week. There's a lot of money and man power tied up if you're wrong, Jordan. Do you know for sure it will happen tomorrow?"

There were no hard and fast rules when it came to dreams. But she knew it hadn't happened yet. If something had happened to Ty, she'd feel it in every part of her soul. Cowboy would have moved heaven and earth be the one in her dream instead of Tara.

The other side of the coin was that she couldn't promise the drug exchange was going down tomorrow, but she felt that Tara's timing was key.

Jordan looked at Bahan, trying to decide how to answer. She'd dismissed the dream about her family, and it had cost her everything. She could live with a pissed off Bahan if she happened to be wrong. But if she was right and didn't act on it, failing Ty would be the one thing she could never live with.

"Yes, Bahan. I'm positive it's happening tomorrow. I'm going to Titus with or without you."

Chapter Twenty-three

Jordan pulled in two narcotics detectives she worked closely with, and Bahan was able to roust three FBI buddies who owed him favors. Jordan and Bahan had spent most of the night going over the plan. She went through it with the team as Bahan drove the unmarked van—for the second day in a row—to Titus.

"Two unidentified male suspects will be meeting with Arlo and Warren Buck inside the diner. One will have long, dark hair, sunglasses, blue windbreaker. The other will be blond with a green fatigue jacket."

"How did you get this information?" asked one of the special agents.

Jordan felt her back go straight, stiffening at the question.

"We got a tip from an agent in deep cover," Bahan said over his shoulder. "There was mention of a diner, and he thinks these two are the delivery guys for the Delago Cartel. Their clothing may not be the same, but it's what they were last seen in."

Jordan turned and met Bahan's eyes in the mirror, hoping her silent *thank you* registered loud and clear.

"History tells us Buck will probably have a few guys with him, bouncers from his club. One of those guys will be our inside cop. Tall. Dark, wavy hair. Don't hurt him," she added.

Bahan pulled into the town's twenty-four-hour department store and parked in the back of the lot. "We're going to take a few minutes, pull our undercover look together. Be right back."

Jordan hopped out of the van with the spray she needed to gray Bahan's hair. "You're going to need to bend down—"

"Hey," he said, "you can't keep up this pace. Slow down. Take a breath."

"I can't slow down. If I do, I'll lose it. I can't lose it. Ty's life is at stake."

"You've got to relax a little, or you'll be too wiped out to get this done. You did a good job pulling it all together at the last minute."

"*We* did a good job." She hugged him, then stepped back. "I couldn't have done any of it without you. You're indulging me on something you don't believe in, I get that, and yet, you're still standing behind me. I won't ever forget it."

"Fuck it," he said. "If you can't do something crazy with guns and drug dealers once in a while, what's the point, right?"

She shook her head at him and laughed. Bahan was right, the tension inside her was coiled so tightly, it felt like the first real breath she'd taken in hours.

All the humor quickly left his face, and he propped his

hands on his hips. "I don't think either one of us is going to forget this night, Jordan. But I still have one reservation. If McGee's life is in danger, we should give him a heads-up. If it were me, I'd want to know."

Jordan shook her head adamantly. "You'd want to know so you could change things, do something different, alter what you'd normally do. If Ty does that, it might not go down like I'm anticipating.

"Right now, I know I can take out the crooked Longdale cop. I don't want to risk Ty by doing anything different to mess it up. If he hesitates or acts too early or gives himself away, it could get more dangerous. I say we go with the plan just the way it is."

Jordan tucked her hair under a curly gray wig and put on some old-lady makeup and clothes. She grayed Bahan's hair and forced him to wear the pants and jacket she'd picked out. She gave him some old-man glasses and was pretty damn happy with the result. She aged them both by at least thirty years.

When the team was in position and they were ready to proceed, Bahan went into the diner ahead of her and picked out a booth.

She walked in a minute later and looked up. Twinkling Christmas lights, a Santa banner, and the neon clock that read 1:36 hit her full force. She stopped abruptly.

Bahan caught her attention and motioned her over with an angry wave. "What the heck are you doing? Trying to get noticed?"

"No. Sorry."

They settled, and the waiting game began. A waitress filled their coffee cups. They ordered, *slowly*. Poked at the food that came, *slowly*.

"This is incredibly nerve-racking," Jordan mumbled. "I don't know how you can eat. I feel like I could throw up."

"If we both go into a diner, order food, and don't bother to eat, someone may wonder what the hell we're doing here. So take a bite, will you?"

Attempting to ease the thundering in her head, she rubbed at her temples. Maybe she *was* wrong. About the day? About the time? Her dreams were never wrong, but maybe she'd confused things because of her feelings for Ty?

Christ, her feelings for Ty. They were stronger now than they'd ever been. What if Bahan was right? What if she'd endangered Ty, because she didn't warn him? A huge lump swelled in her throat, and her heart tumbled right over itself.

"Yo." Bahan snapped his fingers close to her face. "Don't do that. Do not space out on me." His voice was soft and controlled, but it held the dangerous warning she needed to get her head back on straight.

She nodded, channeled the Ice Bitch again, and put the fear behind her. She was *not* wrong. Everything inside her said this was going down today.

The bell on the door chimed. Someone entered. Bahan said nothing, but gave her the nod. Barely shifting, she watched the Longdale cop with blond, spiky hair walk up to the counter and sit on a stool.

"We got a bird in that nest out behind the house." Bahan used the code sentence.

It was less than five minutes before the bell chimed again. The stunned look on Bahan's face told Jordan she'd gotten the details correct. She didn't bother to turn. Didn't need to.

"We got eggs in the nest, too." Bahan said for the benefit of the wire. "Six for sure," he said, indicating the number of suspects with guns. "Maybe as many as seven."

She listened to the sounds of people settling in, calculating the best moment to risk a glance. When she did, she realized she hadn't just gotten most of it right, she'd nailed every last damn detail down to the color of clothing they wore and the seats they chose.

The Longdale cop sat with his back to the others, but it was a good bet he was listening to every word. Jordan blocked out everything but the cop—nerves, fear, thoughts of Ty erased from her mind. Like a machine, she processed the threats. Hand on her gun, she waited for Bahan to signal that Warren was making his move.

Bahan slid a finger across the tabletop, mirroring Warren's slide of the duffel bag.

The payoff was moving.

"Freeze, you're under arrest," Ty's voice sounded from behind her.

She flew out of the booth.

The dirty Longdale cop swiveled, aimed his gun toward Ty.

Jordan pulled her trigger, and the dirty cop slumped to the floor. Bahan rushed Arlo and Warren. Ty jumped one of the drug dealers, wrestled him down. She heard fists connecting with bone and finally, a gunshot.

Christ, no.

What had she missed? What hadn't she seen in her dream?

Neither Ty nor the drug dealer moved. Jordan's world hung motionless for an eternity. She tried to go to him, wanted to rush toward their tangled limbs, but everything inside her froze. A pool of blood spilled onto the floor, and even her heart and breath seized.

Ty finally lifted his head, and the room spun.

Jordan's slow-motion world resumed speed, sounds and movement penetrating through the deafening roar of her heartbeat. People were cuffed, and Miranda rights were given. Local and state backup burst through the doors in full force, but still, she couldn't move.

Untangling himself from the drug dealer, Ty stood and stared down at the man lying in a pool of blood at his feet and then turned his face toward Jordan.

Bahan stepped next to her. "You okay?"

"I will be." She forced herself to look at Bahan. "Can I take the van? I need to get out of here."

"Now? Are you kidding? We've got to report and—"

She felt the dizzying rush of blood drain from her head. Bahan grabbed her arm and hustled her out the door.

Once outside, she yanked the wig from her head and bent over, taking a few deep breaths. The crisp December air slapped some life back into her. "I won't be gone long; I just need a few minutes." She stood upright. "Can you cover for me? I still have the key to my apartment here in town. I'll head there, wash this makeup off, pack up my clothes so that when we leave this time, I don't ever have to look back."

Bahan frowned. "He'll still be here when you get back, you know. You can't hide from McGee forever."

"Maybe not forever, but for right now. That's all I'm asking."

Bahan nodded. "I can give you a little time, but be quick about it. And I need you to leave your weapon." He picked up her hand and dropped the keys into it.

She headed across the street to the bulky, white surveillance van. She reached for the door handle and heard footsteps behind her. She didn't turn around, but she knew by the cadence of the walk and the way her heart raced that Ty was right behind her.

"So that's it? No 'see you around, Ty.' No 'have a nice life, Ty.' No 'I hate your guts, Ty.' You just walk away?"

She tried to ignore the emotion that welled up under the hurt in his voice. "They all three apply. Consider them said if it makes you feel better." She opened the van door.

Pushing it shut, he trapped her between his arms. His breath streaked down her neck, lodging a thundering, vibrating drum somewhere in the vicinity of where her heart used to be.

Every muscle in her body tightened. She closed her eyes.

"Look at me, Jordan," he said, turning her in his arms.

He was close. Too close. He put a hand under her chin and lifted her head.

She forced her eyes open. His gaze was still the most breathtaking sight she'd ever known, but looking at him hurt worse than any physical pain ever had. He was quite simply a painful reminder of what she was. Of what she would never have.

His stroked her cheek.

Damn it, she wanted to be strong, strong enough not to tilt her head and melt into his touch, but she couldn't quite manage it.

"You saved me in there, didn't you?" he asked. "How did you know?"

"Lucky guess."

"No. Lucky dream," he answered. "For me, anyhow."

She looked everywhere but at him. "I have to...um, go. I have business to take care of."

"No you don't. Any business you need to take care of is right here." He weaved his fingers in the tangled mess of her hair and leaned his forehead against hers. "Please don't run from me, baby."

"What's the point, Ty? You want me to tell you that a dream is how I knew you were in danger? And if I tell you that, will you ask me if I'm crazy again?"

"No." He tightened his hold on her head when she attempted to pull away, forcing her eyes directly to his. "Then I tell you I love you, and maybe you tell me you love me, too."

She shook off his hands and forced him back a step. "It won't work."

"It does work. Better than anything has ever worked for either of us, and you damn well know it." He swallowed hard. "I caught the kid who killed Tara because of what you told me. You were right. About everything." He forced in a long breath and released it slowly. "Arron Thomas. He graduated from North Cooper High last June. He was visiting his cousin when they decided to go to the same party Tara went to."

Jordan's breath exhaled on a *whoosh*. Not now, not here, she silently pleaded.

"He said he didn't know why he did it, other than he was using drugs. He felt powerful, like he could get away with anything, but he didn't plan to kill her. That's what he said." Ty's voice broke. "There was no reason. No reason for killing my sister."

Oh, God, she wanted to touch him, put her hand on his

face, maybe run her fingers through his hair. Just one small touch to let him know she was glad they'd gotten some closure.

She simply couldn't take it, and finally, she reached for his hand. "I'm sorry. I don't know if it helps or not, but I know she loved you so much. She still loves you." Jordan debated for a long moment, then said, "Tara was the one who saved you today. She came to me in a dream last night and showed me what was going to happen. I don't think she ever came to me because of what happened to her. I think it was you she wanted to save the whole time."

Ty squeezed his eyes tight, but Jordan had already seen the tears. He put his hands on her hips, like he'd done so many times before, and pulled her body close to his.

"I'm so sorry for not trying to understand more, for not giving you a chance to explain. I had been trying so hard for so long to figure out what happened to Tara, it just didn't seem possible that information from a dream could suddenly solve it. But then I sat down and really put it together, everything you said…" His voice clogged and trailed off.

Pressed so closely against him, she didn't stand a chance in hell of thinking clearly. Or of avoiding the painful, consuming emotions. "Ty, please stop. It's okay—"

"No, it's not okay. It hasn't *been* okay since you left. I can't eat or sleep or function. I've been trying to find you. Twenty-seven phone calls, thirteen texts. You wouldn't answer your phone. Hell, Jordan, you're killing me here.

He crushed his lips against hers, and the need was so desperate, so raw, pushing him away never felt like an option. Her arms wrapped around his neck, and the kiss tumbled quickly from heartsick and needy to fierce in a matter of seconds. His arm squeezed more firmly around her waist and crushed her even tighter against him.

Their lips fused and tangled. He kissed her until she was senseless, dizzy, until she had to pull her head back and gasp for air.

His chest was still heaving when he eased back and studied her for a long moment. "I've thought about you every second of every day we've been apart. I understand you have dreams, bad ones. I get that you don't understand them fully or why they appear, but I'm not scared. It'll never make me stop loving you."

Her heart tumbled when he said that he loved her. But what kind of life could she give him?

"You think you can love someone like me." She shook her head. "But you haven't even seen the tip of it. How dark it is sometimes. How awful, violent, sad it can be. How it drives me to do things, to take chances that aren't smart ones. It would never be an easy, peaceful life with me."

"Baby, we both passed easy and peaceful a long time ago. You think I don't love you enough to stand by you? If you're standing here telling me you're psychic but can't even understand what I feel for you, you're not nearly as good as you think you are."

He dropped his hands. The emptiness of losing contact with him rolled across her.

"I think it's not me who has a problem with the dreams," he said. "It's not me who's too scared to accept things as they are and give us a try. It's you. Quit hiding behind the dreams."

Her bottom lip quivered. Her throat tightened.

"McGee," one of Bahan's agents called out to Ty. "Bahan

wants you inside."

"Go," she said.

"*Fuck*," Ty mumbled. "I love you. I do. I've never been with anyone who's made me feel like this. I want every part of you, even the parts that dream." His lips curved. "Especially the parts that see a gun aimed at me before I do."

He held her head and brushed his lips against hers so softly it stole her breath. And for the first time since she'd been a child, the universe straightened and everything was infinitely less complicated. He loved her. Even with the dreams, he loved her. Because of her dreams, he loved her.

"You. Go. Nowhere," he said with a warning glare. He started to walk toward the diner, then turned back to her, pointing a finger. "We're not done. Stay right here."

"No," she repeated as he turned. "We're not done."

He jogged to the door of the diner.

Once again, she had to admire the sinful perfection of his ass. What were the odds of bronzing those damn blue jeans? And while she appreciated his very masculine form, she wondered why men always thought they were in charge.

She had no intentions of standing around in a parking lot, and she certainly wasn't wasting another minute of her life on Arlo and Warren Buck.

She meant what she'd said—they weren't done, not by a long shot. But now it was her turn to step up. Ty was right; she'd hidden behind the dreams long enough. She may not have been a genius, but she wasn't a total idiot, either. He loved her. She loved him. All the rest was just the messy details they'd have to sort through.

Plus, Ty didn't realize he'd given her something just as meaningful as his love. He'd given her a whole new perspective. Until he pointed it out, she'd completely dismissed the fact that she'd been able to save him because of a dream.

She saved someone she loved because of her gift.

Maybe she hadn't been able to save her family, but she saved Ty. And that, she knew, was worth every dream she'd ever lived through.

He'd made the first move, putting himself out there, risking his heart. He claimed he'd could live with the strangeness that was her life.

Now she'd risk something, too. Her sanity, for starters. Checking her watch, she calculated how much time she had. Ten minutes to get to her apartment. Thirty minutes to shower and pack a suitcase. Ten minutes for the return trip. She'd be back before Ty realized she was gone.

But just to be sure, she'd call him and let him know what she was planning. Then, she decided, they'd be even. Staying in Titus would be damn near as big a sacrifice as suffering through a few random dreams. At least the way she figured it, it was. But if she was going to start a life with Ty, she wasn't going to do it in the grandma garb she was wearing. Nor would she do it in the cocktail-waitress get-ups she had at Ty's place.

The only way she'd stay in Titus would be as Jordan Delany.

Woman. Cop. And dreamer.

Chapter Twenty-four

"Well, that's just great."

Jordan called Ty four times on the way back to her apartment. He wasn't picking up. She knew it was chaos at the diner—Bahan and the other Feds were no doubt drilling him—but if he saw it was her number, why wasn't he answering?

Maybe she needed to call Bahan, see if he could get a message to Ty. Although avoiding Bahan felt like a better plan. Not really avoiding *him* per se, but the next few weeks would be an endless myriad of reports, interviews, and briefings. She needed just a little time to get her head on straight. Her job had been her only concern for way too long. Tonight, Ty had to be the priority.

She was thirsty, hungry, and bone tired, but she powered through a shower and threw on jeans and a blouse. Glancing around the apartment with a surprising amount of affection, she decided she might just miss one or two of the silly roosters.

As crazy as it sounded, they'd become weird little friends who had watched her and Ty fall in love.

It only took a few minutes to throw her clothes into the suitcase. She was struggling with the zipper when someone pounded on the door. Bahan had probably sent someone to check on her and hurry her back to the crime scene.

As soon as the turn of the doorknob clicked in her hand, Ty charged across the threshold like an angry bull.

"What are you doing here? I figured you'd be tied up for quite a while," she said.

He pivoted and pinned her with a look so full of anger, her heart tripped. "Are you okay?" A pang of concern shot through her. "Did something else happen? Did someone else get hurt?"

Fury leapt off of him. He looked like a bomb seconds before detonation. "You mean before or after you took off?"

It took a couple of seconds for the meaning of his words to register, but then she got it. *He hadn't listened to his messages.* He didn't think she was coming back.

"Thought you had just enough time to pack a bag and disappear before I could catch up, didn't you?" he said in an angry growl. "Well, think again." He marched across the room but marched back just as quickly. Ran his hand through his hair. "Do I need to use your own cuffs on you to lock you in place for five minutes?"

She raised a brow. As if *that* would ever happen. "Calm down. I tried to call you. Left a message—"

"Quiet." The harsh bark of the word silenced her. "I'm talking, and for once in your life, you're going to be silent and listen."

He'd misunderstood and was going to feel like an

idiot when he finally heard his messages, but still, her eyes narrowed at his Neanderthal tone. "Ty, look. You don't understand. I just wanted to get—"

"Do you know how many times I've tried to call you since you left?"

Yeah, she knew. He'd made it very clear earlier. Twenty-seven calls and thirteen text messages. But it seemed like maybe more of a rhetorical question, so she kept her mouth shut.

"All I asked was for you to wait for me. Just a little while until Bahan was done with me so we could talk. But you took off. *Again!*"

Jordan moved closer and could feel the hurt radiating from him. She'd become adept at blocking the feelings most people emitted, but with Ty, she just didn't know how to guard against them. "Okay, I get it." She spoke calmly, determined to set him straight. "You're upset because I left. If you'd stop interrupting every time I open my mouth—"

"How can you not want to fight for what we have? I'm sorry for every wrong thing I said, but nothing that happened between us was so big that it can't be fixed. I mean, come on."

To shut him up, she threw her arms around his neck and pulled his lips firmly against hers.

He stood stiff, shocked, then his lips softened.

Her tongue eased into the familiar, glorious heat of his mouth, and she poured everything she had into that one drugging kiss.

His arms tightened around her. He groaned and shuddered. "I don't want to lose you. I can't," he whispered, "just *can't* lose you."

Emotions hung thick and heavy in the air, but they had changed, morphed into something less angry but more desperate. "Look," she said, "I know you're tired and upset, but why didn't you listen to the messages I left for you?"

He moved his hands to her face. "Because I wasn't about to let you run away with a simple *goodbye* on my phone."

"I mean it, Ty." She smoothed her fingers against the front of his jeans. When she felt his phone, she dug it out of his pocket and handed it to him. "Listen to your messages."

"Damn it, Jordan. I'm tired of playing games." Irritated, he snatched the phone from her, punched in the numbers, and held it to his ear. "Oh," he said when the reality hit him. "You were coming back?"

She smiled and nodded.

"You were packing a suitcase so you could stay with me? In Titus?"

"Yes."

"But you hate Titus."

"So imagine how much I must love you."

A deep, coiled tension seemed to rush from his body on a giant exhale. Frankly, he looked like he might pass out. "Thank God," he whispered.

She tugged him toward the couch. "Maybe you should sit."

He dropped down onto the cushions.

Lowering herself next to him, she shifted to make sure she had his full attention. "I love you, Ty. More than you know. More than I'm comfortable with. A whole lot more than I thought it was possible for me to love someone."

"Baby, I love you, too. It almost killed me when I thought you'd left again." He pulled her tight and brushed his lips against hers. "I know we have to go back to the diner, but for a little while, can we please stay just like this?"

She nodded as he tugged her against his shoulder. Exhausted, they settled against the back of the big, old sofa, snugly wrapped in each other's arms.

"You know," Ty finally said, eyes still closed, "this thing is uglier than homemade soup, but Christ, it's comfortable."

Jordan laughed. "I know, right? I'm really going to miss it. I love to sleep on it." She nuzzled into his neck. "But I love to have sex on it even more."

He groaned, and not in the good way. "Great. Now I have to figure out how to buy the damn thing."

New emotions filled the room. Better emotions. In fact, Jordan couldn't remember anything in her life feeling this close to perfection.

After several minutes of quiet, Ty asked, "When exactly did you decide, you know, that you couldn't live without me?"

She smiled against his chest. "The night Lewis kicked me, and you followed me out to Buck's picnic table, you had me weak-kneed. But by the time you took me back to your parents' house and took care of me, I was a goner."

"Is that so?"

"Pretty much." She found his hand and laced her fingers with his. "But the night that Warren—"

"Shhh, It's okay, I get it." He touched a finger to her lips. "You don't have to talk about that night."

"No, actually I do. I saw my dad that night, and I think he saved me. He told me that he was sorry for all the mistakes he made. Even after all these years, it helped. Him taking responsibility helped me understand that I wasn't the only one to blame for what happened to my family that night. He said it was time to forgive and learn to make connections again. I think he might be right."

Emotion overtook her voice. Ty grabbed her hand and kissed it.

"He also said that you loved me and would find me and take care of me. And just like that, I slipped from his arms into yours."

"He sounds like a wise man," Ty said, pulling her close. "I will most definitely always take care of you." He gently touched his lips to hers and kissed her as though he was kissing her soul. At that moment, she knew her father had been right. There was a lot to be said for connection. Especially when those connections came in the form of Tyler McGee.

There would be more police work and there would be more dreams, but the one truth she finally understood was that she no longer needed to dream alone.

Epilogue

Two months later

St. Louis County Police Chief, Ronald Hyde, gripped the microphone on the podium and began to wind down his speech with a theatrical flair.

"These officers are a shining example of what can be accomplished when local, state, and federal agencies work together. I'm convinced the St. Louis Interagency Drug Enforcement Team is the most valuable cooperative effort Missouri has in place to fight drugs in our state."

Jordan made the mistake of glancing at Bahan. He pinned her with an accusing look as Chief Hide waxed on about the importance of working as a team. Hindsight truly was 20/20. She was lucky to be alive. Lucky she'd kept her badge. And damn lucky Bahan had the authority and inclination to report her strengths and smooth over her less than professional behavior.

Guilt made her break eye contact with Bahan and look at Ty. The stony expression carved on his face made her heart ache. The commendations she and Ty received today would never be associated with a victory, but rather a painful reminder of what had been lost.

The way she figured it, they both needed a nice long stretch of sipping tropical drinks and dozing on a warm beach. She hoped that was exactly what Ty had planned for their two weeks off. She'd given him free rein to schedule their vacation anywhere he liked, but God help him if he missed the less than subtle hints about blue Caribbean water lapping at her feet.

Chief Hyde continued on.

"Operation China White confiscated over thirty pounds of heroin. By the time it's cut with additives, that's over a million dollars' worth of drugs off the streets. It was quite a bust."

Yeah, Jordan thought as a final applause spread through city hall, it *was* quite a bust.

Not only had they gotten a substantial amount of drugs off the streets, four drug runners for the Delago Cartel had also been arrested. One of the runners had been offered immunity for turning evidence against the cartel. They'd gotten a lot of good information out of him, but unfortunately, not the one piece of information Jordan had wanted most: the names of the men who'd killed officers Lee and Benson.

Today, the families of the fallen officers had been given posthumous commendations. Quite honestly, Jordan found it agonizing to maintain eye contact during that part of the ceremony. Their families had been handed medals in lieu of justice, and the sting of it sliced wide and deep. Every cop knew the risks, particularly working inside the drug world. But you at least had hope that another cop would have your back, catch the asshole who'd gotten the drop on you. Jordan felt the failure of not providing that justice in every breath.

But despite the fact that this case had almost broken both her and Ty, the knowledge that Arlo and Warren Buck were sitting in cells somewhere felt good. It'd feel even better with a margarita in one hand and Ty's sunbaked biceps under the other. It was finally over, and she was more than ready to get the heck out of Dodge.

Later, back in her office, she packed up her laptop and edited her phone greeting to basically say: *Don't call me, I'll call you.* All she needed now was one hunky Longdale cop in a swimsuit, and frankly, the swimsuit was optional.

"Hey, gorgeous," Ty said, walking into her office. "Kiss me now or lose me forever."

She raised an eyebrow and leveled a grin at him. "Well, then, front and center, officer."

Sauntering toward her, he backed her up as though he was closing in on prey. She quickly became wedged between her desk and a very tempting wall of muscle. He yanked a folder from her hand, tossed it to the desk, and peered down at her. "Is that a direct order, detective? 'Cause my front to your center *is* one of my favorite positions."

He leaned in and kissed her. A sweet, sweet wave of pleasure took her breath away. He tugged at the pins that held her hair in her standard professional bun and then caressed her scalp as her hair fluttered free.

Her eyes closed, and her head tipped back into his hands. "That feels *so* good." She practically purred the words, and his fingers stilled. Her eyes blinked open, and she immediately clicked into his hungry, lust-filled stare.

Wiggling out of his arms, she shook her finger at him. "Nice try. How many times have I told you no hanky-panky in my office?" She made a good pretense of scolding him, but inwardly, she smiled, knowing that if they'd been anywhere but her office…

"Pack it up then, woman. If you insist on killing my fantasy, we're out of here."

She was intrigued. "You have a fantasy that involves my office?"

"Well, not so much your office, but"—his hands sketched an hourglass figure—"but that uniform, goddamn it."

She looked down at her dress blues. Standard uniform for all ceremonies and in no conceivable way attractive. "Have you lost your mind?" She snorted. "I'm covered from my chin to my toes."

"And it's all very…formfitting." He blew out a breath and groaned appreciatively.

"Seriously? In Titus, I walked around in a bikini top and cut-offs for days on end. Big hair, lots of makeup. Perfume. Heels. It never fazed you. And you're saying this"—she flicked a hand up and down her body—"works you up?" She laughed. "You are an incredibly disturbed individual."

He moved closer, hooked a finger in the collar of her shirt, and tugged her close. "That's why they call it a fantasy. Now, if there happens to be red lace underneath all that and you took it off real slow—"

A knock sounded on the door, and Bahan poked his head in.

Jordan jumped away from Ty, her face hot with embarrassment.

Bahan rolled his eyes and whispered, "Get a room," as he stepped inside. "Listen, my new boss would like to meet you. He used to work in St. Louis, then in Kansas City. He's back and was impressed with our task force. I'm showing him around a bit."

Knowing Ty was ready to manhandle her out the door, she aimed a warning glare at him.

She turned back to Bahan. "Sure. Bring him in."

"We're not ever going to leave, are we?" Ty grumbled when Bahan walked out.

"Shush. You know how much I owe Bahan. Two minutes. They'll be here; they'll be gone."

Bahan walked in, followed by an attractive older man in a crisp blue suit—salt and pepper hair, meticulously groomed, expensive-looking shoes. He was FBI, all right. He held out his hand to Jordan first.

"It's nice to meet you, detective."

Bahan jumped in. "Ken, this is Detective Jordan Delany." He motioned toward Ty. "And Officer Tyler McGee from the Longdale Police Department. Jordan, Ty, this is Special Agent Ken Bellows."

Bellows turned toward Ty and shook his hand. "Nice to meet you, McGee. Congratulations on a job well done." He turned back to Jordan. "SLIDE is a wonderful unit. I'll be throwing all my support behind the effort, and I'm proud that our special agents are a part of it."

"Thank you, sir," Jordan said.

"It's exciting to see law enforcement as it should be," he continued. "When it comes to drugs, we're in this war together. Whether you're FBI, DEA, or a city officer, if we don't work together as a team, shame on us, right?"

"Absolutely," Jordan said. Her gaze flashed to Bahan's. He was gonna irritate her about teamwork and cooperation from now until she retired, she just knew it.

There was no anger in his expression this time, however. Instead, Bahan winked at her, and an evil smile spread across his face. "Jordan was just saying the same thing. In fact, she could be our poster child for teamwork. Right, Jordan?"

"Right." She wondered if Bahan had paid Bellows to set her up that cleanly.

"I understand you're on leave for the next two weeks," Bellows said. "Well deserved and well needed, I'm sure. You kids have a nice vacation." Bellows headed for the door, then stopped and turned back to her. "By the way, Detective Delany, did you have family that worked for the FBI years ago? Is that what brought you to law enforcement?"

Not by a long shot. Knowing her father had been on the *wrong* side of the law was probably the single biggest reason she'd pursued her career. That, however, didn't seem like information that would endear her to an FBI agent.

"No, sir. No one in my family is in law enforcement. Why?"

"The name Delany clicked with me." He snapped his fingers. "I worked with a Delany years ago. Good agent. He and his family were killed when his cover was blown. I wondered if maybe you were related."

His words started spinning in her head. "I don't think so, sir. I don't have any living relatives."

"You have an uncle, don't you?" Bahan asked.

Yeah, the son of a bitch who'd refused to take her in after her parents had been murdered. Jordan glared at Bahan for mentioning it. "I had an uncle. William Delany.

We were never close."

Bellows paused with his hand on the doorknob. "No, my guy was Jack."

Jordan's heart thundered. Jack was her father's name.

"We were working together one night, chasing after two local dealers," Bellows said. "We'd been watching them for weeks, finally nailed their operation. We chased them into an empty warehouse and took 'em down. I thought we were clear. With no provocation, and no warning, Delany whipped around and shot a third guy. The asshole was probably thirty feet away, a semiautomatic pointed at us. I never heard a sound, but Delany spun around and nailed the guy like he had eyes in the back of his head."

Jordan's gaze darted to Bahan, then to Ty. A roaring rush of blood pounded through her head.

Ty stepped close, hooked an arm around her waist.

A chill sliced through her and almost froze the most important question of her life on her tongue, but she managed to force the words out. "Do you remember what time of year Jack Delany's family was killed?"

Bellows frowned. "It was horrible. Happened on Thanksgiving weekend. I've never been able to smell pumpkin pie or eat turkey without thinking of Jack."

Jordan inhaled on a gasp. Ty pulled her tighter against his body.

Bellows smiled and shook his head. "I still don't know how he did it, but he saved my ass that night. I asked him how the hell he pulled it off, but the wiseass never told me, just made a joke. Said he must have seen it in a dream."

Acknowledgments

I've heard it said that it takes a village to raise a child. Much to my surprise, I've found it also takes a village to write a book. At least for Dream Huntress it did. Experiencing the love and support from so many different people was one of the wonderful surprises along the journey. Please indulge me while I thank my village.

To my editors at Entangled Publishing, Tracy Montoya and Terese Ramin, thank you for seeing the potential in my manuscript and guiding me through the process of creating a book I am really proud of. Don't ever underestimate the huge spot you hold in my heart. You took a chance on an unknown author and made a dream come true. I will always be grateful.

To my fabulous romance critique partners, Claudia Shelton, Linda Gilman, Tammy Day, Dana Waganer. I'm not sure what divine power brought you into my life, but it had to be more than just dumb luck. We came together because of an interest in writing; we'll stay together because of the honest and true friendships we've formed. Thank you for the chocolate, the purple pens, the retreats, the bingo nights, and the love.

To my other fabulous critique group, Cathi, Michael, Kirk, thank you for being patient with me in the beginning, for all the grammar lessons, and for letting me become a valued member of your group.

To the first unfortunate victims that were asked to beta read, Cindy Nieukirk, Melissa Elmore, Cindy Shelburne, it's very possible I owe you a significant amount of wine and chocolate. And Ms. Neiukirk, I realize there is not enough wine in the world to repay the number of times you've read and corrected things in this manuscript, (or listened to me bitch.) You'll just have to suck it up and realize you wear the BFF tiara for a reason.

To my family, I can only say that I wouldn't have finished one chapter, much less a whole book, without your love. Corey, Cody, Cailey—you are my world. Nothing matters more than you. Thank you for being patient and loving your mommy, even when she locks herself away to write. And Mr. Sharp, you are a dish master, king of all household repairs, and a laundry god. If my ship comes in, your Mustang will be my first purchase. If not, well, you'll still have my undying love—thank you for picking up the slack. Mom, there are no words, just know how much I love and appreciate you. For the babysitting alone, I owe you my sanity.

Thank you to RWA and my local MORWA chapter. I'm not very outspoken, but I'm often in awe of the amount of talent gathered in one room during our local chapter meetings. I sincerely appreciate the opportunities and education you provide for romance writers.

I could go on, because there are so many experts, writing groups, instructors, and mentors I've had the privilege of working with, but I don't want to leave anyone out. If you've helped shape my writing world, chances are you know it, and I thank you.

Michelle

About the Author

Michelle Sharp is a romantic suspense author from the Midwest. Although she has a degree in journalism from Southern Illinois University, she finds weaving tales of danger, deception, and love much preferable to reporting the cold, hard facts. Her goal in life? To team resilient, kick-ass heroines with the sexy alpha's who love them. Her debut novel will be published with Entangled Ignite in summer of 2014. She is a member of Romance Writers of America and Missouri Romance Writers.

Bonus Material

Cut Cemetery Scene

"Come on, baby. Just answer the damn phone." Ty dialed Jordan's number again. He stood beside his truck in the parking lot of an all-night grocery store. A well-deserved six-pack and a bouquet of flowers in one hand, his cell phone in the other.

Her voicemail kicked on. "This is Jordan. Leave a message at the tone and I'll call you."

"God *damn* it." He slammed the phone against his truck then cocked his hand back to throw the fucking thing into the next county. About a half second before it slid from his fingers, he gripped it tighter with the pathetic thought that maybe she'd call back.

He'd spent the better part of the last twelve hours in Blake's office explaining how an anonymous tip had led him to Aaron Thomas. Sleep had closed in on him as soon as he'd slid behind the wheel of his truck. Dozing for an hour in the police station parking lot had helped some, but he still felt like he'd been hogtied and dragged a country mile down a gravel road. The last time he'd truly slept, he'd been wrapped around Jordan. *Great*, now just thinking about crawling into a bed without her made every other ache pale in comparison.

"Damn stubborn-assed woman," he grumbled, pulling onto the road again. So they'd had a fight? Couples have fights all the time. Didn't she get that?

He blew out a huge breath, considered banging his head against the steering wheel. *No, actually.* She probably didn't understand why the one person she'd tried to help, *and* the one person she should have been able to trust, had acted like a complete dick.

But in his defense, most people didn't go around claiming to hear from the dead. Sure his mom had sworn she could still feel Tara all around her. In their house, especially in Tara's room. But he'd never believed her, had chalked it up to a mother who couldn't let go.

Now he didn't know what to make of it.

Especially since… *damn.* When he'd taken Arron down, *something* had happened. Probably just his conscious playing games, trying to keep him from making a mistake he'd pay for forever. But when he'd had his hands wrapped around Arron's neck, he'd wanted so badly to hurt the little fuck and make him pay for what he'd done to Tara. Make him feel even half of the inconceivable pain their family had been through.

Then he'd heard Tara. He heard her voice as clearly as he could hear his own. Just a couple sentences, but none the less a voice of reason warning him, saying things in direct opposition to every emotion he'd felt in that moment.

No. He just needed sleep. He'd needed it then, and sure as hell needed it now before he jumped to the conclusion he'd heard his dead sister's voice. But damn, it *had* sounded like something Tara would have said.

Ty stepped on the gas a bit harder now. Flying along the country roads had been his chosen method of blowing off steam since he'd been a teen. Windows down. Radio up. He'd fucked with fate more than once on these curvy, backwoods roads. Fate had apparently enjoyed fucking him right back. He'd been a hellion as a kid, pulled more stupid teenage stunts than anyone had a right to. But as big of a dumbass as he'd been, he walked away without a scratch. Then ended up burying his baby sister. A girl whose worst offense had been a B minus on a final exam. If that wasn't fates way of kicking your ass, he didn't know what was.

Pulling next to the back fence of the cemetery, he killed the truck's engine and reached for the six pack. He popped the top on the first beer, drank it down without pause. Then grabbed two more and stuffed them in the pockets of his coat. The bouquet he'd bought had ended up on the passenger floorboard, so he grabbed it, got out of the cab, and hopped in the bed of his truck.

In his toolbox, he kept a flashlight and an old rag. It was the same routine as always. Even so, he wondered if there'd be a time when he could come here without every part of him burning with emotion. It certainly hadn't happened yet.

He climbed over the cemetery fence. Most of his visits were at this time of night. Why would anyone come during the day and risk running into someone they knew? Who the hell wanted to make small talk when you felt like your guts were bleeding out the front of your body? The moon was bright tonight, he didn't even need the flashlight to light his way. Finally hitting the peak of the hill, he knelt down at Tara's grave.

Tara Diane McGee
Beloved daughter and sister
A short time on earth, but forever in our hearts.

He swept the rag over Tara's tombstone, pushed away the grass and the dirt. His mom already had a bunch of red plastic poinsettias in the vase with an engraved bell that read—*Love You Always*. So he laid his flowers on top of Tara's stone.

Stepping back, he sat on the little cement bench next to Tara's grave and popped the top on the second beer. Leaning on his knees he said, "Hey, kiddo. You would not *believe* the day I've had." Under the circumstances, he decided there was no one better to tell the news to. Despite their age difference, he'd always shared a lot with her. It was hard not to. She could talk the ears off of a deaf guy. He smiled at the memory, but a tear rolled down his cheek.

"We got him today," he said around the emotion burning in his throat. Then tried to wash it back with another drink of beer. "I wanted to kill him. I might have if I thought that's what you wanted. But… something stopped me."

A brother I worshipped my whole life because of his goodness and strength. A brother who'd never devastate an already broken family with another tragedy.

"I might have been a little… ," he twirled his finger next to his head, "… coo-coo. Because I thought for a minute I could hear your voice. I know that's stupid, but I guess your mind does crazy things in those kinds of situations. Still, it was enough to make me think about Mom. I decided she'd really be pissed if she had to visit you here, and me in jail."

He ran the cold beer can over his forehead in lieu of drinking it. Likely, the outside temperature had dipped below the freezing mark, but his body was producing enough heat to keep sweat trickling down his face. "So... my girlfriend says you've visited her in her dreams." He held up his beer in a toast. "I know, right? That's pretty crazy, too. Maybe we *do* belong together. But see, the thing is, if you were going to visit anyone's dreams, it would be mine, wouldn't it? I've busted my ass trying to catch this guy. You sure as hell wouldn't go to a stranger, would you?"

He took another swallow of the beer then set it on the ground next to him. "And right now, if you could hear me, you'd let me know. There'd be a sign? A whisper? A lightning bolt? Hell, knowing my little sister you'd throw a rock at me, pour my beer over my head." A bitter bark of laughter managed to push from his lungs in challenge. "Come on, twerp. I dare you. Do something, I swear I won't freak. Just—do *something*."

It was true that he'd been here before, talked to Tara on many occasions, it was just this was the first time he'd ever asked her to talk back. *I've lost my damn mind.* But why pretend now that the last 24 hours were anything less than a clusterfuck of bizarre. If he wanted to talk with his dead sister, he'd damn well talk to his dead sister. Fuck it. He picked up the beer, tossed back the rest of it.

"See Tara, it would be a lot easier if you'd help me out here because I don't have the first clue what to believe. Jordan is not the kind to make up something like this, and despite what I said to her, I don't think she's crazy at all." He laughed at the next thought. "And trust me when I tell you, she sure as hell ain't the centered, spiritual, one-with-the-universe type either."

He raked a hand back through his hair. "Ah, Christ. What the fuck am I going to do? I love her, Tara. Have I lost my mind? How can I love someone who claims they have visions and that they communicate with the dead? That's not even possible. You and I were so close, it would be me. If you were going to talk to someone… it would just be me. That's all."

He shook his head, took the next beer out of his pocket and popped the top, tried desperately to swallow the lump choking off his ability to talk. "But the thing is, I don't think I can let her go. Just the thought of not being with her again…"

Closing his eyes, he sat quietly in the still, cold night until the heaving of his chest leveled out some. "So that's it, huh? No ghostly images? No spooky sounds?" he whispered. "Well, you weren't much help tonight, squirt. I know for a fact if you could hear me you wouldn't be able to resist screwing with me somehow."

He stood. "Alright, baby girl. I need to go. Wish me luck with this stubborn woman of mine." He started to leave then turned back. "But if you are visiting her, could you tell her to answer her damn phone." He bent over, kissed two fingers and then laid them on her grave. "I love you."

He stood. In the still night, not so much as a leaf had rustled in the quiet air, but the temperature took a sharp dive toward artic, and the wind blustered around him. The little bells in Tara's flowers tinkled in the gust.

He glanced at the jingling bells, then looked up at the tree leaves and out over the rest of the cemetery that seemed to be resting in quiet and stillness. For the first time tonight, he felt a true chill. Not only in the air, but shooting down his spine and raising the fine little hairs on the back of his neck. When he stepped backwards, his heel hung up on a good sized rock. He side-stepped and stumbled, trying to keep from going down. In the process, he lost his grip on the open beer. He fumbled the can like a possessed football. It sloshed and spewed, soaked the front of him as he landed on his ass.

Stunned, he sat silent for a long second, then smiled. "Well I'll be damned."

Made in the USA
Charleston, SC
11 July 2014